Dark of the
Moon

Also by Janice Daugharty

Going Through the Change

Necessary Lies

Dark of the Moon

A NOVEL BY

Janice Daugharty

HarperPerennial
A Division of HarperCollins*Publishers*

This book was originally published in 1994 by Baskerville Publishers, Inc. It is here reprinted by permission of Baskerville Publishers, Inc.

HarperCollins books may be purchased for educational, business, or sales promotional use. For information please write: Special Markets Department, HarperCollins Publishers, Inc., 10 East 53rd Street, New York, NY 10022.

First HarperPerennial edition published 1995.

Library of Congress Cataloging-in-Publication Data

Daugharty, Janice, 1944–
    Dark of the moon : a novel / by Janice Daugharty. — 1st HarperPerennial ed.
    p. cm.
    ISBN 0-06-097655-1
    I. Title.
[PS3554.A844D37   1995]
813'.54—dc20   94-43892

95 96 97 98 99 RRD 10 9 8 7 6 5 4 3 2 1

For Seward, my spring, and for Susan, my rock.

Dark of the
Moon

I

Soon as I heard the whistle of the six o'clock train at Tarver crossing, I went to listening out for Israel's old piece-of-a-car, sorting its roar from the train's rumble across the woods. And I knew Hamp, at his shine still out back, was listening too, for revenuers, for any break in the humming quiet of locusts at sundown.

I sneaked out of the kitchen to the open hall, looking up and down for Hamp, who was bad to turn up when you thought he was gone. Through the tunnel of sun, blackgums stirring on the back yard seemed the only movement for miles, and in the oaks out front, the seesawing ring of katydids, the only other sound. No sign of Hamp.

Still, my chest felt tight as I eased up the hall and around his long-bodied dog, laying slung like a black overcoat. He opened one eye and twitched his ears, warty with ticks, then went back to sleep, paws flat out before him on the wide boards. Gave off a warm-thick smell, like fever on a baby.

In mine and Hamp's room, up front and off the hall, the clock ticked on the mantelpiece in time with the squeak of rotten floor joists. I thought it said six o'clock. Now that dark was coming quicker with fall, I doubted the clock, doubted the timing of the train, but I didn't doubt what Hamp would do if he ever found out I sang with the boys.

Be that as it may, if they didn't get a move on, we wouldn't never make it to Valdosta by seven, where we were supposed to sing for some charity at the city auditorium. We always sang on weekends, either free for charity or for next- to-nothing at some nightspot. To get experience—that's how I put it to the boys. But tonight was special; tonight we'd be singing with the local big groups. Either way, gearing up to sing on Fridays, I'd feel something loose within me fixing to form.

Once, just once, I'd have liked to be on my way to sing without a knot in my gut. But Hamp would always stop by the kitchen and start his bull: If the boys' sanging ain't bringing in no cash money, they oughta stick to the business. I knew "the business" could turn anytime, turn on them, just like gator-hunting had turned on Colin—Hamp's first born by his first wife—fresh out of the pen. Last week, the same bunch of agents that put Colin in the pen come begging him to hunt down gators across the Georgia/Florida line, gators somehow coming to be the enemy in back yards of houses going up on Florida lakes. Law was like that. And tomorrow bootlegging could go just as honest, just as sour, the sheriff could turn just as quick, sic the revenuers on Hamp and the boys to clear hisself.

Lately, Hamp had got to where he suspicioned everybody, and he kept relocating the still. After those agents come by to get Colin to go hunt gators, Hamp moved it from Tarver to the woods behind the house. Why he kept moving it closer, I didn't know, but it made me juberous. I hadn't never before paid mind to making shine being anything but one more way to make a living. No worse and no better than shooting a deer for dinner.

I'd let Hamp have his way with Colin and J.B.(John the Baptist), but my three were mine to shape or shame. Though the truth was, Hamp wouldn't have let the least ones go sing if the trips hadn't been a good front for running shine.

From the front porch, I watched Israel's car slew dust along the curve of pines and skid to a stop in the stand of oaks. In spite of being loaded, the backend of the maroon Chrysler set level from the six-ply tires and the helper springs put on when they'd souped up the engine. Cars changed on the place about once a month to throw off the revenuers, who the boys hadn't never laid eyes on but had been warned about since they went to peeing off the porch.

Going down the doorsteps, I watched Bo Dink slip over next to Israel on the front seat and make room for me. Little Noah was setting high in the back, scratching his head. Israel and Bo Dink had that hard chiseled look, like Hamp, where Little Noah was all soft and round. Had a tendency to lean forward all the time, like he couldn't see good, or was listening with his eyes. But all their hair was black as the blackest bear's in the Okefenoke out there. Thousands of acres of pines, palmettoes, cypress and gums turning to black-water swamp—pulse of the Okefenoke.

I didn't turn around to look, but always expected Hamp to pop up and order me back inside, my needing to sing a tug on my heart. Three years I'd been singing with the boys— Merdie and the Boys—and three years I'd been looking for Hamp to find out and stop me. Maybe kill me. The lower the sun, the lower the season, the more the feeling seeped into my soul. But he didn't never leave the place, and unless somebody—say, the sheriff for instance—told him I sang, he probably wouldn't find out. Not that the sheriff, Hamp's bootlegging buddy, would think to tell. They talked business or nothing, never messed around outside of Swanoochee County. Strange thing was that when me and the boys sang at Bony Bluff Church, just up the road apiece, I worried least because neither the old man nor the sheriff would set foot inside a churchhouse.

I opened the car door, letting out a ghost of cigarette smoke, and got in. Nobody opened their mouth till we were good and clear of the place, making time up the dirt road.

Israel, the biggest worry-wart in the bunch, smoked and drove, one arm hooked on the steering wheel. For some reason, he'd took a notion to grow out a mustache, straight and black as hog bristles. Looked like he was making up for the hair sliding on his high forehead. He wore it long on the neck and cut high over the ears, and it was gapped up bad in the back from where the barber got hold of him. Come to be gapped up that way because the barber, Alvin Nabors, wasn't really a barber, just another bootlegger with a front.

"Old man was sampling bad when we picked up the load," Israel said.

Gazing out the bug-crusted windshield, I bit on the rubber band between my teeth and bunched my straight black hair in a low ponytail. "Better get a move on; sing starts at seven." When I did get away from the house, I didn't want to be talking about Hamp.

Israel passed the faded no-trespassing sign nailed to one of the tallest pines and tore west up the hardroad, rocks shooting like buckshot under the hot car. The sunk orange sun made his and Bo Dink's faces look like wet clay. "Gotta swing by Tarver to drop the load," Israel said.

"Do it coming back."

Israel's black gaze stung like guinea wasps. "Can't go up yonder with no load of shine."

"Do like I say." The way I talked going to gigs was different from how I talked at the house. There, I'd humble down and let them boss me around, just like Hamp.

I stared straight at the setting sun, road opening fast in stripes of sun and shade. From the house to Tarver, to Cornerville, there was nothing to see but long-leaf pines, scrub oaks, myrtle bushes and palmettoes, now and then giving way to bar pits of shrunk black water, choked with lily pads. Wire grass in the shallow ditches was parched from the long hot summer just come to a close. Tiered streaks of woodsmoke hung above the top-heavy pines from control burning done by the big paper companies, who owned most of the flatwoods now. Hamp and my mama had somehow managed to hold onto their homeplaces, in spite of hard times. And I thought about how we used to burn woods every fall, the way the smoke smelled clean but smothery. Times seemed better then, but they weren't. The nose tricks the mind.

"I'd as soon set at the house," Bo Dink said, "as go sang in front of that big bunch of people."

"Sing," I said. "You gotta start sometimes singing with the big groups if you want to get to Nashville." I had all ideas he was heading down the same wrong road Israel took a few years ago. My teeth felt tight and gummy, like I was biting on a rubber band. "You do your Elvis tonight, Bo Dink," I said.

"God, Ma!"—he laid over on Israel, knee jam up with the hot gutted dashboard—"I ain't no good at Elvis."

"Yeah, you are." Looked like he wanted me to beg him into living. Used to, he loved Elvis better than anything, but now all he thought about was how he looked, what they thought about him at school.

"Ain't that kind of sanging, ain't rock," said Little Noah. "It's church stuff." He was setting flat in the back on a humped bed of croker sacks that hid jimmy-john jugs of shine, packed tight from the cooter hull to the front seat. Guitars surrounding him.

"Gospel—slip it in on 'em." I looked at my fourteen-year-old baby, a mite on the chunky side, with blue eyes and wavy hair of all things, then over all three part-Indian faces. "Little Noah, y'all, let's sing like we mean it tonight."

I always said that, but tonight I meant it more than ever. "Step on it, Israel."

The red needle on the speedometer fanned across the row of

5

numbers, from 80 to 95, and I knew we were going faster than 95. My heart was.

Soon as we got in sight of the auditorium, the boys went to fussing with one another.

"You reckon we at the right place?" Little Noah scooted among the guitars, bad chords strumming about the car.

"Don't stop at the front where everybody's going in." Bo Dink shouldered Israel. "Go yonder at the back where that fellow with the banjo's going."

Israel gunned along the curb, then braked for a dressed-up man and two little girls to cross in front of the car. White smoke from the tail pipe caught up and overtook the car, fogging the group going through the double glass doors.

"Now, you got everybody looking." Bo Dink tilted toward the long curved windshield.

Israel propped one arm in the window, set up tall, and motored along the shrubs to the opening of the back lot where three women in red fringed vests and skirts crossed to the stage door.

"Go on and park the damn thing, for Chrissake!" Bo Dink shrunk up to nothing; legs weren't big around as my arm in them tight dungarees.

"There's the law, Mama." Little Noah slooped low, knees pressed into the back of the woolly front seat.

"Shut up, Little Noah," I said. "Y'all making Israel nervous."

Israel seized up and stopped at the place to turn in, like he was trying to pick out a parking spot. The police car went on by and up the street, between the hospital and the auditorium.

"Go on, Israel," I said, "he ain't noticing you."

He pulled up, the big Chrysler wedging between two teenitsy cars. When he cut the engine, its simmering roar still sounded in my ears.

"I want to tell you something, Ma," he said, arms crossed on the steering wheel. "If the law was to get us up here, we everyone gone set tail in jail, and the old man..."

"I ain't studying Hamp," I butted in. "Y'all get your guitars and get out."

I no sooner got the stage door swung open than a man in a plaid shirt with a turquoise on a string noose popped out of the shadows backstage. "You folks here to sing or to see the show?"

I could hear the boys behind me back off, feet scraping sand on concrete and guitars bumping.

"We're singing." I looked him square in the eyes. "Merdie and the Boys."

Four more men in black rhinestone-studded suits shoved past the boys, then me. "Johnny Cash," the tallest man joked and bowed his black head.

About that time, Katy Land come frisking through the door, smiling ear to ear. Dressed in a white cotton shirt and a long denim skirt and dangly gold earbobs. She was about half my age and half again my size, one of those women made it look like a light had come on—twinkly green eyes and fluffy brown hair that bunched like fur on her shoulders. She stretched high and hugged the one called Johnny Cash and they went to talking and laughing. I knew her good, Katy Land. Got first chance at all the gigs about town; when they couldn't get her, they'd call on us or one of the other groups. Not having no telephone, me and the boys would generally just show up, praying Katy Land didn't. But I had to hand it to her, she could some sing. None of that copy-cat stuff like everybody else. Was I jealous? Some.

She looked up and saw me and said, "Hey, girl, how you doing?" and flirted off with Johnny Cash along the tunnel of curtains. The light backstage was a red-blue color that turned everybody purple, the sound of tuning guitars, banjos and fiddles a hellish rake on the dead air.

The man with the turquoise noose went down a list on a white piece of paper. He was a long-tall man with a sway back and tan hair that out of the purple light would be the same shade as his skin. "Ok, ma'am, you go on down those stairs there and get dressed and we'll call you when it's time."

I set out with the boys following me down the stairs where a swarm of jabbering rose to the down-clop of boots. I didn't need to check; I couldn't have lost the boys if I tried. They'd get used to a place only after we'd been there a dozen times. Toot's, where we generally sang on Friday nights, was like home. They'd march in that smoky, low, candle-lit room, set up, and sing from the heart till two in the morning.

The sway-backed man called after us. "You fellows can go to the end and wait in the men's dressing room."

Well, maybe I could lose them after all. "We'll stand yonder by that side door," I called, taking the last of the stairs to the well of closed concrete, hotter the deeper we went.

"Ma," Bo Dink yapped in my ear, "I can't believe us to think we're good enough to sang with these fancy groups."

I stepped clear as a bunch of giggling girl cloggers in stiff crinolines and red gingham dresses tapped upstairs, brushing my boys to the wall. Then I waited by the open basement door that led up more stairs to the parking lot.

The boys edged down the stage stairs and headed for the outside stairwell where a generator's roar cut the other racket.

Israel gazed up at the frame of dusky sky, more worried about the load of shine than the singing. He wasn't bashful in front of a crowd, but then him and Little Noah didn't sing much by themselves, like me and Bo Dink. There's a difference in having a crowd boo at the group and boo at you by yourself.

We waited for better than a hour in the outdoors stairwell, listening to the set-back thrum of guitars and banjos and the doubleshuffle tapping of cloggers on stage, to the hisses and sighs up and down the stage stairs.

Katy Land, of course, went on four, five times before us. Everytime she got called upstairs, she'd bust out of the dressing room door with her hands on her flushed cheeks, bright as the mirror behind her fired by naked lights.

Bo Dink and Little Noah set on the outside stairs and tuned their guitars, peaceful as on the porch at home, while Israel paced and smoked between the stairs and the generator.

"Merdie and the Boys," somebody called down the stage stairs.

I flapped my frocktail. "Y'all look alive," I said and walked off. I never looked back, even going up the stage stairs, could hear them breathing hard behind me. "Let's sing, boys." A sweet burning built in my chest with every step up, the red light and the puffing no-color curtain, the last divider between me and the crowd, between me and the bright lights. I felt like stopping and shoving the boys ahead, but knew they wouldn't go on without me, and I felt like Bo Dink said earlier—*We oughta stick to Toot's and little crowds where people dance and drink and don't even notice if you mess up.*

I stepped between two of a dozen side curtains off the lit stage and looked out at the faceless heads that could go for chalked aughts on a blackboard. I never sang to people back then, I just sang to the boys to get them going.

They cleared their throats, strapped on their guitars, and tracked in behind me, while the man with the turquoise noose was still introducing us. I knew we oughta wait but couldn't chance stopping because the boys might turn around. The anouncer looked sidelong at us, tromping on, and cut the introduction to "Merdie and the Boys!" and handed me the mike.

The crowd clapped like they would for anybody else, a baby cried out, setting another one off, somebody hooted in the back where a hazy beam of light punched a hole in the dark and hit me full in the face. When the clapping stopped, I thought I oughta say something but couldn't figure what, maybe something I'd heard other group leads say about poor crippled children and how they were so glad to be a part of something so worthwhile, but thought only of what my mama would say when asked why she delivered babies for free out in the flatwoods.

"You do good, you get back good," I said, "we're all in this together." The mike squealed like a marked hog.

I pushed up my sweater sleeves and nodded at Israel. All three boys were gazing at their guitars like they were learning how to play. Those smoked-brown guitars looked more like family than they did. Little Noah's flat lips were lined in blue. He strummed a few bars, and I started singing "Your Cheating Heart" with the mike squealing so that I couldn't tell if I'd chose the right song or not. Had we planned to start with gospel—"Just a Closer Walk With Thee"? To keep Hamp from finding out I sang, my practice come only at church and gigs. I sang on anyhow, lifting my baked face to the light.

The boys caught up on the guitars, weak chords trailing my natural keen whang. One at a time, their voices filled in, singing harmony, the mike quit squealing, and the shallow song seemed to bounce back and scatter to our little group onstage.

Somebody on the front row tittered and I felt faint-white, knees shivering like the guitar strings, but I kept on, tapping my feet out of time, and realized that the song sagged more the closer we got to the end. As Israel chorded down, clapping staggered about the auditorium like static.

I turned and looked mean at the boys.

Israel, with his foot propped on a straight chair, picked wild, looked mad, and struck into "Blue Moon of Kentucky," my usual solo.

I knew we hadn't planned to do that song, but I belted it

out—sounded like I was begging, a tangling whang—till I could sense the crowd standing us, all the time thinking only of Bo Dink's Elvis act coming up and listening to the boys playing behind me, the last of the song leaking down like rain off tin.

The crowd clapped, whether because the second song was good or over or better than the first, I couldn't tell.

"Now, my middle boy, Bo Dink, the good-looking one there"—I turned and pointed, making my voice homey like Mother Carter's on the Saturday night Grand Ole Opry—"he's gone do his Elvis for y'all." I walked over and handed him the mike. He took it like a snake, face welted from the pout of his plump Elvis lips.

The crowd laughed like he was fixing to blow on some jug.

I walked across the long deep stage to the wings and stepped back to watch.

He fiddled around a few seconds with his pick, then lit into strumming and singing "You Ain't Nothing But a Hounddog."

"Oh Lord," I said in my hand. He didn't even sound like hisself, much less Elvis, was stiff and wormy-looking, knee cocked like it was stuck. His guitar strap snagged on his bucking-bronc belt buckle as he slung it to the side.

The announcer, coming fish-eyed from the shadows off-stage, looked at his watch. "One more," he said, like he was doing me a favor.

The crowd never let up laughing, but when Bo Dink got done they clapped. I walked onstage and took the mike. It felt stuck to his fingers.

Little anyhow, I felt littler on that stage; still I held my head high. I turned to the crowd, to the rows of ducking heads, some walking around or leaving. "We got one more to do for y'all." The mike squealed and everybody laughed. "One we do at church sometimes, called 'I'll Fly Away.'" I looked at the boys—eyes down, faces burning under the white light.

Relieved that their part was almost over, they sang better than before. But it was hard to believe that these were the same boys born picking and singing, my boys. I sang out strong, pulling them along, harmonizing with Little Noah's changing alto, but only on the last part did we sound anything like at church, backwoods flat but strong-throated, somebody else's song sang our way.

As we wrapped up, the crowd sent us off with clapping anyhow, but stopped before the boys tromped offstage. Boots thundering to the far-away wings.

"Y'all got one more time to come on," the announcer said to me. "Wait downstairs." His tight face broke out in smiles as he turned and walked onstage.

"They ain't enough damned money in the world to make me go back out there," said Bo Dink, blowing on my neck.

"Since when did you go to getting paid for singing?" I took the stage stairs, feet sideways to keep from tumbling.

"I ain't and that's just the point." He clopped behind me to the basement stairwell.

"You do, cause I say so." I parked in the doorway, let the boys pass through to the chilly air and the hammering hum of the generator.

"God, Mama," Little Noah said, "we ain't never sounded no worse." He set on the stairs and hung his head, staring at his turned-up boot toes.

"You don't know nobody up here in Valdosta." Israel took a pack of Lucky Strikes from his shirt pocket and knocked one out on his thumb bone. "We won't never set eyes on that bunch of fools again."

"I feel like killing myself," Bo Dink said. "*Elvis*. Mama! Elvis is been dead twelve years."

"Bring him back to life." Crossing my arms, I watched the cloggers troop up the stage stairs.

"*You* bring him back to life." Bo Dink took the basement stairs in twos, up.

"Don't you dare sass at me," I hollered. "You know what's the matter with you, Bo Dink?" He kept right on going and I kept right on talking. "You give up too quick. Get back here!"

"Let him go," Israel said. His pocked face looked bruised and hollow. He spewed smoke through his nose, smoke stacking up the stairwell to the band of cloud-spun sky.

"If y'all don't want to go back on," I said, "we'll go to the house and y'all can live out the rest of your born days in the flatwoods." With your daddy, bootlegging, I didn't add.

"Nashville's your notion, Ma," said Israel.

"Ok," I said, starting for the stairs, "let's go."

"I want to go to Nashville, Mama." Little Noah looked up where I stood beside him. I put my hand on his head and screwed it round as I stepped down. His wavy hair felt soft as the day he was born. Scissors didn't touch it till he was going on five.

Out of all of them, he was the one with the least talent, couldn't make it. Israel and Bo Dink maybe. I didn't know. I didn't even know where Nashville was from the house, in which direction—the woods looked alike north, south, east and west—and now Nashville was just a name I'd always heard, a make-believe place, something on the radio.

"Hey, Merdie," a man from the doorway called out. "That your real name?"

"I'm Merdie." I walked over to the big-bellied man blocking the doorway.

He leaned in the frame of light and smoked through the gash in his bushy brown beard. After each serious suck, he dropped the cigarette to his side, thumping ashes. He looked like he was fixing to start laughing, one big pointy-toed boot set sure in the narrow stairwell. "You ain't half bad." He nodded, green eyes closing as he took another draw.

"Thank you." I stood facing him, a good foot shorter. My heart felt like it was bleeding. I looked up at the empty stairs. "You hear Bo Dink?"

"That Elvis crap? Yeah. Ain't to my liking." He sucked on the half-burned cigarette and flipped it to the corner where the generator puffed at chewing gum and candy papers. "Everybody and his brother's doing Elvis. Now, take you...you ain't like nobody else. Could be another K.T. Oslin. Got a manager?"

"No." I wondered right off how come him to make out like being different was so fine, then right in behind it say I could be another K.T. Oslin. Then I wondered what he wanted and knew I didn't have any—not money, not loving.

"Y'all sang much around here?" he said.

"A little. Here and there, fill in."

"Next Friday night be over at the American Legion Post 21 on Williams Street. Seven o'clock. I'll make it good with them." He turned and walked off, sweaty shirt pulling across his big bull back, but he walked like a baby, belly first.

On the second go-round that night, me and the boys went on without Bo Dink. Little Noah and Israel hung back while I sang my heart out for our new manager, who was either long gone by then or lost in the crowd. When I couldn't spot him from the stage, I figured he'd lied, but sure enough, soon as we got done, the announcer traipsed on and announced that Merdie and the Boys would be singing next Friday night at the American Legion.

Following the boys to their nest in the outside stairwell, I felt like shouting the news to Katy Land and the others. Course I didn't. For all I knew, that big-bellied man had told them the same thing and, come Friday night, we'd everlast one show up at the same place.

As we started upstairs to the parking lot, we saw Bo Dink come spidering down. He waved us back and hissed, "Ma, Israel, the law's out there snooping round the car!"

Israel and Little Noah ducked low and turned, boots tapping like my heart on the concrete stairs. Bo Dink right in behind them. Katy Land and the three women in red fringe crowded into the stairwell, blocking the basement door, and the boys lodged around the generator. Shocked faces switched to fake smiles.

I stepped to the foot of the stairs and propped up next to Israel. The women, still grouped in the doorway, started talking among themselves, reshouldering their pocketbook straps, and waited for us to go up first. Katy Land looked like she wanted to jaw with me, but I cut her short. Me and the boys hemhawed around a few more minutes, hoping to go out the blocked door, and wouldn't you know it, the cloggers bunched behind the group.

I started on up, hearing the boys' bootclops against the cloggers' taps. Like me, I figured they were scared to death the law would grab us the minute we reached the landing: a storm of lights and sireens, car doors pried open and croker sacks flung and jugs of clear boiling shine set out to view. But when we got to the top, overlooking the cool dim parking lot, no sign of the law.

The loud bunch on our heels scooted past and struck out across the lot, while me and the boys hung close to the curb, behind a line of parked cars. Israel's Chrysler, facing a strip of trees off the main street, now set off to itself like a wreck on display at the fair.

Israel leaned against a skimpy tree, growing out of the sidewalk. "Let's get out from here, leave the damn car."

Little Noah hunkered, like he was dodging bullets, toward the slanted shadow of the building, where Bo Dink had ironed hisself to the wall, then circled wide and scrunched behind me. "Buddy," he hissed to Israel, "we can't just run off and leave the car here."

"How come you think we buy them old two-hundred dollar cars?" Israel, tall and braced to look brave, stepped from the tree. "Let's go, Ma."

"I don't see no sign of the law," I said. "Besides, y'all want to walk home? Know anybody up here might could give us a lift?"

Nearly everybody had left the lot before Israel cranked up to go, his souped-up Chrysler blasting and smoking.

"Ease on out of town," I said, and he was, so slow that cars backed up along Main street in a string of lights like Christmas. "Bo Dink just thought somebody was checking out the car."

"I seen him." Bo Dink was gazing out the rear glass with Little Noah. "A man with a mustache was bent down checking the tag. Had on a red and blue streaked shirt."

"Go on, Israel," I said, knowing in my heart Bo Dink saw what he saw, but no point in worrying the other boys.

"Tag's about how come them to suspicion us," said Little Noah. "Big old car with a Swanoochee County tag up here in Valdosta always looks like moonshine."

Bo Dink sounded like he was primping up to cry. "Couldn't nobody tell we got a load; somebody must of turned us in." Then looked like he went to doubting. "We setting level— wait! What about the tires, Israel?"

"Shut up!" Israel said. "Any fool happening by could tell we running shine. Tires ain't all they is to it, and we ain't got no tag." He took two or three side roads, some twice—either lost or trying to throw off the law.

I looked back. "See, nobody ain't following us." A couple of cars behind us turned in at the Burger King. Down the side street, puny pine tops made perfect cones on the light-tinged sky, how Little Noah would've drawed them.

"They don't show theirselfs like that." Israel lit up a ciga- rette and held it to the wheel, shaking. "If they there, they'll likely let us get to where we gone drop off, then bust us. Or follow us home one."

I gentled them through town, like I'd gentled them onstage. "Just keep going like you going," I said, and he was mashing the gas, chugging like a stock car before the race.

When we got out of town, shooting east along that foggy,

dark twenty-mile stretch to Cornerville, we didn't meet even one car, not a light to be seen in the fog sealing off the road behind us. The boys were setting quiet. Too scared to talk, I guessed.

Soon as we got close enough to see the red light blinking at the crossroad in Cornerville, Israel slowed, then just about stopped on the Alapaha bridge. Over the gapped concrete railing, I could see the creek-width river, parting the dark woods with a live pewter glow. "Now, I don't know where to go on to the house or stop off and drop the shine," he said.

"Go on," I said, not knowing which away to go either. "Go on and drop the load." If the barber had done come looking for his delivery and it not there, he'd go straight to Hamp and there could be a throat-cutting. Hamp'd swear Alvin was lying, trying to cheat him out of the cash. The delivery man, in this case Israel, always set the jugs out in the bushes along one of the dirt roads, and another man would come to pick them up. Cash changed hands later. A system based on trust, a understood, twisted kind of trust that carried over to trusting one another to kill one another if either got caught cheating.

If we were fixing to get nailed, I'd as soon it be out in the woods as at the house where the revenuers would get Hamp and J.B. too, causing a bigger ruckus. At least we'd try to get shed of the shine, maybe clear the boys with Hamp.

J.B. camped on the homeplace in a house trailer, parked by the still. Every evening, come dusk, he'd go out and circle the trailer and still with sewing thread, so he could tell by the sag or break in the thread if anybody had been messing around. Come morning, he'd check the thread and check for tracks in the raked dirt of the circle, and sometimes, specially if he was drinking bad, he'd shoot a good round of buckshot in warning.

Israel drove on through the blinking red light in Cornerville, where even the new Minit Market was done closed. You could buy beer there, except on Sundays and election days, but if you wanted legal liquor, you had to go to the joint on the Florida

line, two miles south. Not that Swanoochee County was voted
"dry"; nobody couldn't afford a liquor license. Back in the
sixties, when Hamp got big into shine, the county was dry, and
you could make a killing in whiskey, but now dope had the
bootleggers smelling the patching. A lot of them had switched
from outsmarting the law with shine, to outsmarting the law
with dope. Not Hamp. He kept his mindset from the good-old-
days like a woman does her hairdo.

Nobody was hanging around the red light, where boys were
generally bad to gang up at night. Not a soul around the flat
brick courthouse or the cement block store across the way.
Israel drove on, louder than fast, past the Methodist churchhouse
with its white steeple poking through the fog, past the same old
hip-roofed schoolhouse I went to as a girl. Then he picked up
speed on the lonesome, open road to Tarver.

All those dirt roads, forking off from the hardroad, went by
initials or names of bootleggers, and the boys knew right where
to drop what load: Old J.B. Cowart Road, Alvin Nabors Road,
C.C. Road, and so forth.

Israel, easier now that he was in Swanoochee County again,
looked back once and cut down the fourth road on the right,
bucking over a washout in the sandy ramp. Headlights opening
the ribbed vee of pine trunks. Just before he got to the Florida
line, he veered left, skirting the graded ditch, and braked,
pitching us all towards the dash.

I rolled down the window to the cool pine smell of the dark,
buzzy woods.

"Ok, boys let's unload and get gone." Israel's sound white
teeth were shining in the fuzzy orange dash light. What little
smiling he did looked like he was laughing at hisself, at the
messes life could make. He got out, Bo Dink sliding right in
behind him, and Little Noah grunting and shoving at the car
seat, then stumbling out—too chunky to be quick on his feet.
Bo Dink reached around him and went to slinging croker sacks
to the ground, while Little Noah walked in circles, trying to

look busy.

"Here, fatso," Bo Dink said, passing behind the first croker-wrapped jug. Little Noah took it and passed to Israel, who hobbled off to set it among the fanned palmettoes in a pine clearing. If you looked at those old heavy glass jimmy-john jugs they'd break.

Hamp's two oldest boys had been putting in to use plastic jugs and hauling bigtime like everybody else, get in with the big gangs and quit little-town dealing with the sheriff. Huh uh! Hamp, at sixty-five, wasn't fixing to change, and I knew, knowing J.B. and Colin, that they were up to more than changing jugs. I couldn't put my finger on just what, but something was in the making.

When the boys got the last jug unloaded and chunked the croker sacks in the car, they brushed out their tracks with a gallberry and got in to go, breathing easier as Israel turned around and took off toward the hardroad. Still not a soul in sight. I felt sleepy, wished I could doze during the ride from Tarver to the house, but I had to stay awake to keep Israel awake, knew I'd be up for good when I got to bed. I didn't sleep much since I'd started going through the change.

I looked back at the gravel, red in the tail lights, and rested easy that nobody had followed us. Bo Dink was curled on the bed of croker sacks with his hands folded under his cheek, and Little Noah was setting with his head on his knees. "You sang real good that last time we went on," I said to Israel, whose eyelids drooped like he was dozing.

He lit a cigarette, didn't answer, cut his red eyes in the mirror. All our eyes stayed blood-shot from those smoky dance halls and staying up. No smoke in the auditorium tonight; his red eyes worried me. (I always got to worrying more late in the night, like when I did get still I had to come up with something else to do.) "You believe somebody's still tailing us, don't you?" I leaned a little closer, like it would make us close again.

He aimed the lighter at the socket and jabbed it. No need for me to stay awake; Israel wouldn't fall asleep driving now, not while he was scared and mad. I yawned and laid over on the door, the engine jarring in my ears, but my eyes kept flying open. My sleepy time was over.

When we got home, the old dog come barking from the woods behind the house, and I felt satisfied that J.B. was looking down the barrel of his shotgun at us. The least boys crawled out of the back and scattered across the yard, pissing on the humped oak roots, while I went on inside. Then Bo Dink and Little Noah come in and went to their room.

First thing, Little Noah turned on the tv to one of those all-night ghost shows where a woman screams and a monster grunts. The boys must have seen the same one a dozen times. I'd moved the tv in there from the kitchen when I figured they weren't never going to turn the dern thing off anyhow. Least I wouldn't have to watch it. I'd give up trying to wean them; they'd watch it no matter what. And moving it in their room had made Little Noah feel like a king. He could wallow in bed while watching cartoons and game shows.

Maybe watching tv would keep him from storying so much, I'd decided, keep him out from under my feet too. Else, he'd be drawing and showing me his pictures. Pictures I'd loved when he was little, but now that he was growing up—my big fat baby—I was in hopes he'd quit drawing so much and start studying his lessons.

Israel come on in, plucked off his boots in the hall, and went in the bedroom too. They all slept in the same room, Bo Dink and Little Noah in the same bed, and generally fussed till they fell asleep.

What I needed to do was move Israel in the middle room, between the boys' room and the sideroom, off the back porch. But I kept junk in there, trunks of old clothes and pictures—not just mine, but Hamp's dead mama's and his first wife's—and cleaning it out would take more time than I had. Besides, that was the one place I could take a bath and be by myself, and sometimes when I couldn't get to sleep for Hamp's snoring, I'd wander off and doze on the single bed among the treasures of the other two women, my junk inheritance.

Israel bellered, "Cut off that shit so I can get some shut-eye." The tv blared loud, then got low, loud and low again. Bo Dink started fussing at "Fatso" for hogging the bed. The monster grunted.

I did my business, slid the slopjar under the bed, brushed my feet and snuggled under the quilts. The room smelled like fresh deer and wood smoke, dark except for firelight dancing on the tongue-and-groove walls. I laid listening to Hamp snore in the other bed. His on one side of the tall room, mine on the other, the fireplace in between where a litard knot he'd set fire to earlier had rolled to the edge. Used to, he never got cold; lately he built up a fire whether he needed one or not. One of these days, I figured, he'd set fire to the house and burn it down around him.

Thinking about the house burning, it come to me that my mama's house was still home to me. This was Frieda Jean's, Hamp's first wife; his Mama's house before her. I even used their pots and pans. Did my business in Frieda Jean's slopjar. Took over mamaing her two rough, scrapping boys, me nothing but a youngun myself.

My mama had pitched a fit, said the first wife died of worryation—Hamp claimed she died of heart trouble—but daddy thought my marrying was a good idea, Hamp being industrious and kin, no loafer like so many of the sawmill men that hung around daddy's store, playing poker till the timber ran out and the sawmill moved on to the next woods settlement. Well, Hamp still weren't no loafer.

Turning to face the outline of his bloated body, round-toed brogans set by his bed, I thought about the big-bellied man, our new manager, and wondered if he was after me or after money.

I smiled. Neither one. One look at us and he'd know we didn't have no money, and me, I was dried up.

Hamp hadn't touched me since right after Little Noah was born. Whether because his prostates were bad or because I wasn't young and pretty no more, I didn't know. And used to...used to...he'd bend me over the bed or sail in on top of me and poke me full, taking what was his. No love meant, none took. But he was proud of me then, like he was proud of his land. Proud of his boys—roosters, he called them. Proud when I got swole up round and went out mornings to hang clothes on the line, a barefooted girl with boy-babies hanging to her frocktail. Him and all six brothers might be standing around the grapevine, swapping notions, and he'd strut and pack his shirt while they all watched me. I was young and half-pretty, proof of the mustard he could still cut.

He was still snoring like a bull frog, but I was too tired and anxious for day to get up and switch beds. So, I laid there, running off thoughts in my head till the east windows over Hamp's bed turned from black to gray. My last thought before I dozed off was of what could go wrong to keep me from the American Legion next Friday night, and I counted the weeks till Jean Stover's baby would come due.

The old rooster woke me, crowing a circle around the house; every morning he made his round like the hands on a clock. Just as the sun broke through the turning leaves of the woods, I heard J.B. and Hamp quarreling out in the kitchen. They got loud then low, the way they'd done every morning come sunup since I could remember. But this time, I figured, they could be hashing over some real mess.

I got up and slipped on the first frock I come to on the broomstick rod in the corner at the foot of my bed. Put on my shoes and combed my fingers through my hair, then tipped out and up the hall. Old floor boards would creak under a ghost.

"Who's that?" Hamp hollered.

"Just me." I went to walking fast to the watershelf, running water and dashing it cold to my face. I dried on the sour towel, hung it on the nail and went to the kitchen.

At the cookstove, I put on fresh coffee and started the grits water boiling. Hamp made his coffee too strong, claimed mine was too weak. "How you, J.B.?" I said.

"Ain't worth a shit." He was crouched, smoking, on the long bench, with a full hubcap of cigarette butts before him on the eating table. His face was squat and stuffed, black hair growing low on a slick white strip of forehead.

Creek-Indian run strong in all the Lees, especially Hamp—busyeyed and blooded, solemn to the bone—but every now and then there'd be a throwback, like J.B. and Little Noah. Where Hamp, Colin and Israel were sharp-faced, dark and hard, J.B. and Little Noah were pale, soft and chunky, quick to make light of what was dead serious. Bo Dink took after me, stringy and tough as a pineywoods rooter.

Hamp rocked his chair from the hot ticking woodstove, to his end of the table, glittery black eyes grazing me. "Somebody come messing around the still last night."

"Broke the thread clean in two," J.B. put in.

"Gotta move it." Hamp placed his hands on his legs, like he was fixing to raise up, but reared instead.

Nothing new. I whacked off some slices from the side of smoked bacon a old man at Needmore had paid me and mama with for doctoring a growth on his neck.

J.B. crossed his pudgy arms on the table. "Let's load it up on the two-ton tonight and set up on the Herring old place for a change."

"We'll move it in broad daylight." Hamp's chair legs clanked to the floor, jarring my window full of daybreak over the sink. "Besides, we ain't moving it all that far."

"Old man," J.B. said, "you making a mistake. Can't keep moving it closer to the house."

Hamp's sleep-thick voice got gruff. "We'll move it where I say move it, and we'll do it by day—keep from making folks

23

suspicious."

"Man, you can't do that..."

"Always have." Hamp stood up, shoulders stooped like a shrunk giant's. He poked off down the hall to the yard, where the light was thinning gray over the woods.

"He's gone get everlast one of us landed in jail." J.B. swung around on the bench. His legs looked shorter with his low-riding dungarees. "Well, I ain't moving my housetrailer this time."

I went on sifting flour for a fresh waiter of biscuits. I'd get breakfast done, then have to keep it warm for them to mope around till they got hungry, my own boys straggling in as they woke up.

J.B. headed out, muttering. "Horseshit revenuers!"

I wondered if one really had followed us home. "Can't talk nasty in my house, J.B.," I called after him.

He peeped around the door. "You want to go with me, Merdie?"

"Where?"

"To pieces." He laughed and let go of the door facing and stomped out the back.

While my boys were eating, I went out front to the old two-story barn to milk the cow. The shingled loft, smokey gray against the bluing sky, was sunk into the rotting rafters on the north end.

Inside my milking stall, the dirt was steeped in cow piss, strong as straight ammonia in the packed-down air. As the sun leveled across the woods, yellow bars of sunshine rolled up in the cave-brown light, turning with dust specks.

I squatted to milk without a stool, squeezing one full warm udder, then the next, milk spraying on the bucket bottom till it foamed to the tune of muffled rain. The ripe smell of milk covered the rot of ammonia and hay. When the freckled udders shriveled in my hands, I let go and caught two more, and my red cow, Filly, switched my face with her wiry tail. "Hoo now," I said. She shifted, jerking the spongy tits in my fists. I patted her rump, went back to milking. She was the best company on the place, the only other female for miles. It made her jittery when I milked squatted down; all I had to do was get the stool from the corner and set, take my time, and she'd gentle. She knew me better than any one of the men that set quarreling around the breakfast table, and I felt bad for not taking my time, but I had to go on calls with my mama that morning. We had three women ready to drop babies in the coming month.

When I got done, I set the bucket of warm sudsy milk on the corner shelf and went out to the shed facing the side lot to get a bucket of shellcorn for Filly—make up for my slack. Hid from the front of the house by a fencerow of cherry trees, I could hear my boys tussling and quarreling on the front porch, then Israel's car crank up and spin out up the road, toward Colin's place. I set my bucket down and crossed the lot to the cherry with a broke limb, hanging this side of the wire fence, tore it loose from the gray silk skin of the trunk and chunked it over. Cherry leaves are pure poison on a cow.

Soon as Filly got done eating the corn, I turned her out in the side lot where the ferny dog fennels were turning wine. She waddled through the gate and hiked her tail and let go a steaming pile, then started grazing ahead in a patch of clover, the last, I figured, before the winter freeze. Already the morning air was cool and thin, the crickets tiring down to a tight keening cluster in the grass, and the sun had started to arc a little south.

II

I closed my eyes to Sunday breaking blue in the two windows over Hamp's bed; I opened them to the same shade, like denim fade in washwater. I must've just dozed off.

Hamp's bed was flat instead of humped, and my heart was whumping, a backlag of racket ringing in my ears. I set up and listened, holding my breath. Nothing but a few birds chirping in the woods. I started to lay down again when a loud boom went off behind the house, the dog barking wild. Somebody let out a holler.

My face went to tingling, like a foot gone to sleep. Deer season hadn't started yet, so I knew it wasn't deer hunters. It was one of mine, either shooting at a deer or at one another. Or maybe the still was being blowed up. I jumped out of bed, slipped on a old frock, and ran out in the hall.

Israel and Bo Dink were heading out the back, a few steps ahead of me.

"What the...?" I hollered, but they just sailed off the porch, barefooted as yard dogs, and trotted across the yard, taking the woods path to the still.

The dog kept barking like he'd bayed up a snake.

I lit out behind them, bare feet smacking the packed dirt, damp vines and gum leaves swabbing my face as I took the trail. The smell of buck passed in warm waves, ripe and thick, over the cool woods.

As I got close to the new spot where Hamp and J.B. had set up the still, I could hear them shouting at one another, and I figured they were about due for a knock-down dragout.

Bullous vines and bamboos shed on the path, a rusty purple shower whispering down. I ducked under a holly limb, the soles of my feet picking up its thorny leaves, but I kept on going—heart galloping against my ribcage—till I could see the crook of copper pipes above the box-shaped vat. Blue gas flames flared end to end under the rusted bottom and glinted off a cluster of glass jugs set at the mouth of the pipe. I eased up on the clearing, scared of what I'd find.

Hamp, hid in the woods behind the still, was yakking at J.B., and the dog, stalking the trace of gums, looked like he was swallowing barks and coughing them up.

Coming around a persimmon tree, I just about bumped into Bo Dink and Israel. They were standing off and watching J.B., who stood to the right of the bush-whacked palmetto clearing. Water trickled from a black hose hooked to the last pipe, a slow puddle spreading among the palmetto stubbles. In front of the still, a patch of dirt was tore up from where somebody'd been tussling.

J.B. had the stock of his shotgun braced against his fat-padded shoulder and was squinting along the barrel. Looked like he was aiming for the tall silver propane tank at the head of the vat, against a background of tree trunks and blurring fall leaves, gold, orange and brown.

From the woods, I heard a rustle of dead leaves, like a

armadillo rooting, and one long heaving grunt. And then I saw the branches shaking on one giant blackgum.

J.B. got a fresh hold on the shotgun and went to spouting out cuss words, his stuffed face sweating oil.

"J.B.!" I hollered, stopping next to Israel. "What you up to?"

He didn't answer.

Bo Dink and Israel cut their eyes from the shaking limbs where leaves sifted down, to J.B., gun cocked and ready.

"Turn him loose, old man." J.B. stood stiff, bare feet planted in the mud. He had on a black t-shirt and dungarees that rode low on his narrow hips. A band of white skin shining at the waist like a coachwhip belt.

Hamp stepped from the dark woods to the morning light and stopped behind the bullet-shaped tank. His white face pceped over the shoulder of a man with a mustache, in a red and blue strcaked shirt.

"Oh, Lord!" I covered my mouth.

The old dog went to barking faster, louder, lunging at the man whose legs hung like khakis on a clothesline. Brown eyes buldged in his beef-tallow face, hair sticking up like a funny-paper character's. His neat mustache was the same tan color as his hair. Looked like he might be closer my age than Hamp's.

"That's him," Bo Dink whispered, like he'd just seen Santy Claus. "That's the man I seen snooping around the car in Valdosta."

"Hush up," I said, creeping toward J.B.

He hollered, "Turn him loose," squinting at Hamp and the man.

Hamp's arms were latched around the man's chest, and the man's arms dangled over Hamp's like they were broke. Two sets of legs jigging side to side and back, they danced from the simmering still to the edge of the brightening woods, and again behind the propane tank. The revenuer's eyes seemed to change colors, and now took on the dead light of the puddle that spread from the trickling black hose. His chest looked sunk-in

28

and weak, and up against Hamp's broad body, the man looked somehow not too important— not like a revenuer. A disappointment.

From the time I was little, I'd seen a blue-dozen revenue men come by my daddy's grocery store to check on him ordering so much sugar and mash. Daddy looked like he plum enjoyed that—kept them wondering right up to the last minute, just before they got ready to haul him in. And then he'd show them the bill of sale where he sold sugar to the honey men, trot them out to his own honey house and hives, and laugh as they shied from the bee swarms. He'd walk them through the swamp, around gators and moccasins, to show off his pen of wild hogs. Hogs he baited, trapped and sold—what he didn't give away in hog meat. He even had the revenue men help hold the boars while he marked them, cutting out their nuts and chucking them across the board pen or putting them in a bucket for supper. Mountain oysters, he told them. They would turn green as the myrtle bushes. We never once ate mountain oysters, to my beknowest, but we would have if those revenue men had took my daddy up on his offer to stay and eat. Daddy was bad to pick at people, but revenue men weren't people to us, though those men were different from what we called regular revenuers. This man right here, checking out Hamp's still, was a real revenuer, the kind that snoops around at night. And I reckon I figured a revenuer would look big and boogery, but this one was little, scared to death.

"Turn him loose so I can shoot him." J.B. shifted and stood flat-footed in the black mud.

"Ain't no killing gone take place." Hamp's gruff, shaky voice thundered about the clearing and bounced off the woods.

"What you gone do with him, old man?" J.B. laughed— something mad struck loose.

"I got him." Hamp got a fresh hold on the man.

"I say, what are you gone do with him?" J.B. kept the shotgun on them, but his elbows got slack.

Hamp's face was shore-up to the other man's, both tall, about the same height, but Hamp was holding him up so that just the toes of his tan suede boots touched the scuffed dirt.

"What about it, old man?" J.B. went to grinning, his wide lips stretched across his soft bearded cheeks.

Hamp looked like he was studying, or listening for something behind him in the woods. But he kept a grip on the man like he was using him as a shield against J.B.'s double-ought buckshot.

"You ain't got no choice, old man, but to let me shoot him." J.B. sounded like he was trying to humor Hamp into reasoning with him. "We turn him loose and your shine business is hist'ry." He nodded at the gurgling still, copper pipes glowing as the sun struck suddenly through foamy clouds.

Hamp jerked the revenuer's head like Howdy Doody's and snatched him up, stepping back to the trunk of a blackgum. The tree shook and squirrels sprang branch to branch through the changing woods. The dog followed Hamp and his catch, barking and lurching.

Hamp got still. "A dead man draws buzzards and blow-flies."

J.B. squeezed the glinting gold trigger and shot above Hamp and the man, and the leaves of the blackgum scattered to the bluing sky and drifted down; the dog slunk away, then circled, barking.

Israel and Bo Dink backed up, faces tallow as the revenuer's. I stood there. "Put the gun down J.B."

His white jowls went stiff against the braced stock, eyes on the revenuer and Hamp, lapped like paperdolls.

Hamp looked straight at me, the force of his head making the man look too.

"Turn him loose, old man," J.B. said. "I gotta kill him." Mud swole over his feet.

Hamp's fingers turned purple as he gripped the man tighter around his stove-in chest. "I got him."

The man grunted, first sound he'd made.

"Everlast one of y'all's crazy." I stepped up to the line you could just about see drawed from the sight of the shotgun to Hamp and the man. White thread tangled on my feet from where J.B. had set his trap the night before; I tore it off and went to winding it up.

J.B. shot above Hamp's head again, a headaching blast, and I backed away, my ears stopped up good now, then ringing free enough to hear something crazy come out of Hamp's mouth.

"I got him, gone keep him," Hamp said.

"How you gone do that, old man?" said J.B.

Hamp lifted the man and backed up.

J.B. laughed, bent over and went to coughing, stood and aimed again. "You gone nuss that bastard the rest of your born days?"

Hamp looked like he had to think about that, his big feet right behind the man's, planted now, like forever, in the rotted leaves. "Merdie and the boys will."

J.B. looked down the barrel another minute, then cut his eyes at me, at Bo Dink and Israel with their mouths open. Then he started laughing, bent double, and lowered the gun.

"Run go get my hog rope, woman," Hamp hollered. Seemed like now that he'd decided, he come alive. He didn't look at me, but down at his thick arms locked around the man's chest, which looked like the air had been let out. The man's head lolled like it depended on Hamp's to hold it up. His eyes were wide, hadn't blinked in all that time.

I wondered if maybe he wasn't already dead.

"I said go get my rope, woman," Hamp yelled.

"I will," Bo Dink said, who never volunteered nothing. He scuttled off through the woods, hopping palmettoes, toward the house. The old dog quit barking, went to wagging his tail, and struck out behind Bo Dink, like we'd switched from danger to games.

I couldn't take my eyes off Hamp, off the man, the first real revenuer I'd ever seen. And just what were we supposed to do with a revenuer? But like Bo Dink, I reckon, I was glad there might not be a killing. Sorry as he was, I knew Hamp's heart wasn't in killing neither.

"Go on to your trailer, J.B.," I said.

He set in the mud, laughing, shotgun across his denim legs.

Hamp toted the man up to the vat and sighted down the heat-wavy pipes of the still to the end where a trickle of shine, like mica-laced water, ran slow in a jug set to catch it when it come: 200 proof, first catch—pure shine—to be cut from the last running to 100-proof.

By the runoff time of the shine, I figured we hadn't been out there more than fifteen to twenty minutes, but it felt more like a hour. Hamp's new set-up, with the shotgun condenser, would run off a batch in no time, another batch working in the buck vat, ready to run. How come Hamp to call the condenser shotgun was the dozen or so tubes carrying steam through the big pipe. Looked like the cluster of barrels on a old-timey Gatling gun.

We all just stood there watching Hamp and the man, while listening to the slow, trickling tune of the shine. The revenuer's eyes cut from me to J.B., then to the side, like he was trying to get a good look at the face against his, him and Hamp like two people getting their picture took.

The crows cawed, the squirrels scamped back to the tattered tree, not another sound in the brightening woods but J.B. laughing, the vat heating, and the jug filling, till Bo Dink come up, slapping branches and beating the dirt with his bare feet. When he got to us, he stopped, blowing hard with one knee cocked, and held out the rope to his pa.

Hamp stepped up, wearing the man like a apron. "Bring it here, boy."

To keep Hamp off Bo Dink, I took the coil of rope and walked slow ahead.

J.B just set there, laughing and staring at the mud swelling between his legs.

Up close, I could see the revenuer's chest moving up and down under Hamp's locked hands.

"You bunch of pussies," Hamp hollered over my head, "get over here and help your ma hog-tie this here revenuer."

Israel and Bo Dink caught up, and we eased along together, as Hamp walked the man to meet us.

"Get his feet first," Hamp said, grunting as the man grunted.

The revenuer's weak-coffee eyes cut from us to J.B., then at Hamp, lips parted like he wanted to say something. What got my attention was the fine brown hairs jumping on the hollow of his throat.

"Ain't got my pocketknife on me," Israel said, tying the man's ankles together in double knots over his dusty suede boot tops.

Hamp strained, arms still locked. "Bring the rope up and tie off his hands." He let go quick, the man's arms dropped, then he clamped his arms over again.

Israel brought the rope up to tie the man's wrists, now forced together in front, rope trailing along his quaking khakis.

Bo Dink with his mouth open held to one end of the rope while Israel looped it round the revenuer's wrists and tied a double knot, then yanked down to test it, jerking the man and Hamp forward.

Now what? I wondered.

J.B. had quit laughing and set watching us. "Got you a pet shorenuff, old man." He laughed like he was wore out from laughing, but had struck up a interest again.

"Set another jug yonder," Hamp shouted, jumping with the man, "then get your ass out from here." He picked the man up, boots clear of the ground and dangling.

J.B. got up, mud sliding off his legs, stomped across the puddle, and set the overflowing jug in the mud with a smack. Then, legs spraddled, like he didn't want to get nasty, he set another jug under the free-singing trickle and stalked off through the tromped-down dog fennels and cat-claw briars where they'd dragged the still through the woods yesterday.

"Got him good, Pa," Israel said. "Now you can let go."

Bo Dink kept holding the end of the rope and looked like he didn't know whether to let go or not—had just ended up that way.

Hamp walked the man across the clearing to the path, still welded to him, while Bo Dink backed along, holding the end of the rope with just enough slack to keep it from dragging across the mud mix of water and shine.

As they shuffled ahead, me and Israel come in behind, and I could smell fear and sour buck and something else along the path. Now that I wasn't so worried about a killing, I got mad at Hamp and the revenuer. Mad. I could smell and taste mad like pennies in my mouth. How in the name of God were me and the boys supposed to babysit a revenuer and sing? Singing at church tonight was out; Friday could be out. I watched Hamp shuffle the man towards the house like a dead gator snugged to his chest.

In the yard, Bo Dink backed around the far end of the clothesline, dodged the washpot, then the pole tripod, and around the crumbling brick well, us all following like mules on a line. "Where you want him, Pa?" Bo Dink swagged the rope before him as he backed up the doorsteps.

Hamp grunted, lifted the man and toted him up the steps to the back porch. His face turned old-petunia purple.

Bo Dink backed along the porch, glancing now and then behind at the open hall. A dull slice of light cut the house in half.

Feet scuffing hollow across the floor, Hamp stood the revenuer on his feet, still holding to him, husky Sear's denims bagging on his flat behind.

"Put him in the sideroom," I said, going around the dog and the boys, and standing away from the door. The room was dark as a cellar. Without thinking, I'd put him in there, like company. And it looked like the narrow room had been built in case we caught a revenuer: across the hall from the kitchen, where we stayed most of the time. No windows. My babies' room. It still had the cot Little Noah slept on last and still slept on sometimes. Anybody else took a notion to nap went in there; I wouldn't let them lay down on the beds during the day after I made them up. I hoped the sheet was clean.

Hamp lugged the revenuer into the room, up to the bed, and let him go, both of them breathing hard. The man stood there stiff, so did Hamp, like now they were apart they didn't know what to do next.

"Lay on down," I said, coming just inside the door.

The man turned—seemed bigger now that they were separated—and hobbled around on his roped feet to face Hamp. Hamp stared at him, elbows cocked. He jerked his head. The man looked at me and the boys and the dog, standing in the doorway. Then he set, still watching us watch him in the dim cool room.

I crossed my arms, wondering how long we could all stand there. Could we go now? My mouth tasted like dirt.

Hamp turned around, shoved past us, and ambled out. "Get him settled in, Merdie." He went to wash his hands at the watershelf, and water gushed through the drain to the dirt on the outside wall of the little room.

Israel stepped out in the hall. "I gotta run down the road for a minute...check on something."

"Like hell you will!" Hamp tromped to the door, wiping his white face on a white towel, white the way white is when you're bout to faint. "Get your gun and go to setting guard." His eyes were black glittery and fixed. "You too, boy," he said to Bo Dink. "Merdie, trim the rope so the revenuer can lay down a spell. Here." He chunked me his pocketknife and shambled off to the kitchen.

Bo Dink and Israel pounded down the hall to get their shotguns, come back and squatted, one on each side of the door.

Staring at the end of the rope coiled on the floor, I went to the bed and trimmed the long pieces, sawing with the knife blade, and chunked it aside, then cut the rope below his wrists and above his feet. I could feel him breathing quick. My eyes flew up and met his, clear green and sharp, not brown like I'd thought. His face was square cut, a smooth beige with that kind of colorless bloom that fear brings, a good face, even-featured and brotherly but not the kind of good looks you daren't trust.

"One slip of the knife and you go free," he said low.

"You mean you—you go free."

"No," he said, eyes darting at the door. "You let me go and turn state's evidence, your daddy and the others serve a little time and you go free."

"Hush up," I said, my eyes darting too. "Hamp's my husband."

After I got done, I turned around and went out. "I'll go fix breakfast and y'all can take turns eating," I said to the boys.

Hamp come out of the kitchen with a leftover biscuit and a strip of sidemeat. "He talking in there?"

"No," I said and pushed past him in the door.

He moped off to the back porch and set in the cowhide rocker, brogans turned on their sides.

My rooster hopped up on the porch, catching the edge with his waxy-gold claws, flapped his wings and crowed. After so much quiet in the house, it sounded like Gabriel's horn.

"Get out from here, you son-da-bitch!" Hamp stomped the floor, jarring the windows.

The rooster flew up, squawking, and landed in the watershelf runoff where Princes Feathers grew, the same crimson color as his cone. He flapped his blue-black wings and crowed again.

"Bo Dink," Hamp said—just as calm. "Shoot that son-da-bitch for me."

Bo Dink stood up, turned around and stuck the barrel of the shotgun in the door at the revenuer. His hands were shaking, his hips about as wide as a boy doll's.

"No," Hamp hollered, leaping up, "the rooster, you fool!"

I come out of the kitchen with a dishrag in my hands. "You shoot my rooster, Hamp Lee, and you're a dead man." My nerves had had it.

Hamp chunked out the rest of his biscuit to the mud bed of Princes Feathers and stomped down the doorsteps, watching the rooster and a flock of white hens gather and peck it to crumbs.

By dinnertime, stone-dark clouds peaked like mountains in the east and spread to a thick gray hull of sky. Flies swarmed over the back porch, hall and kitchen. Everything in the house felt damp and sticky, smelled like rats, and my brassiere was glued to my breasts. We could look out for a cold front to come through after the rain.

Two meals. I'd cooked two meals and spoon-fed the revenuer. Gave him water every hour, scared to death I'd forget.

Hamp had come back and pulled up his rocker where he could watch the revenuer through the gap between Bo Dink and Israel. They set, leaning against the wall on each side of the door, knees drawed up, taking turns dozing. Both shotguns lay on the floor—Bo Dink's finger hooked on the trigger.

The revenuer laid still, looking up at the aged tongue-and-groove ceiling.

About two o'clock Little Noah finally got up, ambling sleepy-faced down the hall, and stopped when he saw everybody camped out before the sideroom door. "What's going on?" His changing voice cracked the even sound of slow rain on tin.

Nobody said a word, like they couldn't decide who or how to tell it. Rain pelted the tin like acorns and misted the hall.

"Your pa caught a revenuer." I was carrying a glass of water into the room.

Little Noah stopped in the doorway, gaping. "I bet that's the same one Bo Dink seen..."

"Hush up," I said, knowing what he was fixing to say. I slipped one hand under the man's warm neck—his hair felt like chicken feathers—picked up and put the glass to his lips. When I felt his head hold steady, I cupped under his chin and water trickled to my hand. "Go get you some dinner," I said to Little Noah. "Chicken gizzards and greens."

Little Noah looked from me to the man, his sleep-shrunk eyes speaking instead. He didn't have on a shirt and his chest was dimpled fat. A patch of dark fuzz was starting between his swole breasts, and I knew how come he never went bare-chested like the other boys. He rubbed his eyes, stepped back, and looked at Bo Dink and Israel. Hamp, snoring in the rocker, scraped his feet on the floor, snorted and snored again.

The revenuer gazed up at me, like a man just come to from a lick on the head. "He who comes to the table first eats best."

"Hush now, you're feverish," I said. "That's *Into whatsoever city ye enter and they receive you, eat such things as are set before you.* New Testament." I dropped his head and turned my back on his puzzled face. Let him think I was stupid if it would shut him up.

I followed Little Noah to the kitchen, where the light on made the hall look darker.

"Ma," he whispered, "don't you bet that's the same fella...?"

"Hush up and set down." I got a plate and started helping it from pots on the stove. "J.B. tried to shoot him; your pa said we'd keep him here instead."

"Mama," he hissed over my shoulder, "how we gone do that?"

"I don't know." I dipped him a big helping of stringy turnips, rich green and tart as vinegar in the musty air.

He seemed to think all at once how the revenuer might affect him. "This mean I can quit school?"

"No."

He scratched his head, thinking. "Well, I could shore be a help to you if..."

"No." I stared him in the eye. "You're going to school."

"Ok." He turned around. "But I gotta..."

"And I gotta cow to milk, wood to tote, washing, cooking, babies to deliver..."

"Ma"—he set on the long bench, waiting for his food—"how you gone look out after him and you a woman?"

I knew he was thinking about the revenuer getting away from a weak woman; I was thinking something else. I remembered that even revenuers have to be-excused. "One of you boys go take the revenuer to the outhouse."

III

On Monday the weather was chilly and bright, sun strong through the open hall, making me a little less juberous. But I still felt bilious from not enough sleep: all night I'd been back and to, to the dark, airish sideroom, covering up and watering the revenuer. Everytime he started his sass, I'd give him some riddle to mull over. To my beknowest, he didn't try his stuff on anybody else—reckon he figured me being a woman, I was soft-hearted. Or weak.

The boys wouldn't set foot in the room; they camped out by the door. And soon as it got daylight, Bo Dink put in to go to school. He hadn't never been much for going on Mondays, him or Little Noah. Like Israel, I expected Little Noah would quit once he turned sixteen. So far, thank the Lord, Bo Dink, going on seventeen, was hanging in there.

Hamp let Little Noah go that morning but made Bo Dink stay home to set guard, while he watched from his rocker till long about nine. Then he mosied off to the still, and Israel left, leaving Bo Dink, puffed up, to guard and take the revenuer to the outhouse.

I gave Bo Dink strict orders to sidetrack his daddy from killing the revenuer if he come in before I got back, and then sneaked out and headed for my mama's to go on calls. Saturday was our regular calling day, but after walking all the way over to Jean Stover's, we'd found her gone. No message, nothing. I was mad about having to go all the way back to check on Jean, and scared too of what might go wrong with me gone. Even so, it felt good to get out of the house. But much as I loved Mama, much as I couldn't hardly wait to get to her house, once I got there I couldn't wait to go. She thought I was curious cause my head was always in the clouds, and to me she was curious with her feet flat on the ground.

Generally, Mama would come pick me up in her car, but last week she'd got in a bog and had to leave it till the woods dried off. I was just as glad to be going on foot, keep her from coming by the house and finding us with a revenuer. She'd bought the car after Daddy died out of what they'd skrimped and saved, and seemed like she never could figure where the old Chevy would get stuck. Was forever trying to make it over swamps and logging roads, to the honest-to goodness Okefenoke.

On a Georgia map, the Okefenoke looks like a big blue puddle that stops just out of Fargo, Florida-line side, but really it sloshes over into the flatwoods connecting Clinch to Swanoochee County. Woods so flat and swampy you can't see out, can't see in, or into one another's doings. You go to walking and happen up on your neighbors: people shock-eyed and dark, like they've taken on the color of the swamp.

It's real hard to give the layout of a place and its people when you've lived there all your life, when the land's flat and the people, for all you know, are just like everybody else in the world, when you've been walled-in by trees and never seen a place from above or away off, because then you think of the place only as how it figures in your life.

I took the long way around to my mama's, hearing the crows calling over the cypress slews. The sun had almost cleared the bushy pine tops and was showering down on the dewy green needles. Misty spider webs glinted, strung tree to tree, like fishing line. Off in the palmettoes, where the woods got thicker, squirrels barked and spiraled up the scattered sweetgums. I had two ways to get to my mama's, both paths wore clean by my feet over the twenty years I'd been married to Hamp, and I just about took the short cut. Wished I had.

I hadn't gone far when I heard voices that sounded way off, carried on the wind, and a fast chopping, like a young boy just learning to use a axe—glancing licks that don't count. But listening hard, I decided that the noise was coming from close by, and since nobody didn't live around there, I got curious. I turned back to my right and creeped around a turkey oak where wild hogs had been rooting for acorns. The sound got closer. I walked easy till I come up on a clearing set off in a stand of pines. And then I saw four women's heads sticking up above a patch of split-leaf plants that looked like full-grown okra.

I'd know that bunch anywhere—Colin's Lucy and her girls. Didn't have to see their faces. I'd know them by that certain loose, bedraggled hang of heads. Too lazy to be wild, they were wild-looking, with hair the color of canned Christmas snow.

Off to theirselves on one end of the patch, two of the girls leaned on their hoe handles and mumbled. Both cheeky, white and listless, like their sister on the left, who was keeping up a steady beating motion with her hoe. Hair striking like sun on a mirror.

Grayer than blonde, Lucy stood at the other end of the patch, resting on her hoe handle. "Y'all stop that jabbering and get to work." She ducked and stood with a plastic jug and went to swigging.

One of the girls doing the talking sassed back but started hoeing around a shaking plant.

"Don't chop it down, nut," shouted Lucy, high-stepping through the spiky leaves to the girl. She popped the girl's jaws. Her head didn't even bobble. She just stood there, blue eyes closing like a tilted doll's.

"You got ery idee what one of them things is worth?" Lucy turned around and started searching through the patch for her own hoe.

The girl went back to work, cussing every other breath, long straight hair sliding over her face.

A breeze blew up over the woods and the surface of the patch shimmered like oil on water.

Marijuana. I knew that's what it was and I hadn't never laid eyes on no dope before. Okra, Lucy wouldn't have been hoeing. Wasn't a industrious bone in her body, her girls' neither. They'd set around all day at Colin's little shack up the road and watch tv, the girls nibbling on potato chips and swigging cocoalers, Lucy slugging whatever liquor she could lay hands on. The place a mess. I hadn't never seen them hit a lick at a snake in the five or so years they'd been with Colin. But give them something to get into, something might bring in some cash or make them feel like they were into meanness, and they were go-getters.

Lucy's girls had been after my boys since they got there. Didn't go to school and went with anything in pants. Last time they come to the house for dinner, the oldest one set out on my porch, leg cocked on the arm of a rocker, and set fire to strands of her clear, coarse hair. Wore shorts up to her split. Bo Dink and Israel gazing like she was some movie star. (Little Noah hadn't took a interest in girls yet.)

I ducked behind the oak, listening to them grumble and fuss, a light coming on in my head. So, that was what Colin and J.B. had been up to. Dope! Hamp'd die. No, he would kill them. He was bad against dope. And I had to agree with Hamp— moonshine wasn't nothing next to dope. Everybody in the flatwoods messed with moonshine; we were noted for it. If the law happened up on a patch of dope next to a shine still, they'd pick the dope to come down on everytime. Now, I had a whole new set of worries: if dope was out in the flatwoods, the law would be looking closer. And what if my boys got into dealing dope? What if they already were?

I slipped around the oak, nerves in my kneecaps jumping. I halfexpected to run up on some more dope, figured J.B. and Colin had marijuana in spotty patches all about the woods. Uh, huh! While Colin was in Florida, gator-hunting, he'd put Lucy and the girls to work. So, that's how come they hadn't been to the house lately; Lucy might get tanked up and talk. I hadn't thought much about them not coming, cause generally I didn't mess with them and they didn't mess with me.

As I come out of the strip of woods between my place and Mama's, I could hear bees swarming. Their singing seemed to hover with the sun over the side yard between her little frame house and Daddy's old store. The smell of honey pulsed thick-sweet and drawing.

Mama was standing before the row of white bee hives set along the edge of the west woods. Dressed in green twill pants and a brown plaid shirt, a felt hat covering her bushy red hair, she looked like my daddy. "Don't come over here," she hollered. "Bees don't know you." She claimed the bees knew her by smell, like pets, and would sting anybody else.

"I'll wait here." I stood watching as she eased to the next white box and lifted the souper, setting it on the grass, then picked up the bee smoker and puffed twice inside the brooder. Smoke rose blue to the fan of sunshine coming through the trees, like the glory rays off Jesus in the picture at church. One by one, she lifted trays of cones and stuck them in a shiny bucket, put the tops back on the hives, and tipped with the bucket to the back porch. Setting the bucket on the floor, she hurried along the side of the unpainted house.

"I'd done give you out." She sailed her hat to a twig chair on the front porch. Her brick-red hair was matted on the crown and bushed around her keen face.

I went to itching. "I had a little holdup at the house." I didn't want to go back through it all, hoped she wouldn't ask.

"How bout giving me a hand," she scolded—her rough voice didn't go with how little she was. She began gathering from the edge of the porch a jar of honey, a mess of collards, wrapped in newspaper, and her black doctor bag that old Dr. Pennington died and left her.

I crossed the yard and took the bundle of greens. Why did she always make me feel so useless and lazy? Why did I let her?

We walked off through the dewy grass ditch to the clean dirt road, her swinging the bag by its flaky leather handle.

"Car still in a bog?" I asked.

"Fool thing!" Her short bow legs made long strides, quick steps that dug the toes of her brown brogans into the panned dirt.

We hadn't gone two yards before she stopped, listening while she gazed across the fenced-in field on our left. A swarm of wild bees buzzed over one of the pear trees. "Let me run go get my bell and saw," she said. She set the bag and the jar of honey in the middle of the road and went to walking at a half-run back toward the house, freckled elbows pumping.

My God! I thought, if I'd been the one held her up, she'd have harped on it for a week. I didn't know what Hamp might get in his head to do to the revenuer and me not there. I needed to get done and get home. "Come on, Mama!" I twisted in the road. "Damn bees!" She made a little dab of money selling glue the bees put out to seal off cracks in the hives; found a place in New York through *Market Bulletin* claimed they used the waxy glue to seal cracks in music fiddles. She didn't even like honey, didn't sell it now, and like so many of the beekeepers' wives in the flatwoods, she'd become allergic to the stings.

I heard the tinkling of her bronze hand bell from the rear of

45

the house and watched as the bees settled in a cluster on a bent limb of the pear tree.

She straddled the fence off the yard, walking fast through the field of goldenrod and rabbit tobacco. Hand saw down by her side, she sneaked up on the tree and started sawing the limb with the bees on it, a cluster that hung like frosted ice. Then she carried the whole limb, off from her body, stepping high and light back the way she come, to set it on the ground before one of the hives.

Directly, she come grinning up the road to where I was, her scrubbed face red. "Got'em." She picked up the jar of honey and the black bag and set off walking, a step ahead.

Yeah, Mama, I felt like saying, you can out-walk me, out-do me, out-think me. I don't care. I don't want to be like you and stay here till the sap's sucked out of me. But I didn't say anything. I'd go on being something for women in labor to hold to while my mama delivered their babies, and if she had her ruthers, I'd do the delivering after she died. Huh uh.

"Reckon that gal's gone make it two more weeks?" Mama asked.

"I don't know." I didn't care, just so it was after Friday, just so I got done and got back before Hamp killed our company. Bo Dink could be smoking dope on the porch, for all I knew.

"Nine times out of ten, they drop when the moon fulls," she said. "But you know that, don't you?"

"That's what they say." Those women should keep up with their periods, not make us have to guess and check moons.

"You and the boys sang at church yesterday?"

"No'um." On Saturday she'd asked if we sang Friday night. I decided to turn the talk around to her. "Mama, you need a Jeep."

She looked back, searching my face.

I stepped up beside her, in line with her eyes. "Mama, I ain't looking for the Bigtime," I lied. "I just need to get off from the house now and then."

"Ain't nothing wrong in that."

"But I can't lie and say I want to take over your birthing business for a bunch of fool women."

"That's nature for you, Missy," she said. "But if you know they're fools, you're not, and that puts you in charge."

"Mama, you don't know how bad things are getting at the house." Then I told her all about Colin and J.B.'s dope patch, how scared I was the boys might get to dealing dope if we stayed.

She gazed off at the steady *ta-ta-tat-tat* of a Lord God. The giant red woodpecker looked stuck to the riddled trunk of a dead poplar. "I been knowing they's dope in these woods," she said, "but from what I been seeing on the tv, they's dope everywhere."

"Well, I still can't run the risk of my boys getting mixed up in J.B. and Colin's dope doings. We've got to get out."

"They's more ways out than taking the hardroad." She knocked on her head with knuckles made big from regular popping. The older she got, the more she talked in riddles, and I knew the answers but let her go on. I'd do what I wanted to do, always had. She hadn't stopped me from quiting school and running off with Hamp, and after I had babies, she made over them like it was her idea. Dropped by the house daily. Till they got grown. Till her and Hamp had a falling out. Big bully that he was, he acted scared of my mama. Now I knew why he was scared—when she laughed at you, you felt like a worm. She'd laugh if I told her about the revenuer.

Dobbie Stover's dogs come yapping from behind a junked car set down on its rims in the rank grass where crickets seemed to gather from the close woods. All around were old tires and trucks and drums, a woodpile of fresh sawed logs on a bed of pine bark. A axe stuck up in a leaning block near a scatter of raw split wood, the smell of tar sharp in the heating sun.

I spotted Dobbie's pulpwood shoulders as he slunk around back of the half-painted house, seeing us come up. It made me mad the way he treated us like the law or some preacher come to beg him to go to church. The last baby we delivered for Jean, he puffed up and said, It's about time everybody took care of their ownself, and I knew he was trying to get out of paying us, blamed Jean for putting his pride to such a test. Men!

Jean's two little white-headed girls, wearing long white shirts, slipped out on the front porch and stared over the half wall under the punched-out screens. One was gnawing on a finger.

"Hey, you girls," my mama said. "Ain't y'all cold?" She tramped on up the wobbly block steps to the porch and set the honey on the screen ledge.

I laid the collard greens beside a little girl's black patent shoe and some wadded britches covered in dog hair.

The girls took off running, barefeet slapping through the house where the sun from the back streaked through. "Mama, Mama," they hollered, "it's Grannie come to see you."

Everybody called her Grannie or the grannie woman, meaning midwife, and everybody in the county loved her, except Hamp, who called her the widow woman. (Her name was Dell, but I could count on the fingers of one hand how many times I'd heard her called by her given name, always felt funny even calling her Mama, and generally, to cut down on confusion, I'd say my mama.) They hadn't started calling me anything yet, and I didn't look forward to taking her names.

"Y'all come on in," Jean hollered from the back, then come waddling through the house, holding her high belly.

Every pregnant woman around placed their hands flat on their bellies when my mama got near them. More and more at church, I'd been noticing them doing it to me. (My mama didn't go to church; I went just to sing and to get the boys to go.)

"We come by on Saturday," Mama said. "Course you was gone."

Jean's drab blonde hair hugged her round red face like it was damp. "Yeah, we had to go to town. Get groceries."

"Your blood pressure's up," Mama said, putting her bag on a slick-nasty brocade chair. "Here, you girls hang onto this for me." Mama handed each of the little girls a necklace of raisins from her bag.

One girl scooted up on the chair and set, twitching her toes and gnawing raisins, while the other gnawed a finger instead of the shriveled brown necklace and leaned on the chair arm to watch.

Mama took the blood pressure cuff and the stethoscope Dr. Pennington left her with the bag and went over to Jean, who'd plopped loose on the couch.

Jean laid out a arm, the other one crooking automatically over her eyes, while Mama wrapped the cuff round and listened through the stethoscope.

"Huh," Mama said. "Ain't the worst I seen it. You laid off the salt?"

"Some," Jean said, eyes covered, head resting on the couch back. The corners of her thin mouth twitched.

Mama watched her face. "Hog meat?"

Jean's lips moved.

"Lay off the salt and hog." Mama moved the stethoscope down to Jean's pooched belly.

The axe on the woodpile went *kr-rak kr-rak*, clean strikes and splits.

"Little fellow's heart's just a-knocking." The back of Mama's neck was grooved where her hair curled up. "Moving much?"

"Driving me crazy." Jean set up, smoothing her green flared smock over her belly. "Dobbie says he's gone be a reg'lar rooster, kicking like he do in the middle of the night."

Mama put the stethoscope in the bag and went to mashing Jean Stover's swole ankles, purple stretched skin on cracked dried feet. "Well, you tell Dobbie for me, I wouldn't look for ery boy. Carrying too high. Showing all signs of another girl."

49

"Oh Lordy!" Jean sniggered.

The wood chopping stopped.

Plundering in her bag, turned away from Jean, Mama pulled out two bottles, both whiskey-bottle brown. "Health department sent a bunch of stuff for me to pass out." She held up the biggest bottle to the window and shook it, squinting at the rattle of tablets. "Sulfur for impetigo." She handed it back to Jean, passing the little bottle with a black rubber-top dropper from left to right hand, then on to Jean too. "Cod liver oil for the bowlegs." She cackled out. "You got plenty of aspirins?"

"Some." Jean, holding the two bottles in one hand, leaned over to look in the bag.

"Here"—Mama was still pilfering and rattling in the bulging bag and passed back a clear bottle of white tablets— "have some more on the gover'munt."

The little girl gnawing the raisin necklace climbed down from the chair and draped her tube-like body across her mama's lap. Jean picked at the child's hair with her free hand. "You got erything to dose the lice with, Grannie?"

"That youngun got a case of the headlice?" Mama turned, hands on her hips.

"Both of 'em do."

"Well," Mama said, "you bout as well cut that head of hair off then."

Dobbie snatched open the back screen door, his face red and puffed up. "Ain't nobody cutting my girl younguns' hair. Answer to me if they do." He turned to the bucket on the watershelf and started swigging water from a metal dipper.

"Well," Mama said loud, snapping her bag loud, "they ain't gone get shed of no headlice till you do."

"Let's go, Mama." I headed for the door.

"Got the damned lice from that bunch of niggers up yonder at that Head Start shit in Cornerville." Dobbie come walking our way, looking mean at Jean.

"Now, Dobbie," Jean said, sliding out and off the couch.

She snickered. "Blames everything on the coloreds," she said to us.

"Gotta blame somebody." Mama was on the porch, eyes green with youngun mischief. "Nigras don't have headlice."

The children streaked out between me and the open door, and Jean caught the least one by the arm and dragged her back, squealing.

"Jean, beat that youngun's backend!" Dobbie stood god-like in the sun tunnel of the hall.

"Let's go, Mama." I walked off into the yard, slapping deerflies from my legs.

"Don't jerk her arm like that, Jean." Mama stood on the doorsteps. "It's apt to come clear out of the socket."

Jean let the little girl go, and she laid on the floor, kicking and squalling. Dobbie hollered at her to shut up.

"Get back in here, Addie," Jean called to the other girl over Mama's head. "You gone get on a rattlesnake in that high grass."

Addie dashed through the palmetto bushes and gallberries and around the house.

"Let her be," Mama said, watching for Dobbie strutting toward the porch. "Better off out there than inside." She didn't say with him, but looked at him with fire in her eye.

Dobbie stood in the living room doorway. He stripped off his wide brown belt, and Jean backed while the girl on the floor spun like a turtle on the road.

"You lay ery hand on that youngun, Dobbie Stover, and I'll sic the law on you so fast." Mama slammed the screen door hard. "From here on out, I'm checking younguns too, taking what I know back to the county."

She never took what she knew back to the county, but everybody knew my mama, knew she had some dealings with the county; the health department not long ago had give her a set of baby weighing scales to show how much they thought of her doctoring in the flatwoods. That trained nurse didn't fool me, she was scared to death to come out there, left the dirty doctoring to my mama.

"Jean, if you get to ailing, send somebody to fetch me, night or day," Mama called. "You hear?"

"Y'all be coming back." Jean always said that to keep us straight—neighbors, not business.

"Mama," I whispered, stepping over a rain-filled tire, "you can't mess in people's doings that way."

"Hush up," she said, marching through deer tongue and wire grass, "you're still in training."

The second day of a cold front is always coldest, and by Tuesday, Bo Dink went back to school with Little Noah, leaving Israel to take out the revenuer, while I fed him, kept him covered up, and rubbed Vaseline on his rope-burned ankles and wrists. He'd about been better off with his boots on, but I took them off and put him on a pair of Israel's heavy wool socks. Israel and the revenuer were about the same waist size, so I even got a changing of Israel's clean dungarees and a shirt. He pitched a fit, said he'd as soon let some mangy dog sleep on his clothes. Then he left, mad—a good excuse to keep from helping with the revenuer.

With everybody gone but me and you-know-who, the kitchen was quiet, a mess of grits-and-egg-gommed plates scattered on the table, one biscuit left. I ate it, turning on the radio to a old Ernest Tubb song, "Walking the Floor Over You," and washed down the doughy bread with the last of the boiled-down coffee. Tubb's singing sounded like he'd started off too low or was just practicing; Israel could sing that song a sight better. I strained and scalded the fresh milk I'd just took from Filly and left the jars out to cool while I washed the dishes and tried to figure what to cook for dinner. A big pot of lima beans with ham hocks and more biscuits.

Starting with the boys' room, I straightened the beds, turned off the blabbing tv, and opened the windows to air the smell of rank socks. I didn't try to pick up their clothes, strung over the bedsteads and floor and chester drawers. I'd learned away back there wasn't any use in trying to do much, not with a bunch of men on the place. Once in a while, Little Noah would take a notion to make hisself useful, clearing the dishes off the table and such, but he was so big and clumsy he broke all my glasses. Besides, he'd eat up my leftovers. I thought about a daughter, but was glad I never had one. She'd have ended up like me, slave to every Joe come along.

Disremembering that I'd slept in Hamp's room last night— what with the revenuer in the sideroom—I started in the middle room, my junk room, to straighten that bed, but the door was latched from the other side. The door knob had come off a while ago and I'd run a nail through the thingamajigger that turns the knob, but still half the time it wouldn't catch and the door would swing free and flap in the jamb. So, I'd put a screen door latch on the other side, kept it hooked, and was forever having to go around and unhook it if I wanted to pass through. The only way in and out of the middle room was through the boys' room, or the sideroom one, and that latch had me going the long way round to get to my housework. Don't know why that one room ended up without a door to the hall— guess back then, when the house was built, Hamp's daddy had enough trouble getting it level, much less worrying with doors. Most nights I went back and to through the sideroom, facing the kitchen, but the boys were plum used to my wandering, didn't pay me a dab of mind if I walked through and them buck-naked.

Soon as I straightened mine and Hamp's bed, I stripped off my house frock, balled it up and chunked it under the ones hanging, put on a pair of Bo Dink's wore-out khakis and blue shirt. Used to, I'd have washed everything dirty on the place. But housework got ahead of me a long time ago, and I hated staying inside, even on days when the weather was bad.

Around two, J.B. come in with Hamp to eat and poke fun at
the revenuer, said he wondered how long before the law would
come looking. Set Hamp to thinking, so they decided after
dinner they'd go out and move the still closer to the house.
Pretty soon I'd have to walk around it to hang out clothes.

J.B. had just last week got drunk and run off his wife,
Jeanette, and the younguns, and now she was back. So, J.B.
would stay over there close home for awhile—except to eat—
and I figured it was just a matter of time before Jeanette would
come with her four younguns to eat too. During the day she had
to work at the telephone office in Valdosta, and some nights,
so she sent the oldest boys to school, the least ones staying with
her mama in Cornerville. I'd put my foot down a long time ago
about keeping hers or Lucy's brats— I'd raised mine, they
could raise theirs. No more taking care of younguns. And now
here I set with a revenuer.

Late that evening it turned sure enough cold, so I brought
him to the kitchen while I cooked. I tied the piece of rope I'd
cut off before to one of his legs, the other end to the leg of the
woodstove. Then I wound a strip of clothesline around his body
and the back of the chair. Before long, his thin hollow face
started taking on some color from the heat.

"You bout to roast?" I said, greasing Frieda Jean's cast iron
frying pan to go in the oven—keep it from rusting.

He didn't answer, looked off at the door like a sulling
youngun and locked his knees. He hadn't said much since I'd
played crazy—looked like now he'd lumped me in with the
rest— but I reckoned with me feeding him regular and the boys
taking him regular to be-excused, he didn't need to ask for
nothing. His eyes stayed on us, ours stayed on him.

I was getting plum used to him; he had a ripe must smell like
a deer. I spoke up loud, like you would to somebody old: "Soon

as Israel comes back, I'll see to it that you get a bath." If he was looking for something fancy, he was in for a big surprise: Hamp wouldn't put in a bathroom. Said he wasn't having nobody shit in his house.

"Incredible," said the revenuer. "This is incredible."

"Thank you."

"Actually," he said, switching from hard to soft, "what I meant was, I find it difficult to believe you're married to Hamp. You're so young and vital."

Revenuers, I figured, must have a list of fool ways to try and get free when they get kidnapped. First, he tries to get me to turn tail on my whole family, and now he's trying to turn my head. I started humming and flamming pot lids in the stove drawer.

Next, Lord help! he put in trying to talk like us. "You could shore better yourself, to my way of thinking."

I went to singing, staring out the window over the sink, and he went to mumbling to hisself, then: "Hey! Hey you, lady! If you know what's good for you, you'll cut these ropes and let me go. How long do you suppose it'll be before a search party shows up here?"

I switched back to humming again, so I could hear him. I was curious about what he'd say, and truth be told, I was scared too.

"You don't think I work alone, do you? Huh?" He waited and I kept on humming. "I have to radio in every hour on the hour, or my department will send someone to my stakeout."

Liar. If that was true, they would have been here by now.

"Do you think that a government man can just disappear and no one look for him?"

Still I didn't answer.

He jerked the foot tied to the woodstove, rattling the door on the front and sending grinding quivers up each joint of lacey rusted pipe to the ceiling.

I turned around, facing him. "You've been pretty lucky so

far—Hamp didn't let J.B. shoot you. But you keep that up and I guarantee you he will."

He got still. "Listen, lady, I'm not a bad man, I'm just doing my job. Let me go and I won't hurt you." His face looked as honest as mine.

I heard the school bus coming up the road and could tell he heard it too. He set up, listening. "Ain't nothing but the school bus," I said.

He still watched the door, hopeful-eyed.

"Alvin-the-barber drives it, another revenuer-hating boot-legger." Up the hall I saw the bright gold bus pull through the lane and the boys get off, Bo Dink striking out to the lot, and Little Noah shambling on in.

"Little Noah's here to take you to be-excused." I'd been noticing the revenuer squirming and setting sideways for the past hour but was making him wait.

"A smart woman like you must see how degrading this is...and the pain from these ropes..." He raised his roped feet and hands. "My guess is you're a Christian."

I hollered, "Little Noah, come take the revenuer out to be-excused."

Little Noah come in, starving to death, and I told him he could have some bread pudding when he got back. He led the revenuer out, and the way they both toddled off down the hall reminded me of how the boys used to rock Hamp's Mama's chair from the porch to the kitchen, day in and day out, after her stroke. You could tell they were tired of her, maybe deep-down glad when she gave up the ghost.

I was looking through my greens for lice and bugs, trying to hurry before the backbone boiled down in the pot, when all hell broke loose outside. Somehow the revenuer gave Little Noah the slip, tore out at the outhouse and hobbled clear to the front yard before Bo Dink and Little Noah could tackle him. They all three shuffled in, hassling like dogs. We got him settled in again in the sideroom, scorched pork smoke boiling out of my kitchen. I'd have to start supper over and hope Hamp hadn't caught wind of anything.

Then that night, while Bo Dink set guard, dozing, the revenuer made his second get-away. Somehow he'd untied the ropes on his hands and feet. I'd left on the light in the kitchen, me trying to get some shut-eye with Hamp snoring for all he was worth, and I heard the revenuer creeping up the hall and peeped out just in time to stare him square in the eye.

Israel's face popped out from the door across the hall. "Where you think you going?" he hollered, and Bo Dink jumped up and throwed the shotgun on the revenuer and said, "Where you think you going?" too.

Little Noah lumbered out, shook up and white, and went to switching on lights, a dull, cold stillness settling over the hall like midnight at a wake. And then they put in to rouse their pa, to figure out what to do next.

But once Hamp got good and asleep, you could roll him off the bed and he'd keep snoring. It was like he'd pulled down shades over his eyes and set some clock in his head that said go to sleep at eight and get up at five. Last summer, when the brick chimney in the boys' room crashed down in the middle of the night, Hamp never heard it. Sounded like the end of the world.

Israel, still holding the shotgun on the revenuer, kicked open the gaping door and shouted, "Hey, old man," getting louder and louder when Hamp kept on snoring.

"Shut up, Israel," I said, shoving around him in the door and crossing the room to Hamp's bed. I slapped him across the face and backed up. He turned, facing the other way, quit snoring, then started again. I waited a minute, then stepped up, reached around, and slapped him again, this time a hard bop across the nose with the flat of my hand. His eyes flew open and he rolled to his back, holding his nose. "Who the hell hit me?" he mumbled.

"Nobody," I said, "I just shook you. The boys need some help with the revenuer."

He shot up from there, mad and addled, and out in the hall with his britches held in front of his dingy boxer shorts. "Son-da-bitch!" he bellered. "I oughta gone on and knocked him in the head." He looked at Bo Dink's shotgun, looked down at his britches, then at the revenuer, who was standing there freezing.

Tin was cracking overhead like ice between teeth.

The revenuer shook his head and turned around, side-stepping along the dull silvery wall to his room. He didn't say a word, like we'd all been playing a game and he'd lost, fair and square.

Bo Dink, Israel and Hamp got to talking and come up with the likely idea to tie the revenuer's hands behind his back. Me and Little Noah couldn't stand the thought of that—he looked so peaked and pitiful—so I made them tie his elbows where the heels of his hands would just touch. They were too sleepy to fuss, so they set him down and tied his feet and wrists again, then ran a rope through the crook of one arm, around behind his back to the other. To sleep, he'd have to lay on a knot.

Soon as they went off to bed, leaving Israel to set guard, I worked the knot over to where it would rest between the revenuer's right arm and side. His hands were shaking, fisted on his chest. He kept his eyes closed, breathing quick and even through his mouth. I covered him up good and went to make sure the spigots were dripping so they wouldn't freeze up and bust.

By the third day, Hamp looked like he'd got blind to the revenuer, so I took to bringing him to the eating table, tying one end of the long rope to his ankle, the other end to the table leg, where I could eat and feed him at the same time. Course, J.B. had to show hisself.

"I shitting-shore got me a big buck last night," he said,

hanging over his full plate and getting ready to cram. "Pow! Right between the eyes."

"How many points?" asked Israel, working with his spoon around J.B.'s elbows.

"Fifteen, twenty, thirty—hell, I don't know, man. It was dark."

The revenuer set up straight, staring at J.B., now shoveling lima beans to his mouth. "30-30," J.B. said, catching a dribble of chewed beans with his top teeth. "Slick as a whistle."

"Bring us a mess," I said, trying to put a cap on his trying to shock us—no real right answers with J.B.

"Uh huh," J.B. went, chasing a mouthful of beans with half a biscuit in one bite. "Blowed his brains out."

The revenuer, beside me, shifted, raised both feet and set them down hard. "Bow season, when does bow season start around here?"

Hamp stopped chewing; Israel set back, eyeing me; J.B. put the biscuit down neat on the edge of his plate like he didn't want it to sop.

"Bow season?" J.B. said.

The revenuer answered with a plain "yes."

"You mean like bows and arrows, injun hunting?" said Hamp—not really a question.

"Yes." The revenuer, no fool, set up till his back looked like a board.

J.B.: "You ever done any of that?"

Revenuer: "Yes."

J.B. snorted, Hamp coughed, play choking. The revenuer looked fired up. "What's so damned funny about sportsman-ship, may I ask?"

"May I ask." J.B. repeated, snorting at Hamp, bowed over his plate. "You hear that, old man? Got us a sissy here, a sissy revenuer." He elbowed Israel, who fidgeted but didn't take his eyes off me. "What say we whip his ass?" said J.B.

"Shut up, J.B." I got up for Hamp some more tea. "Shut up

or else."

"Ok." J.B. held up one hand, his black eyes set on the revenuer, who stared back, blowing through his nose.

"Let's get the shit out of here, old man. Got a still to see to." J.B. put the last part to the revenuer, like he was daring him to dispute Hamp's power.

After they left that afternoon, just me and the revenuer by ourselves, I got sorry for him. Man didn't know when to shut up. Washing dishes, I saw him try to reach the knot on his right side with his left fingers, wrists twisted till the undersides laid together; everytime he'd get close, the rope hooked to his right elbow would yank the knot and elbow away. He looked like a cat chasing his tail. When he saw me watching, he set up proud.

"You want me to help you straighten your ropes, put your wrists back together?" I asked.

He just set there, staring off at the door, fingers wrapped round his crossed arms.

"Ok, you look a sight easier like that anyhow." I hadn't noticed what I was doing, had my arms crossed too, undersides together.

"You want to listen to the radio?" I said.

He didn't answer.

I turned it on anyhow, half-hearing some wild, fast truck commercial, then the weather—thirty degrees tonight—then news of a big drug bust in Lowndes County, and where President Clinton was going for Thanksgiving, some six weeks away.

Nobody hadn't been by since we caught the revenuer, except the mailman—stopping his gray pickup at the box by the road, picking up or dropping mail, then driving away. And I figured my mama's car was still in a bog. The big rain we had on Sunday probably had her friend Tinion's truck stuck too, trying to get her out. They'd have to wait till the woods dried off.

By then, I'd got to where I could take the revenuer to be-excused. Didn't bother me—not with my bunch of boys. Reckon he'd have liked to pee on me, but that was the one time he kept a civil tongue in his mouth. Looked like it would get away with him though, me seeing and handling his privates.

That evening, I took his long pale thing out and pointed it like I would a hose to water cabbage sets, it warm and tense in my hand. He cleared his throat, looking off, glassy-eyed. I waited. He cleared his throat again and shifted, me hanging to his shrinking wienie. Maybe I was holding it too tight. "You want me to let up a little?" I didn't look at it. He nodded. I let go, grabbing it closer to the root with my thumb and finger, and in a minute he let fly. I shook it off and poked it back in his britches and zipped him up, us both looking off while I led him back through the cold light glancing off the bright sand yard.

"Some things you gotta get used to, revenuer," I said, staking him out again at the woodstove.

He looked straight at me. "My name is Mac."

Well, bless pat, in two hours time the revenuer was singing a different tune, like a mocking bird, and anybody didn't know what he was up to would've took it to heart. For all his blustering and blundering, looked just like he was taking a shine to me.

I let him run on at the mouth that evening, cause truth was I liked a little attention good as the next gal. And he was right sharp, right at first—none of that "You got a fine figger for a short gal," or "Anybody ever told you you got pretty hair, or eyes, or a fine behind?" Nosir, he aimed straight for the head, going on about how smart I was, how "perceptive," how "intelligent," how he had never seen one woman turn out so much work in a day. But if I had been smitten by the revenuer— which I wasn't—that would've been his big failing too. Who but some man had a interest in how a woman could serve him would go on and on about how handy she was around the house? And like the rest of his kind, he soon worked around to bragging on my hair and face and what-all. But he was good at it, a regular poet.

"You know," he said low, hanging to my heels while I gathered eggs, of all things, from the hay nests around the wood blocks under the house, "your hair picks up just a tinge of copper in the sunlight."

"That so?" I'd play like I was won over so he'd keep jabbering. Had a olive-green army blanket shawled about his shoulders and caught at the neck with a safepin.

The evening sun played bent shadows of us from the dirt to the house, set high off the ground. It was nearly warm out in the open back yard, where the trick sand, which looked white but turned gray on your clothes and skin, spread level to the woods. Now and again, a breeze would lift from the blackgums and pines with a cold shudder of leaves, then settle into the kind of still warmth that leaves your face freezing and your body sweating.

Israel, beneath the tin shelter by the stove-in arbor of the grapevine, was tinkering under the hood of his car, and every once in awhile he'd get in and race the engine, a smoking roar scattering across the dual tire trenches cut by the house. Run-down outhouses of every kind and description—a tar-papered tobacco barn, a log cotton shed with crumbling dobbing, a outhouse with knotholes like cow eyes, and a smokehouse with shedding shingles—set among the pecan trees decorated with logging chains and fan belts, parts of old cars and fifty-five gallon drums, whatever my bunch could tote up, whatever they could find.

The revenuer toddled behind through the wire gate of the chicken yard, me reaching around him to latch it. "Do you ever cut your hair?" he asked.

"At my age, where you reckon it'd come down to if I

didn't?" I flounced on through the fussy chickens and ducked into the henhouse.

"How old are you?" he said, dodging around my old rooster humping one of my speckled hens. Aggravating rascal was forever showing up in the chicken yard, not a hole to be found in the diamond-pattern wire.

"Last birthday, thirty-seven." I darted out of the hen house and roused the rooster off the ruffled hen and headed him toward the gate; black feathers flying, he fluttered and squawked and kited up just short of the board rim of the chickenwire, then circled back around the yard after one of my Rhode Island Reds.

The revenuer stood watching from the shade of the umbrella chinaberry. My milk cow had nibbled the bud of the tree when it was just a switch, causing it to bush out even and round. "You certainly don't look thirty-seven," he said, watching Israel, good and out of earshot, duck under the hood of his Chrysler.

I stooped down, going into the hen house again, and smiled to myself.

The revenuer was standing smackdad in chicken shit, chalky stars that dropped fresh each night from the chinaberry roost. "Most women start to show some age by thirty-seven," he said. "You know, kitten-claw marks below the eyes. Crêpe-papery cheeks. Too much sun."

I went on plundering in the hollowed straw nests set in tobacco stick frames, picked up a egg, still warm and yeasty, and placed it in my wire basket. "I been out in the sun my whole life."

"You don't say."

I could see him through the cracks of the rotting boards, watched him watch Israel working up a temper under the car hood, then shuffle toward the hen house and stoop in the doorway. In that army blanket cape, he looked like a sorry magician fixing to pull another trick from his hat. "Probably, your diet of good home-grown food," he said.

"I don't diet."

"I meant..."

Israel swung past the chicken yard, toward the house, with a greasy carburetor in his hands, glowering at me and giving off a smell of gas and a disgusted glare: his car didn't work and by-God somebody was gone pay and being I was his mama, I oughta see to it, like keeping time going by winding the clock, that his car never quit.

Well, I did care if he got his car running—it was Friday and we had to sing—but I trusted him to get it fixed or die trying. He was that good at mechanicking. Besides, another old car was always setting handy, behind the pecan trees. No worry about that.

He stomped across the backporch and into the kitchen and the loud *lam-a-lam* of metal on the eating table set the old house trembling, and the revenuer picked up talking where he left off. "It's hard to believe you could have grown boys like that. Your body doesn't show it."

Of a sudden, I felt self-conscious, my whole body airing up, and wished he'd quit checking me out. I shoved past him in the low door and set my basket by the gate and dumped the dirty water from the car gas tank cut down for a chicken trough.

The revenuer, leaning on the trunk of the chinaberry now, was talking low, then he spoke up. "Can you hear me from there?"

Oh Lord, what if Hamp happened out of the woods and heard him, what if he stopped him talking and left me with nothing to look forward to but...but Hamp and the boys and supper to cook? Suppose none of the cars would crank and I couldn't get to the American Legion to sing. "I can hear you," I said. "I just know what you're peddling and I ain't buying."

"Let me assure you," said the revenuer, bowing his chest like my rooster, "that I never say a word I don't mean."

"Me neither." I turned on the spigot, rusty water ribboning to the trough—pump needed waterlogging—then turned to face him and caught his eyes and felt plum staggery.

"Don't you ever stop and carry on a conversation?" He nodded to the shade set off by the shifty sun like a stage.

"I can talk on my feet, go ahead." I turned the spigot off.

"If it bothers you, I'll be quiet," he offered.

"Might as well talk as set silent. Unless, that is, you might be smart enough to figure on Hamp and them hearing." Lie, and he knew it. From the chicken yard, you could see the house, the loft, the woods where the still set behind the blackgums. Little Noah and Bo Dink were watching tv to keep from taking in stovewood. "Go on, talk, helps get your mind off your misery."

"Speaking of which...could you loosen these ropes on my wrists? They're cutting to the bones."

"Not just this minute, I can't." I picked up my basket and prissed out of the chicken yard, hot thrills rushing through my body that didn't show I'd birthed those grown boys.

IV

can't say how come, but having the revenuer around gave me the guts to stand up to Hamp—well, a little. I had never been the quiet type, but what I generally fussed about was muddy boots and houseflies, pissing off the porch and bottles chunked under the house. After I stood up to Hamp about the rooster and about tying the revenuer's hands behind his back, I got the nerve to stand up to him about my Friday-night singing.

All day I'd been gearing up to lay down the law. I'd took the revenuer right along to do my milking, so cold I had to bundle him up like a Indian in a blanket—him bargaining, flattering, begging pity, and then rearing. I'd greased his ankles, wrists, and elbows twice that day. I'd took him with me to gather eggs. I'd tied him to the woodstove to cook. But I wasn't about to take him to sing. And I wasn't fixing to set-tail at the house and nuss him neither.

Like I said, me and the boys were halfway expected to fill in for Katy Land at Toot's on Friday nights, but if we didn't show, they didn't care. Some other group was always waiting, stood as good a chance as us of getting to sing.

Hamp and J.B. were out and in all day, staying just long enough to eat and poke fun at the revenuer. You could tell Hamp wished he'd let J.B. shoot him, then he would've saved face with J.B. and been shed of one more mouth to feed.

Late that evening, Hamp come in again, his planed face purple-pied with cold. He washed up and ate, then sallied out the back.

"Hamp," I called, coming out of the kitchen to the back porch where the sun was setting low, orange and cold, "you gone have to look out for the revenuer tonight."

He turned around on the edge of the yard. The copper pipes of the still winked through the tangle of shed bullous vines.

"The boys have to sing up yonder tonight." I rolled my hands in my apron. I felt like saying right out that I was singing too, but knew better.

"Let'em go on without you." He started to walk off, tall body making a heaped shadow on the rain-pecked dirt.

"I'm going with them."

He tilted his head, looked mean at me, made to walk off again.

"I'll leave him here by hisself."

"Ain't no such athing." He turned around, side-stepping toward the sun-blazed brick well.

"I'm going." I'd come this far, I wasn't fixing to back down.

He looked off across the east woods where the sun struck just the treetops. Didn't look mad, didn't look glad. Then his strained face turned crimson. "I swear and be-damed! I reckon I oughta let J.B. shoot him, be done with it."

"Maybe you ought to." I didn't mean it, but I wasn't letting him pull that one on me.

"Always something..." He snorted like a bull and stomped

across the yard to the house.

"I'm going on soon as the boys get back from the sawdust pile."

That's where Hamp had started burying the jugs of shine since the revenuer come.

"I bout as well go on and knock that son-da-bitch in the head." Hamp stomped up the steps and into the kitchen.

The revenuer was tied to the woodstove, arms twined like a church lady's. Stiff-necked, he gazed from me to Hamp. "Hey!" he said to me, "you're not leaving me here with him by myself."

"Hush up," I said, then went on talking to Hamp in the door. "Might oughta take him to be-excused before you put him to bed." I let Hamp get good and in the kitchen, then edged out around the eating table, feeling the revenuer's eyes on my back.

I looked behind me and saw Hamp beholding the revenuer, and the revenuer beholding him. They hadn't hardly spoke since the revenuer come. Hamp was bashful with strangers since he changed, and that was probably how come he didn't want to get saddled with the revenuer. That, and not wanting to get stuck with doing a little something around the house.

My heart was pumping in my throat. I felt mean, I felt right, I felt hot. I didn't know if I was really going till I heard the car up the lane and went out on the porch. For a fact, to my beknowest, Hamp hadn't never killed nobody, but he would jump on a man in a minute. I had no way of knowing how far he'd go. He hadn't never hit me. Maybe he thought hitting me, like having things to do with me, would be more trouble than it was worth. Maybe he hadn't hit me because a good stropping gal to keep house was hard to come by in the flatwoods.

"Merdie," he called down the hall, "you go and I'm gone put this son-da-bitch out of his misery."

Now I knew how come me not to never make him mind the babies. Going up the hall, I could hear his big idiot feet slapping the floor behind me to the porch.

"You hear me, woman?" he yelled.

"Hey, hey lady!" the revenuer called, stomping the floor and rearing. "Get back here!"

I walked straight for the car.

"I'm gone knock him in the head." Hamp picked up a rocking chair, like a play-pretty, and chunked it in the yard— wood cracking, chickens squawking and fluttering under the house where the old dog laid looking out.

Around all that racket, I could still hear the revenuer taking on, and sounded like he was rocking his chair clean through the house, yelling, "Hey, lady! You, lady, get back here!" Thought I heard something like, *Don't make me have to kill nobody*, but it could have been the other way around, and besides the revenuer would have said it proper. I decided it was just my conscience talking.

The boys set mum, watching, while the idling car sputtered, backfired and spewed smoke.

"Go on, Israel," I said, getting in and slamming the door, my teeth gritted so I thought they'd crack like the chair.

Israel stared across Bo Dink and me at Hamp tromping down the sun-bright hall with his elbows pumping. "Ma, you ain't fixing to let him...?" Israel asked.

"Go on, Israel." I turned my back to the window.

Israel eased the car in first and pulled around the cluster of oaks, slow like he thought I might change my mind and get out, then puttered up the dirt road, his and Bo Dink's faces like wood Indians.

"Yeah, go on, Israel," Bo Dink mumbled. "We ain't getting into this."

"Shut up," I said.

Little Noah squirmed, kneeing my seat. "Aw, he ain't really gone do it. Remember that sorry old bird dog he was always gone kill."

"Shut up, Little Noah," Israel said, "that dog got loose."

I ain't never been no scareder, and I almost got out halfway to the hardroad and walked home. "Go on," I said, pulling my hair around in a ponytail. "No, back up." We'd passed the logging road that went to J.B.'s place.

"Ma'am?" Israel stopped the car with a squeal of brakes.

"Run me by J.B.'s."

He backed up slow and cut in where palmettoes rustled cold at the base of the pines. When we pulled up in front of J.B.'s trailer, I got out.

"Be back in a minute." I left the door open and hurried across the weedy brown yard, stepping high over brick bats and bottles and junk. Coming off the cool air of the north woods, fresh shit smelled strong from where J.B. had hung a croker sack between two pines, like a swing, for them to set on and do their job. Said he didn't want to fiddle with no septic tank or outhouse, him having to pick up and move everytime his pa took a notion to relocate the still.

The tv was running wide open, the younguns were tussling, and J.B. and Jeanette were fussing, making the windows of the blue trailer shake. Something glass hit the wall and shattered to the floor.

I knocked and the door flew open, and there stood J.B. with his shotgun aimed at my face, like their fussing had been a front.

"I come to see Jeanette a minute." I looked past him into the sun-flooded trailer. "Jeanette!"

"Come on in, Merdie, if you can get in," she hollered with her mouth full. Two snotty-nosed boys darted to the door and stood staring around J.B.

"I ain't got but a minute," I called.

J.B. backed into a chair before the door, eyes trained on the tv. The boys disappeared, feet grinding on the floor.

Somebody switched the tv channel from laughing to talking and J.B. jumped up and yelled at the younguns—done forgot me.

Jeanette slouched to the door, brushing her black bangs from her forehead. "Merdie, I ain't seen you in a coon's age." Tall and stout as she was, she always craned her thick neck like she had to look up to talk.

"Jeanette"—I got one word out. She strained to hear around the racket, her broad face jutting up and out. What sounded like a pot hit the floor inside, rolled and settled, humming on its bottom. I tried again but she still couldn't hear me.

"Y'all younguns cut it out!" she shouted and clung to the door, fingernails bit to the quick. The racket rocked on. Time was moving; for all I knew Hamp could have done knocked the revenuer in the head.

"Jeanette," I said loud, "I need you to do me a favor." I hadn't never asked her for a dime.

Her mouth flew open; she peeped down at me.

"I need you to go over to the house and set with Hamp and the revenuer..."

J.B. hooted, rearing in the chair.

I tried to ignore him. "You know about the revenuer?" I asked Jeanette.

"I heard." She laughed, nervous.

"Well, I gotta go with the boys to sing and I need you to mind the house till I get back."

"Merdie, I swannee..." She looked at J.B., some secret between them. "I'd be glad to help out, but I just come in from work, got these younguns with a cold and..."

J.B. jumped up, grabbed his shotgun from the corner behind his chair. "I'll set with the revenuer." He laughed wheezy, bunched fat shaking under his white t-shirt.

"J.B., you set foot out that door with that shotgun," I said, "and I'll turn you in, dope, moonshine, and all. I mean it."

Mad must have showed on my face. He propped the gun in the corner and set again. I didn't know if I would do it; I didn't know if I wouldn't. I was too tired and too mad to be messed with.

"Merdie," Jeanette said, bending close, "J.B. ain't bad, you know? He's had a hard life, what with his mama dying when he weren't nothing but a boy. Old man loco like that... J.B. can't help the way he is."

I knew that bunch at the telephone office had been swapping that Phil Donahue psychology bull again: nobody could help the way they was. I took a ten-dollar bill from my pocket—the only money I had to my name—shook it at Jeanette. I'd kept it on me when we went to sing to make me feel like somebody with a right.

She looked at J.B "Well I reckon I could..."

"Old man's apt to lay him low," J.B. snorted.

"Shut up, J.B." I said "Jeanette, keep Hamp off the revenuer."

J.B.'s jowls, set against the sun through the filmy windows along the west wall, looked·like the yellow calico cowl on my rooster's neck.

"And don't leave there till I get back," I added, shaking the ten-dollar bill.

Jeanette took the money, and I knew she'd give it to J.B. for cigarettes and beer—gave him every dime she made. She was weak like that, but she'd bow up at Hamp like a man. Good. Keep his mind off the revenuer. And I could count on her to keep anything from happening. If it hadn't already.

Israel like to never found the American Legion on Williams Street where we belonged to sing. You could drop him off in the middle of the Okefenoke and he'd find his way out, but take him to town... And I was up tight over the revenuer and Hamp, over Hamp and Jeanette fussing and fighting like they'd do. I did try to keep peace when she come over, but one time Hamp turned over the eating table, food and all, because of her sassing him. Much as anything though, I was worried that our new manager wouldn't show. Had we give up Toot's for some new place didn't know us from Adam?

We had dropped off the load of shine along one of the side roads out of Tarver, and I hadn't said a word about us being late. The boys were nervous enough. Bo Dink and Little Noah couldn't understand why we didn't go on to Toot's where we at least stood a chance of getting to sing. Israel looked like he didn't give a flip if we sang or not, just so we didn't haul no shine to Valdosta again. None of them mentioned the revenuer again. I reckon they figured he was history.

The sky hung low with scrappy, gray clouds, and the cold had let up the way it'll do in South Georgia—warming up just long enough to rain, then turning cold again.

The building, off a side street in Valdosta, was dark-looking, despite the street lights. Cars and trucks were parked in every spot on the lot dotted with shedding crêpe myrtles.

As Israel drove back and to along the rows of cars, looking for a parking spot, I was so nervous my hair felt like it was pulled too tight. He drove around the last row, and I saw our big-bellied manager smoking on the stoop under the red canopy. He stared at us, looked like he recognized the car, dropped his cigarette and mashed it with the toe of his snake-skin boot. Israel parked and switched off the car, but our manager still stood there, his beard bushed out across the bottom half of his face.

I was beginning to feel that sweet stinging in my chest, my face tingling like it'd do just before I sang, but below the stinging, my gut rolled thinking about the revenuer. I felt like I'd left a sick man with a murdering nurse. I hadn't never really been selfish before, always put my whole family ahead of myself. Well, I thought, I'm still doing it. But the boys couldn't go on living to where they'd as soon deal dope as shine, to where they'd as soon shoot a revenuer as a rooster.

First thing, when we got out of the car, our manager jumped us for being late, then waddled up the walk. He had a little skip in his long strides, one toe snagging and sliding ahead, like a dance step. We followed, not knowing if he meant he was through with us or was leading us inside.

While I talked to him, Bo Dink and Israel set up to sing on one end of the dim room, which looked like a house with all the walls and ceilings knocked out. Tall domed windows were set between thick wood rafters. Little Noah stayed close on my heels. "Run on, honey, help the boys," I said, turning to the manager. I could feel Little Noah breathing on my neck. "Run on," I said. He cleared his throat and clomped off to the stage, swinging his guitar as he stepped up. The boys acted like they were scareder of our manager than they were the crowd, which was bigger than we were used to at Toot's, but not all that different: drinking and smoking and eating, not paying much mind to our manager telling me off, or the boys fumbling around the jumble of stools and mikes and cords strung across the platform. I figured after the bright lights and the crowd at the auditorium, the boys would be ready for anything, would take a lynch mob over that crowd with nothing to do but gape and hoot.

Now, our manager set in to fussing about us making up words to go with tunes. My face burned like it did one time at school when my picky third grade teacher got on to me for mashing ants with the toe of my shoe during recess. I didn't know I wasn't supposed to, still didn't. She sniffled and said I ought to be ashamed of killing harmless insects. I'd been raised slapping mosquitoes and yellowflies, killing anything that could kill me. And youngun though I was, I knew she was picking on me because I didn't have pretty manners. Her and her pretty manners wouldn't have lasted a day in the flatwoods. After she died, after fire ants come to plague us, I wondered what that mealy-mouthed old lady would've said if she'd seen me pour boiling water on anthills.

Our manager went on smoking and fussing while I stood off with my arms crossed. Gas space heaters, spotted about the room, hissed blue and low behind all the racket. Every now and then, a warm wave would pass over the airish room. I didn't tell him I hadn't listened to the words on the radio, I just made up my mind to listen from now on. It was me learned the boys the wrong words, and now I was messing them up, had that to add to my guilt of leaving the revenuer with Hamp and Jeanette. Oh, Lord, she'd make him wish Hamp *had* knocked him in the head.

"You ever heard of K.T. Oslin?" our manager said, bending to hook up two black cords trailing from the platform. He didn't wait for no answer, just started fussing about us not holding notes and not singing out.

"Ok." He stood quick, brushed his hands on his shiny black pants, and stepped up to the mike and tapped it. Staticky knocks sputtered from the jutting speakers along the walls, loud in the round of babble. Everybody got quiet, a low mumble like bees, and looked at the front of the room, at us.

"Well, folks," our manager started, talking into the mike like he was kissing it. "I got a real bang-up treat for you-all tonight." He looked at me. "Get on up here, Merdie." He talked in a made-up country voice.

I stepped up and felt like I was still stepping up as I went to the mike pole. I hadn't never been talked straight at by anybody introducing us.

"Folks, this here's Merdie," he said.

He made room for me.

"Merdie here's from all the way up in Tennessee," he said. "She's sung clear all over these United States of A., got a record fixing to come out next spring. Y'all make her welcome."

He stepped back, clapping high, right over my head, his tick-tight belly brushing my arm. Everybody out there went to clapping too, the waitresses stopping in the midst of the close round tables with their trays of beer bottles and glasses held high. Our manager strutted off the left side of the platform, one boot toe snagging and sliding, and stood off to watch, still clapping like he had a spell on all the clapping hands in the room. Sure enough when he stopped, they stopped. They scraped chairs around to watch us, and the waitresses went on, setting out drinks where the flames of squat candles picked up on the glass in overlapping light. Overhead, cigarette smoke looked like low clouds settling stillness just before a rain. The heaters hissed.

I unhooked the mike, its static keeping time with my heart. "Me and the boys would like to start out with a old-timey tune dear to my heart." I didn't have no notion what it was, knew the boys didn't neither, but it would be one I at least knew the words to—something old from the Grand Ole Opry. Next time, we'd be singing some of the new stuff. My face was on fire, the sweet stinging gone. "Ever now and then we get a hankering to do some oldies and y'all look like a bunch could prechate 'em."

The crowd clapped and I knew I could lie with the best of 'em if that's what it took; I knew too that this big, strutting manager was just what the doctor ordered. We were on our way. The only weakness I could find, showing he wasn't quite so sure of hisself, was the break in his gait, the sliding dance-shuffle of that one big foot. I started singing "I'm Walking the Floor Over You," Israel's only good song, and listened for him to join me. But he just stood there, picking his guitar, so did the other two.

I'd get done with one, the crowd just a-clapping because they thought I was somebody and they thought I was good—which I was now I'd got to believing it—and every time, with each new song to bring the boys in, they'd back off and let me sing, filling in just on the chorus.

During break our manager went to talking down at me again, fussing because I didn't sing clear, putting down my whang or my looking at the floor instead of at the people. Then he'd go right back on and blow me up to be somebody. I got plum swimmy-headed. The boys looked like they were glad to be tucked along the wall where the light didn't hit.

We got done around two in the morning, and I figured that

was the last of our manager, but he shuffled up from the room behind the platform and shelled out three ten dollar bills from a doubled-up stack in his hand and told us to be back here next Friday-night. I had all ideas he'd kept a hundred for every ten he gave us. I didn't care. I signed a autograph for some woman with fat brown hair in one of those ten-cent-store autograph books. "Merdie Lee," I wrote, then said it out loud. As the woman walked off, the manager told me from now on, I was plain Merdie, and for me to call him J.J. He didn't never mention the boys.

When we got in the car and got going, I gave a ten apiece to the boys, and it looked like it tickled them. Bo Dink and Israel got to teasing me about the lies, said they'd never known me to lie. Proud. I could tell they were finally proud of me. For lying! Halfway happy and sick, I let it go, and all the way home made fun of our manager to make them happy. And deep down, I did feel good, wide-awake and talky.

At the house, Jeanette met us on the porch, rubbing her sad brown eyes. Her happy face didn't go with her eyes. She could have a big time just eating and talking; even whining she looked happy, except for the eyes. Nothing she liked better than a good fight with J.B. to give her something to whine about. Yellow-faced in the porch bug-light, she whined about Hamp trying to run her off, about the revenuer rearing and begging, how she had to be at the telephone office by six in the morning.

"My feet's so tired," she said, craned her neck and yawned, then backed to the settee Hamp had knocked wopsided during his fit.

Now, I was beholding. And if I let her set, I'd be stuck talking all night. "J.B.'s going to be looking for you," I said and yawned.

She struggled out of the settee before she got settled good

and yawned too.

I yawned again to keep her going. That was mean of me, but there were only so many ways to get shed of Jeanette.

She looked like she was under some spell. Her eyes were closing. "Believe I'll be going," she said.

I couldn't say thank you and remind her she'd done something for me—that wouldn't work. The most natural thing in the world to say to somebody who had done you a favor, a favor that changed your life. I was drunk on how the night had gone, not just the singing, but how the worst that could have happened at home, hadn't happened. Everything would be ok from here on out.

Jeanette was talking again, about to set on the settee again. "Merdie, tell me, how come y'all to end up with that revenuer?"

Oh, Lord, now she was trying to get close with me. "Israel," I hollered out in the yard where he was leaning against one of the oaks, "how bout taking Jeanette home? She's too wore out to walk."

She rolled her shoulders and moped off the porch. "Well, just looks to me like they ain't no way around a killing."

Little Noah and Bo Dink were already in their room, already had the tv running.

I went down the hall to check on the revenuer, thinking how right Jeanette probably was about the killing, but somehow fear would't stick on top of joy. He was laid out like a corpse on the cot, but his eyelids were twitching. "You need anything before I turn in?"

He opened his eyes, stared right through me.

"You mad with me for leaving you, huh?"

He didn't say a word, curled his long fingers on his arms, rope tugging at the elbows.

"Want me to grease your arms and wrists again?" They were chapped red, almost bleeding, made my stomach gnaw to look at them.

He still didn't answer. The room was quiet, the noise of the tv stifled by the junk room between the boys and us.

"Awright." I started out. "You don't want to talk, we won't." I couldn't stand him being mad, didn't know how come. I turned around. "I wouldn't like to be left with Jeanette and Hamp neither." I set on the bed, right at his feet.

He squirmed away, to keep from touching me.

I ran my finger under the rope on one ankle; his skin felt hot and damp, even through the wool socks. "I have to go sing Friday-nights, might as well get used to it." I waited. "I sang tonight, I sang real good." I smiled, couldn't help it, felt stupid, light and satisfied. "I gotta learn words to the songs, though. My manager says." Guess I wanted him to know I wasn't just another girl singer with a dream. I thought about that lil ole half-good gal had been singing Katy Land's songs, swaying and squinching her eyes just like Katy, and Katy'd crawled all over her for not being herself, which as Katy said was bad enough, but copying somebody else made her a nobody. That's how the revenuer made me feel.

I'd never said I sang to a living soul. "My manager made me out to be some bigtime singer, said I had a record coming out in the spring. Said I was from up in Tennessee." I waited for it to register in his cold, lightless eyes. "I never let on different."

He didn't move a hair, looked helpless and sick, for once not blabbing. And I thought about the ants I'd poured scalding water on.

I knew he thought I was crazy. I got up and straightened his pillow and set again and felt silly but couldn't stop talking. Course, I wasn't sleepy. "You like good singing?"

He turned his face to the wall.

I could smell my cooking on him strong, and that seemed strange, but he was no stranger now. "Ok, I'll let you alone." I'd never felt stupid before, and his look made me feel like the worst kind of liar.

I turned off the lamp on the pine chest and started out,

saying, "Good night," and closed the door behind me. I was so glad he was still alive, still there.

Long about that weekend, Bo Dink went to showing hisself. I mean worse than ever. Always bad to lay claim to a certain tube of toothpaste, a towel, haircombs—my this and my that— he come in the kitchen late Saturday evening, toting his own box of Sugar Pops. The kind of cereal that has funnies on the box for poor Little Noah to ogle over.

"This here's my box of cereal," Bo Dink said, "and nobody better not be caught eating out of it." One hand was on his waist and him blowing, body cocked from the knees like a spring.

I was rocking by the door, while the revenuer set by the woodstove, trying hard not to look at one another. All day I'd tried to be friendly, and he'd treated me like some dog. Enough of that.

It was nigh dark, still too light outside to turn on the electric lights, but too dark without them.

Bo Dink got a bowl out of the dish drainer, took a jug of milk from the ice box, and loped to the table. He swung his skinny legs over the bench and set, steady griping about the sorry food I'd been cooking, about the smut from the woodstove on the ceiling, about the revenuer. "I'm sick and tired of helping out with him," he grumbled. "Why we can't be like everybody else is a myst'ry to me."

I kept on rocking, watching as he ripped into the box. He was always finding fault with what we had, kicking chairs because they were old-fashioned, fixing to bring the house up to date. Ashamed of us, was what he was. One time I found where he'd been hiding PTA notices sent home from school, got sorry for him and went to one of their meetings, taking him with me. And from the time we got there till we left, he never once spoke to me. Acted like he didn't know me. I didn't want to go in the first place. Truth be told, I figured in the USA, people put too much faith in education and psychology. Pat treatments for all the world's troubles. And if I could have been what Bo Dink wanted, I wouldn't have, because when he got through that stage, he'd go through another one, and I'd have to change again to please him.

"Don't you reckon we look funny to other people," he said, "having a dadburn revenuer around?" When he saw I wasn't fixing to answer yay nor nay, he poured the pellets of brown cereal in his bowl, smooth forehead curling as he peeped inside. "No dadburn prize!" he said, daring me with his wide eyes. Then he poured the milk on his cereal, starting in on my milk cow. "Been eating bitterweed again," he said, turning up his nose. Spoon clicking on his teeth, he went to gobbling the stuff down.

The sun through the window over the sink hit him in the eyes. "Looks like you'd hang a curtain up there," he said.

I could feel myself heating up. My rocker creaked. The revenuer set still and sulky beside the woodstove with a low fire purring in time with Bo Dink's crunching. He mumbled something, ate another mouthful, and looked like he was plum pacified. Then the band of sun dropped, throwing the room in shadows.

"Ain't nobody gone turn on the light?" He set there, waiting, then mumbling to hisself, swung off the bench and stomped around in front of me and yanked the cord on the overhead bulb. White light showered down and pushed back the fuzzy orange light.

Bo Dink's long shadow folded from the floor to the wall as he crossed to the bench, set again, and went to eating while reading the funnies on back of the box. "Don't look for me to be eating none of your slop tonight, Ma," he said. "And if you looking for more firewood out of me to warm his backend by, don't." He nodded at the revenuer, who set gazing from Bo Dink to me, grinning more than frowning.

I still didn't speak, went on rocking. I'd wear the flinder

rackets out of Bo Dink if I got started.

"Anybody touches this here box is gone answer to me," he said.

I heard the hall floor screak and looked up to see Hamp standing in the doorway. His black bug eyes roved over me and the revenuer, coming to rest on Bo Dink, who was still grumbling. My whole body went stiff.

"How come y'all burning the lectricity already?" Hamp said. "Ain't dark yet." He took three steps and stopped in the middle of the kitchen. His big hand shot up, yanked on the light cord, and the room quickened dark.

"Hey, I can't see," Bo Dink bellered.

Hamp took one giant step to the table, reached across, and popped Bo Dink's jaws. "That woman there's nussed you with the earache a many a-night, and don't you forget it." Hamp tromped out.

I stopped rocking, the revenuer let out a breath, Bo Dink went to sputtering cereal and milk and bawling—"Ma, Ma." He swung from the bench, crying as he come around the table, wrist clamped over his mouth.

"Don't you ma-ma me," I said, rocking again. "I don't blame your pa." I did blame him. I could have killed him for me and for Bo Dink. I could have killed him for blowing up the little stuff and not paying the big stuff the boys did one bit of mind. I could have killed Hamp for bringing the revenuer in to upset the satisfaction of my sorry life.

V

The revenuer was mine now, that was clear.

Come Monday again, I set him out to sun on a five-gallon can while I hung the wash. I pinned up a white sheet between him and the still, barely hid behind the blackgums. Wouldn't be right to tempt a dog with a bone he couldn't get to.

A blue smoke was rising from the still through the tree tops and blending blue with the lake-like sky. Trees like a rim of reflection on water. Where the yard met the woods, grass was trying to grow—now that my boys had got up some size and had quit digging for treasures and the dog had got too old to dig, brown strands snaked to the well. But my back yard had got to where it smelled like hog slop from the souring mash and sugar that went in the shine. Every so often, Hamp would bang a bucket or clink some jugs, and the revenuer would try to peep around the sheet.

He was mad—not that he talked much now anyhow. You

could see it in his eyes, the way all morning he'd been looking cross and jumping up before I told him to. Trying to show how much of a prisoner he'd come to be, how bossy I was.

Hamp had stopped by the washer on the back porch, while I was feeding shirts through the wringer, and said, "I oughta gone on and knocked him in the head," and I thought the revenuer was fixing to bust the ropes and tear out after him.

During the night, he must've tried to get loose again. Only way I had of knowing was by the rope burns on his arms and wrists—just about bleeding from where the thorny braiding had sawed into his flesh—and how he'd worked one wrist on top of the other, knot sticking up on top like a big rough scab. His arms set high and proud on his puny chest. Made me so sorry for him I forgot to act mad too.

Out at the clothesline, I heard a car coming from away off. I stood listening and watched the revenuer's eyes dart toward the back of the house where a dun strip of north road showed through the dried dog fennels and green pines.

Hamp meandered between the blackgums and stood in the shade and gazed at the gap of road, his strong face sallow in the shadows. Directly, he creeped on up behind the sheet and peeped over at the revenuer, all of us trying to figure which way the car was coming from. How close. Sounded like it was getting nearer on the straightaway, then faded out on the curves.

"Probably deer hunters," I said and hung up the revenuer's red and blue streaked shirt. Looked funny on my clothesline, like I'd raised some enemy flag.

At last, a brown car slued on the curve and braked in front of the house, sun bouncing off the glass bubbles on top. "Just the sheriff," I said.

The revenuer leaped up, knocking over the bucket, and Hamp busted through the sheet, it draping on his head like a A-rab.

"Get him in the house," Hamp barked in my face and dashed

the sheet to the dirt.

The revenuer went white and dodged around the wash pot. Hopping toward the woods, his socked feet gouged bunny tracks in the damp sand. Hamp grabbed a wet towel from my basket and chased him down in the blackgum shade, looped the towel around the bottom half of his face, yanking him back.

The sheriff out front set idling like always—burning that county gas.

I followed Hamp, circling toward the house, him leading the revenuer by the tail of the towel, the revenuer just a-moaning and straining and walking at a sideways strut, his gorged green eyes cutting toward the woods. How come the revenuer to pick the woods over the front was a mystery to me.

Hamp shoved him to the corner of the house where the watershelf hooked to the sideroom. "Israel," Hamp hissed, knocking on the porch floor. "Get out here with your shotgun."

Israel was there before you could count to three, shotgun pointed ahead. He ducked under the watershelf and hopped off the porch and stuck the barrel in the revenuer's chest. All three of them stomping around in the Prince's Feathers Hamp's dead mama had set out.

"Now, keep him there," Hamp said, brushing his hands and walking off around the house.

I could hear Bo Dink, done out on the front porch, talking to the sheriff, both their voices carrying down the hall to where the revenuer was sliding in the mudhole.

"Sheriff wouldn't do nothing nohow," I said to the revenuer, then to Israel, "move that thing." I knocked the barrel to the side, and Israel gritted his teeth at me and stuck the point right in the revenuer's face.

Israel hadn't never showed no mean streak before, but now his eyes turned hard, made my hair feel singed at the roots. The revenuer got still, backed against the brittle, grayed boards with sunbursts of tar. He closed his eyes.

I didn't want to see my own son shoot nobody, and I didn't

want to see that poor man, revenuer or not, with a hole in his head. When he closed his eyes my heart heated up. It had been easier to not like him when he talked. I went up the back doorsteps, brushing my feet like I'd generally do, and looked down to where Israel had the revenuer hemmed up. I knew right then that Israel was more Hamp's than mine.

The radio was running in the kitchen, where I'd left it on, trying to learn words to new songs, specially K.T. Oslin's. I'd been hearing her all along but hadn't caught on that she was nobody special, just music, strange because it was new. And all music, which I'd loved since I was little, seemed dead there for a minute. No, I wouldn't give up trying to get my boys out and away from Hamp. Here we finally were making some headway, got a manager and all, and I start finding out my boys ain't interested in what I'd tried so hard to get for them.

I went up the hall, facing the chilly breeze and listening to Bo Dink talking to the sheriff. Ten years ago, Israel had set on the doorstep just that way, looking up at the sheriff, where if he'd been standing level on the yard he could've looked down on that sawed-off, black-headed son of a gun. My biggest boy taking it all in, all the meanness in the sheriff's slick mind, and then changing—a crossover from boy to man, a crossover from good to bad. That's when a gun come to mean something to shoot a man with, same as a deer, and that's when moonshining took on a whole new meaning for me. Israel never crossed back over that line.

Sheriff Crosby stood on the yard with a dusty church shoe propped on the bottom step, his close-set blue eyes staring hard up the hall, past Bo Dink. Sheriff didn't never look at who he was talking to.

I stepped to the wall, listening.

When Hamp come around the corner of the porch, the sheriff shoved his hands in his pockets and backed up, his short shadow falling long across the steps. "Hamp," he said.

"What can I do you for sheriff?" said Hamp.

The sheriff crossed his arms and strutted his pot gut, the way some men do their chests. "I come to get your boy here to do some lectioneering for me."

"That so?" Hamp leaned against the porch with his legs lapped.

The old dog wandered up the hall, sniffed me, and passed to the porch where he sprawled in the sunshine next to Bo Dink.

"Fine weather we having this morning," the sheriff said, looking anywhere but at somebody. "Yeah, I figgered Bo Dink here could take my car and pick up the voters, furnish 'em a pint of your shine and a five-dollar bill to vote for me."

Same way he'd started with Israel. I stepped out to the porch and stood against the wall. "Sheriff."

"How you, Merdie?" He never looked at me. If you were to see him off somewhere without the badge and didn't know who he was, you wouldn't think he was nobody.

"I'm fine," I said, "but it don't make no difference. Bo Dink's not for hire."

Hamp eyed me. But I had him over a barrel, I figured, because of the revenuer.

"Ma!" Bo Dink piped up. "I am for hire, I want to."

The sheriff stared off at the woods where the sun was coming up over the trees to the clearing of the yard only to go down beyond the trees behind the house, a vain course. "Pay's good, Merdie."

"Ain't that good," I shot back.

Hamp laughed, raked his fingers through his lush black hair. "Get on back in the house, woman." He propped his foot on the edge of the porch.

I just stood there, a little scared, where generally I'd have done what he said. How come? Because I always did what he said, because I couldn't very well tow a bunch of grown boys off who didn't even know to want to go. And now Bo Dink...

"Bo Dink, you got better things to do than set and listen to such." My head felt full and light; my mouth wouldn't stay shut. I come in a wan of bringing up the revenuer, but the sheriff wasn't on the level nohow, and the revenuer weren't no more than a dog, some game.

What the sheriff generally did was to take "a little dab of money" from all the flatwoods' bootleggers for heading off the revenuers and for letting us know when they were coming— if and when he knew—and anybody running shine through his county could count on having to leave a little something, say, a couple of hundred rolled in a snuff can under some dumpster, for example. Don't call me, he'd say, call up my brother and leave word. But in this case, Hamp was a little thicker with the sheriff, sold on halves, had to give him a cut of every red cent he took in. The sheriff didn't never have to get his hands dirty, stayed in office, because if he went, we went out of business.

"I reckon you come to square up on what's due you," Hamp said to the sheriff, like he could read my mind and wanted to change the subject. All three kept their backs to me, and the old dog, now sleeping belly-up behind Bo Dink, raised all four paws like he was dead.

"Yeah," the sheriff hewhawed, "it's shore a fine day."

"Go get my money bag, Merdie." Hamp didn't make no move from his spot.

I'd handle Bo Dink later. He wasn't fixing to work for that sorry sheriff. I walked off down the hall and into the cool bedroom, dark coming in out of the sun, and got the floursack of money from under the head of Hamp's bed and took it to the porch. "Here," I said.

Hamp turned around and reached for the bag. "Now, get on back around the house and see to your wash."

The sheriff stood still. "Y'all ain't seen no signs of no stranger by chance?"

Hamp stretched open the mouth of the bag and dug out a fold of cash. "Can't say as I have."

The sheriff turned beady eyes on Hamp. "I hear you." He tee- heed and strolled off apiece. Crossing his arms, his narrow shoulders hiked and cast a heaped shadow on the slice of sunned dirt between the oak shade and the house.

Bo Dink eased up and straggled down the hall, his face white as cold oak ash.

I could hear the clock ticking in the front room, the radio running in the kitchen, and Bo Dink stepping light on the squawking rotten spots of the floor. The sheriff's car was puttering low, sending drafts of exhaust fumes across the yard with the warm acid smell of chicken. Out back, the rooster crowed, his five-note call throwing up the hall like a puppet's.

"Say some gover'munt man's out looking for his partner s'posed to be staked out here in the flatwoods." The sheriff backed to the porch again; his neckless head screwed round like a screech owl's. "I figgered maybe he come out here and J.B. got the jump on him."

"Well," Hamp said, standing flat and licking his finger to peel off bills from the fold in his hand to the stack on the floor, "you know J.B. Don't never get the drop on nobody. Always looking, but don't never get the drop on nobody." The dingy white sack was tucked under one arm.

"I hear you." The sheriff laughed again.

Hamp went on counting, blooded lips moving like he was sweet-talking the money.

The sheriff shifted, watching my milk cow graze on the lot. "I told that gover'munt fellow some agent or other come by and said he was going toward the line, up around Moniac or someplace. North Florida. That's where all the meanness takes place. That's what I says."

I could smell his hot hair oil, rank in the piney sunshine.

Hamp still counted bills on tops of bills—all hundreds—in the sun strip on the floor.

"They looking for the body," the sheriff said.

Hamp stopped, studying the money, then slapped down a extra two hundred. "Well," he said, picking up the stack and tugging the string tight on his money bag, "they ain't gone find ery body round here."

The old dog set up, watching the sheriff take the money, pointy-eared shadow taller on the porch floor than the two men's.

"I hear you." The sheriff counted the money with a quick riffling of the thumb and poked it in his pants pocket. Then he turned and faced the porch. "Tell Bo Dink I'll be looking for him next Tuesday." His face was solemn, eyes fixed in a blank stare at his close temples.

I knew he had a stranglehold on us, on my boys, and I had all ideas Bo Dink was lost to me too, to what I wanted for him, and just like Israel, was in with the sheriff. "You want the revenuer," I said, "go round the house and get him."

"Get in the house, woman!" Hamp chunked the money bag. I caught it.

The sheriff stood for a minute, stunned-looking, then grinned, and holding both hands in the air, shook his head and tripped off across the yard to the idling car. "I ain't heared nothing. I ain't heared nothing. Don't never mess in no family doings." He got in, slammed the door, and screwed the car through the stand of oaks, carving dust alleys up the road.

Hamp wheeled and tromped up the steps, black eyes blazing mine. Everything in me said run, but I backed to the wall and braced myself. His notched fist shot out, loomed and held midair, like he couldn't decide how best to punch me, then swung wide and slammed the wall to my left. The whole house shook. My teeth rattled. I kept my eyes on Hamp's, glittery in his blooded face, flashing back that old mocking power over all he claimed.

"I'm gone kill him and be done with it." He struck out down the hall.

"You lay hand on that man and my boys and me are gone," I hollered, coming off the wall and dashing in behind him, just in time to see Israel poke his shotgun under the watershelf and aim at Hamp.

Hamp halted, cowering, and ducked into the boys' room.

I could hear singing on the radio, and I knew I'd learn new songs, even write some myself, good as K.T. Oslin's. The boys weren't lost completely, but my heart felt like it was wringing blood. I'd got Israel on my side but with doings as dirty as the sheriff and Hamp's. I wanted more than that.

On top of everything else, Jean Stover's baby picked late that evening to come.

The boys had got off somewhere, like they'd do after a fight, and since Hamp was mad, he hadn't come in for supper. Fine by me. I was mad too, mad and ashamed of a stranger witnessing all the trash that went on in our house, Hamp lording his old power over me and my boys acting like heathen. The revenuer's forehead was swole in a blue knot from where Hamp must have throttled him when he lassoed him with the towel.

I come in a wan of cutting the ropes that evening, but I didn't. Whether I was scared or wanting to keep the revenuer there, for whatever reason, I didn't. "Don't look like you'd keep yanking on them ropes," I said, smearing black Ithmaol on his rope burns. I kept my head low to keep him from seeing my shamed face, and fumes from the ointment rose like kerosene to my aching head. My eyes caught his, checking me out, and I saw something I hadn't never seen before.

"Don't pity me." I slid my chair back from the woodstove where we set. Didn't have no fire. It was warming up to rain and already big drops pecked on the tin roof like the chickens were feeding up there.

I crossed to the cooktable and turned on the radio, looking out the window for Hamp in the dusky woods.

"You're to be pitied," the revenuer said.

That was the second time he'd spoke to me in two or three days. "You're a pretty one to be talking," I said.

"At least I'm tied up." He tugged on the rope with his bent

arms to show me and made a pained face. "You could leave if you wanted to."

"I hear you." I got mad at myself for picking the first words popped to mind, the sheriff's, who I was ready to kill because I couldn't kill nobody else, and the boys looked like they were getting deeper in with him. I wondered where he fit in with the dope doings.

"You could cut these ropes right now," the revenuer said, nodding at the butcher knife by the radio, "then both of us would be free." He fidgeted like a man used to talking with his hands.

"I wouldn't set some revenuer loose, no more than a rattlesnake."

"You're so shut-in here, you don't even know what's a crime and what isn't."

"I know bootlegging's against the law, so was killing gators. *Was*, ain't no more." I said. "And I know both's a living like anything else, feeds a lot of hungry younguns out there." I turned off the radio, stalked out, and spied my mama's chromeless car pulling up on the front where rain drops drove like shattered glass through the tent of oaks.

She laid down on the horn, then got out of the car and called over the roof, "Merdie!"

I tipped along the wall, up the hallway. Oh Lord! If Hamp come in and caught her here, it would set him off again. But I could tell by the way her red-stained face poked over the top that she was in a hurry.

She spotted me and hollered, "Jean Stover's Addie come up awhile ago. Come on."

The rain fell harder, beating on the tin. "Just a minute," I yelled. "Let me get my sweater." I took off to my bedroom, jerked a sweater from the wire clothes hanger and sent it zinging across the floor as I let go. I stopped. What about the revenuer?

Tugging on my sweater, I tore out for the kitchen. "Get up,"

I said, "we gotta go."

I didn't know if he thought I'd made up my mind to set him loose or what, but he stood on his feet and went to hobbling in behind me, boots scratching fast up the hall.

Both of us were sopping wet by the time we reached the car. I opened the back door, he slid in, and I got in beside him.

My mama turned in the seat with her arms tucked under her chin, bleached-out eyes merry and wild. "Don't look like no sweater to me. What in the world?"

"Some revenuer J.B. scared up at the still," I said, shaking out my hair. "Go on, and not through the woods. I don't want to get stuck."

She laughed—"Looks like you already are"—still charmed by the revenuer.

"Name's Mac, Ma'am," he said, bowing his drenched head.

"Name's Dell, Mister." She bowed back. "Grannie to folks what matter."

"I'm grateful to you, Grannie. Now, if you'll just head north, I'll show you where to turn off and take me to my pickup."

"He touched or something, Merdie?" She still didn't look at me. "I ain't got time to mess around with no revenuers. I got a baby coming any minute, me and Merdie do."

His eyes quizzed me, rain dripping from his brown eyelashes. "I don't get it."

"Man, ain't you learned yet?" Mama said. "Revenuers ain't welcome in the flatwoods."

"Listen," he said to her, "if you'll just stop up the road, I'll get out. You don't have to drive me anywhere."

She drove off, hitting the ruts hard, setting high with both hands on the wheel. Staring through the rain while the windshield wipers trifled with the downpour. We hadn't gone a half-mile when she stopped at a washout in the road, tapping the steering wheel. "What about right here, revenuer? Merdie, turn him loose."

From where I was setting, I could see a eight-foot gator wallowing across the gaping washout in front of the car. Water streamed like melted copper from the sandy gulley to the black-water ditches either side. Tree frogs in the pinewoods were outsinging the rain.

The revenuer, who couldn't see the gator for Mama's head, turned his back for me to untie the ropes. When I didn't, he turned again and followed my eyes, neck stretching like a pond scoggin's as he watched the gator nose into the streaming molasses ditch on his side of the car.

I didn't go to make no monkey out of the revenuer, I just didn't have a choice.

He shuffled on in Jean Stover's house behind me and my mama, shaking like a dog, and I reckon he expected to happen up on somebody to take him to the law. We left him on the couch, facing Jean's bedroom, and rushed on over to her bed, piling old quilts and newspapers on the mattress.

And if you've ever been to a birthing where the woman didn't carry on, you know you wished she would. Jean Stover wasn't hollering when we got there, wasn't hollering when we left.

Mama cackled at the revenuer as she passed through the darkening living room to the kitchen, and cackled as she passed through again, on her way to the bedroom where I was helping Jean to the bed.

"You coming in right handy," she called back to him and waved a shiny case knife like a witch's wand.

His head was resting on the back of the couch, the two little girls gawking on each side, forgetting their mama who they could see if they lost interest in the stranger and looked behind.

The only way you could tell Jean was having a baby was by her hard, heaving belly and the high feverish pitch to her eyes. She just laid there, looking up.

My mama come around to the side of the bed where I stood, feeling useless, and slid the knife under the mattress. "It'll cut the pain, Jean honey." I always felt like a quack when she did that business with the knife, but I knew she didn't believe it neither, believed only that it gave those poor women something to believe in...something to dwell on. Jean Stover's knees were jacked under the white sheet. The light of the naked bulb above drawed to the white and made the living room darker, the outside black.

"I ain't gone holler." Jean puffed. "Don't want to scare my girl babies into not never having none of their own." She kept one hand, palm up, over her eyes. Her lips parted.

My mama shook her head. "Bear down, Jean." Then she ducked between Jean's legs under the tent we'd rigged so we could leave the door open to the living room and watch the revenuer.

He was setting to where he could see straight under the sheet if he had a mind to look. But he kept his head back. And if Dobbie was to come in and catch a man looking at his wife's privates, he'd kill us all dead, I knew that. But we couldn't move the bed, didn't have time, and if the revenuer set in the chair by the door, we couldn't keep a eye on him.

The rain come harder and the house inside seemed cramped and light, the bedroom like a fire in the dark, with Jean Stover the center, stomach thrusting under the sheet.

"I can't hear myself think for all that rain." Mama popped from under the sheet like she was real interested in the weather. Her kinky red hair looked brighter in the white light, loose like she'd just washed it. She wore it pinned back above the ears, and her face looked shiny and tight, younger without its normal redness. But then, she was just fourteen years older than me. "Bear down, Jean, and you can holler. Younguns ain't studying you, can't hear nohow over all that rain."

I looked out at the dark living room, where the watery gray glow of the window backlit the revenuer's head. The girls were showing him their catalogue paperdolls. Every now and then he'd twist around on the couch, moving his knee up careful to keep from brushing the paper babies to the floor where the little mamas kneeled. At first I thought he was trying to keep from looking at Jean, but then I caught on that he was looking out the window for somebody passing, maybe trying to make out where he was, where he could run to.

"Mama," one of the little girls said, skipping into the room, "that man wants to know have we got a telephone."

"Honey, tell him we ain't," Jean whined, lifting her hand and showing red-veined eyes, like blood from the hid pain breaking through the whites.

"Go on, honey," I said. "Tell him we're almost done."

"Selfish, ain't he?" Mama said, coming up just in time to watch the little girl dash back to the darker room. "Merdic, leastways we know the revenuer's a man." She cackled out as she ducked under the sheet again. "Bear down, Jean, give me a little holler, here it comes."

Jean grunted like somebody punched her in the stomach.

"Here it comes," Mama said, "all the way, bear down. Let her hold to you, Merdie," she added.

I stuck my left arm out over Jean's chest, but she turned her head, wrist flying from her eyes to her mouth. She grunted again. My right arm I generally saved for work around the house, but my left arm was just as strong from all those years of women chinning up on it. Stayed sore.

The rain beat harder, the window over the bed sliding paint-black with rain.

When I looked again at the living room, the little girls were gone, and Dobbie stood face to face with the revenuer, one thin and straight, the other thick and round, both black shadows before the backdrop of muddy light. The revenuer's sharp mustache twitched, fingers fluttering like feathers on his chest.

Thumbs hooked in his hip pockets, Dobbie looked like he was listening, then started to laugh, rearing back with his belly bobbing.

The revenuer stepped closer, almost touching bodies with Dobbie. All at once, he quit laughing and shoved the revenuer back to the couch and looked in at us. The wind howling around the house picked up where his laughing quit.

"Mama," I said, inching toward her under the sheet. I tapped her on the head.

"It's coming." The sheet shirred from the point of her head. "One more push, Jean, the head's out."

"How come y'all to set that horseshit revenuer where he could look in on my wife?" said Dobbie in the doorway. "He yours, Merdie?"

"Not now, Dobbie," I said, staring past him at the revenuer on the couch. He set facing us, his neck stiff.

"Get out from here, Dobbie Stover," Mama said from under the sheet.

I stepped close and stuck out my arm for Jean to clutch, but she kept one wrist over her mouth, the other arm by her side. Her face was red, what was showing, like it might bust.

Then the baby cried, a keen wail like the wind dying.

Mama flung the sheet away and held the baby up by its feet, a scrap of flesh, all stringy-white and blood-streaked, trailing from the scalloped cord between Jean's legs—nothing new and nothing close to human yet.

"It's a boy, Dobbie," she said. "A mean, stinking boy." She whacked the baby on the peach-size rump and laughed while he cried.

Dobbie's lips pinched off a proud grin; he turned, eyeing the revenuer, then doubled over laughing.

I'd wondered what kind of excuse Dobbie Stover would come up with this time to keep from paying us. Now I knew. He might even sue us.

Jean dropped the arm from her mouth to her chest, and I saw the bright red print of her teeth above the wrist.

VI

The weather was no longer changing over the flatwoods. It was winter, a blue cold settling over the green pines and gray gums, dead still and waiting. Matching shaggy heads, cypresses towered over the woods and swamps, old from the roll of ages. Robins dropped in to drink from the watershelf run-off and thrash in the frost-nipped weeds between the house and the lot. Greedy crows cawed over the pecan tree next to my clothesline.

I didn't put out a washing that Friday, like I'd generally do when the sun was shining, mainly because the deer hunters had cranked up that morning and covered the woods, scouting the roads in their fancy new trucks. Nothing like how it used to be on first still frosty mornings of deer season.

The big house would be brimming with men, in from deer hunting. A buck would be hung from the tripod out back, swaying by the heel strings with its sharp head dangling from its ripped red throat. Rack of horns scraping the ground like the branches of a dead oak. A blue-dozen hounds yipping and lapping at the blood soaking into the rich dirt.

Mornings started so early, so cold, they were almost purple. Water splashing on the back-porch watershelf where the men washed up. The big boys, sleepy-eyed, would dandle their feet from the bench at the eating table, and my least ones would whine, hanging to my frocktail while I cooked, tired before the light broke day.

Back then, the moonshine business had been a sideline, what pulpwooders, loggers, timber and turpentine men did for extra cash. Something between them, a spirit of daring handed down, not dark like now.

Hamp was bad to run around in those days, left me setting at the house to brood and wait. Waiting for him to come home and eat supper, kept warm for hours. When he did come in, rank with whiskey and women, if I said anything, he'd say, *You married a man, didn't you?* Then he'd take care of me—"keeping me up" was what he'd called taking me to bed when I was mad. *Gotta keep a woman up or she'll get old.*

But he got old ahead of me, leastways older. And now the house was quiet except for the tv and regular fights with the boys. And if a deer got killed, it was at night with headlights. Most of the land around had been leased to hunting clubs, and they were up and down the roads, all over creation, from October to February, shooting wild in the woods, with Hamp raising cain. No love lost between him and the hunters, between him and the big paper companies that took his land; land left by his daddy and divided up among him and his six brothers, who sold their share to Hamp and moved away. Hamp bought them out with borrowed money, couldn't keep up even the taxes, and soon lost all to the bank except the homeplace. Then the auction, then the take-over of the paper companies, Hamp's swole-up, swaggering pride going little bit by little bit, like the blocks of land, till it was all gone, and in its place, what must have been there all along, a damped-down madness.

Away back, I'd come to the notion that men since Adam had made up a bunch of ideas to keep women in line to show off to other men, to make women feel guilty if they didn't cook, scrub, scratch men's backs, go to church and pledge the flag. So, I'd about quit feeling guilty, but I was still scared of Hamp, did what I had to. And when I started singing, it was a little like sneaking a drink or a smoke or running around. Singing at church was ok in other men's books; not Hamp's, because church singing could lead to worse. Hamp was smart.

Now, on first day of deer season, it wasn't just the buckshot I dodged—I hated deer hunters. But not for the same reason Hamp did: he hated them because they took away his say-so about who could and couldn't trespass on what used to be his land. Land he still claimed. Besides, with the hunters out there, Hamp had to be double careful running off a batch of shine. They might see the smoke or walk up on the still and turn him in.

That morning, he stayed out there on the lookout; I stayed close to the house, quick as I got done outside.

When the first shots rang out and the hounds went to yipping, the revenuer, staked out in a corner of the milking stall, flinched and gazed, trying to spot where the shots come from.

I could feel the milk draw up in Filly's bag, so I let loose of a udder and stroked her smooth belly. "Hoo, now, just them old deer hunters. Ain't gone let 'em mess with you."

The revenuer shifted in the dry hay behind me. I could picture what was going through his head—they might happen up and help him, or he might tear loose and thumb a ride out of the woods. "They come from all over, some from around here," I said. "But I wouldn't look to them for help. J.B.'s a sweetheart up against that bunch."

Still he looked off and listened, now and then shuffling his roped feet in the whispery hay.

I'd learned the words and the music to K.T. Oslin's "Wall of Tears," and this time I meant to practice. That evening in the kitchen, I picked the tune out on Little Noah's guitar and sang it till I got it down pat. Least I could practice now, what with everybody scared to come in, scared they'd have to help with the revenuer. Besides, Hamp had roamed off in the woods with J.B. to check for deer dogs baying along the branch—aimed to kill a few and set a example for the deer hunters.

The revenuer set watch in his chair by the woodstove, my singing loud in the closed room. A keen lonesome sound. Foot on a chair to prop the guitar, I watched his face, his hollow eyes. He was too quiet. Had he took sick or give up? His hair had growed out long, not like Israel's, but shaggy around his ears and scrawny neck. The skin on his elbows and wrists was festering from the rub of the ropes. This wouldn't do.

I leaned the guitar behind the door. "You looking shaggy," I said. "Want me to cut your hair for you?"

"I'm not going anywhere. Am I, Merdie?" He didn't say it exactly hateful and it was the first time he'd ever said my name. It sounded different from how everybody else said it. Even when our manager introduced us, he said my name long and loose, like a joke or country-curious. The revenuer said it like a song.

"I don't reckon you are, but a good haircutting might make you feel better." I crossed the room to his chair, sun through the window at my back raying round us. "You looking holler-eyed."

He scrubbed his chin with his shoulder. "Cut it."

I got my cutting scissors and a towel and wrapped the towel about his shoulders. I could feel the knobs of bones as I smoothed it flat. He gave off a heat like the woodstove. "Want me to move that chair over a little?"

"I'm all right. Get to cutting."

His hair was soft but heavy, like layers of duck feathers. I cut above his ears, then at a slant around his head, finishing the crown by snipping even rows between two fingers. When I let it go, it stood up. Next, I combed the front on his bony, forehead and cut the bangs above his straight eyebrows. Shivers of hair, like glass, caught in the long lashes of his sunk eyes. He smelled like fresh-picked cotton; his narrow shoulders seemed shrunk and pitiful against the ones I'd been used to—Hamp and the boys. But really he looked too perfect, tan-colored from head to toe, hair, mustache and all, like the Dick Powell paperdoll I had when I was little. Flat-stomached and even-featured. I felt sorry for him, specially when I looked over his shoulder at those fevered elbows and wrists.

"All done." I blew at his neck and ears, took the towel off and raked up the hair, then threw it in the woodstove, a high scorch stink filling the kitchen. "Don't want to chance sweeping it outdoors and you taking a headache when a bird builds a nest with it."

He cocked his head and coughed a laugh. "Where'd you hear that?"

"My mama."

"Quack medicine."

"Sassafras tea to break out the measles, cherry bark for yellow jaundice, willow bark for the headache. If you got a wart or mole you don't want, pick up a old bone and touch it; if you get snake bit, dob it with dried beef gall." I laughed like we were above all that. We weren't. "Typhoid—split open a toad and hang it around your neck till it turns green. That's the truth."

"Truths around here, like lies, are strangely uneven."

"I didn't lie to you about going to Jean Stover's."

"Turned around, what would you have thought?"

"You're not mine to let go."

"I'm not Hamp's either." He sucked cold up in his head.

"You catching cold?" I said.

"Rope. Allergic to rope." He sneezed, tried to wipe his nose on his shoulder, but wiped his jaw. "Are you singing tonight?"

"You smoke?" I asked.

"Used to." He laughed. "Had to quit a few weeks ago."

I went to my bedroom to get some Vicks Salve and my pink flannel nightgown, got some pink thread and a sewing needle, and went back to the kitchen. "Got a ruffle here on my nightgown don't do nothing but trip me up." I ripped the ruffle off and cut it in strips. Then I wrapped the strips longways around the ropes on his elbows, under and over, and fashioned them into casings with a neat whip stitch.

I could feel his breath, smell the fever, stale, see his chest rising and falling.

"Are you singing tonight?" He sounded hoarse.

"Yeah." I broke the thread with my teeth, looking up into his eyes. The hair on his arms was raised on chill-bumps. He was feverish all right. The whites of his eyes were red-stained and cornered with pus.

"Does that mean I have to stay here with what's-her-face and the old man?"

I laughed and started whipping up the rope casings around his stacked wrists. "Be glad, she won't let him kill you."

He grunted, breathing through his mouth. "Hamp's not the only threat—maybe not even the greatest threat."

"You mean J.B."

"J.B., Dobbie Stover, your sheriff. Your mother, for all I know." He sniffled again. "I've got a feeling Grannie has more power here than the Georgia governor."

"She does."

"So far I haven't found anyone eager to keep me alive so I can high-tail it out of here and report them for kidnapping and bootlegging."

"True," I said. "But if you're worrying about the neighbors, don't. They're looking to J.B., if not Hamp, to do the job."

"And if J.B. or Hamp doesn't?"

"Then you can worry."

Done sewing, I stood over him and unbuttoned his shirt. He reared back. His breath smelled sweet and warm-thick. I dabbed Vicks Salve in my hands and rubbed them together over the heat of the woodstove. A eye-burning menthol cloud swole over the kitchen. Then I started stroking the salve into his chest; he lifted his crossed arms for my hands to glide under.

"Aren't you a little worried about Hamp coming in and finding you doctoring his prisoner?"

"Hamp won't be back for awhile. Besides, he wouldn't mind," I lied. If Hamp come in now, he'd have a fit. Following the planes and swells of his chest, I kept stroking, his brown chest hair matting hot under my hands. Again I thought of his body next to Hamp and the boys' and felt he was somehow not as much a man, a mite deformed.

"You too little to be a revenuer," I said.

"What's your idea of how a revenuer should look?" He talked with his head back, his bony chest bowed. He sniffled.

"I don't rightly know nomore. Maybe the boogerman." I stuck my finger into the sucking warm salve and wiped a glob in the other palm, then worked both hands together till it was warm and runny. And again, I rubbed the salve into his hot chest over the first coat that had turned clear and slick as beeswax. His arms, tired and raw, now rested across his chest. "Guess I never thought about what one would look like," I said, "just heard tell of them all my life."

He set up, his face close to mine. "You people really are ignor...innocent. You're not putting on, are you?"

"I don't know what you mean." I knew he meant ignorant. I buttoned his shirt.

He flapped his right hand on top of his left arm. "What I mean is—you don't know—you don't think of a whiskey revenuer as human. Do you?"

"No." That was a lie, I did.

J.B. and Hamp come in a little later, and J.B. went to poking fun at the revenuer's pink rope casings. "Why didn't you go on and tack some lace on there, Merdie?" He pulled up a chair and studied the revenuer's face, a grin smeared ear to ear.

He'd let up since I'd warned him, now looked like he'd forgot.

Hamp stood in front of the open icebox, swigging buttermilk. Holding the fruit jar from his white mouth, he said, "We got two of them son-da-bitch's dogs, left 'em in the road."

I wondered if he remembered it was Friday night. This time I wouldn't say nothing; I'd just send one of the boys for Jeanette.

J.B. was talking crazy to the revenuer, like he would to anybody else. "One time a whole carload of revenuers run up on my ass, me hauling a load up around Pearson. Had me a old fifty-two Chrysler, and that sonofagun would some run." He wheezed a laugh. "I walked off and left them bastards. And you can believe it or not, but the *pure* mercury in the speedometer run out on my feet." He drew a line across the toes of his boots. "Got the scars to prove it." He hooked the toe of one boot on the heel of the other, toeing down and heeling up.

"J.B.," I said, turning from the cookstove where I was frying the first mess of squirrels since last winter, "hadn't you better be getting on?"

He stared at me, then at his boots, one halfway off, and tugged it on and straggled out.

Hamp acted like neither J.B. nor the revenuer was on the place. He slammed his glass on the cooktable and started out. "Tell that bunch of pussies when they get in, I want some post oak to build more standards for the two-ton. I'm heading out with J.B. for the Swanoochee to kill some more dogs."

"Hamp," I called out, "the revenuer's caught cold, can't blow his nose."

Hamp snorted, slammed the door.

I went over, picked up Hamp's white handkerchief I'd left on the revenuer's lap, and held it to his nose, let him blow and wiped it.

"Thank you," he said. "Why do you stay here?" His eyes were watery and bright.

I laughed. "I got younguns, man."

"They're grown."

"Little Noah ain't but fourteen."

"Take him with you."

"Where?"

"Wherever."

"On what? My looks?"

"Your talent."

"I'm trying to." I started to step away but his right hand lifted. I thought he was trying to wipe his nose, but when I picked up the handkerchief again he caught my fingers.

"Undo the ropes, Merdie. I've got family worried about me."

"I can't help it; I don't want to know."

"I've got a son too."

"Don't talk to me," I said. "Get up and let me take you to be-excused before I go."

He stood and shuffled out behind me to the back porch bathed in cold bluish light.

"You need to go to the outhouse or just pee?" I said.

"Just pee." He sniffled, wiped his mouth with his shoulder. "Ahh."

At the doorsteps, I stepped down and waited for him—right foot down, yanking the left, feet together, starting over again, down all six steps, till he stood flat on the packed dirt—then I walked on ahead across the slant shadowed yard.

When we got to the brown bushes off the lot, hid good from the house and the road, I turned and unzipped his dungarees and pulled out his long pale wienie.

He spraddled his legs, much as he could, sniffled and stared off at the lot, seeming to go into a deep study.

In a minute, I felt his warm wienie shiver and then stream hot piss on the dead weeds, making a crackling sound. Smelled sharp and feverish. When he got done, I shook it dry and started to poke it into his pants.

"Merdie, don't..."

"Don't *what*?"

"Don't put it up," he said, like he meant the it to be a him, in a voice low and hoarse and not for nobody else but me—no, us. "Hold it awhile longer." He breathed faster, harder, looking around toward the house, off at the loft, at me.

The whistle of the six o'clock train at Tarver crossing sounded out over the woods, where above the new moon hung, a gash in the cold blue.

My face felt hotter in the cold outside than by the fire. This wasn't the same as cutting hair and doctoring; if Hamp heard and saw this I wouldn't never make him believe I was just relieving the revenuer's bladder. I looked around too, at the head-high dog fennels behind, the woods ahead. Not even a breeze in the blackgums where the still set. Swanoochee Creek, where Hamp and J.B. had gone, was a good two miles to the east.

"Hold it tighter," the revenuer said, closing his eyes.

I squeezed and felt it grow thicker, harder, longer, rubbery strong, but with a velvety warm feel, and pulsing alive. Directly, he tipped his head back and moaned and spurted clear white jets to the brown grass. The whole time I'd held my breath, hot all over. Now, I looked at my hand, at his milk on the dead weeds.

"Thank you." He stood up straight, his wienie shrinking and peeping between the teeth of his zipper, runny around the little eye, like it was sick and cold and anxious to go back inside.

Weren't no different from his nose.

At the American Legion that night, I sang "Wall of Tears" by myself, picking along on Little Noah's guitar. The boys hadn't never heard tell of no K.T. Oslin. After that song, they did like I used to, making up words to some tune picked up on the radio, then belting out the old stand-bys. They sang like they meant it only when I chose those old stand-bys, and I'd stayed after them all week to listen to the radio. I felt mad and guilty, mad because they hadn't listened, and guilty because here I stood with Little Noah's smoked-brown guitar, him loose-handed behind me.

Our manager looked like it did him some good that I sang that one by K.T. (that's what he called her now), and the crowd purely loved it, he told me during our first break. But about halfway through the night, I got to noticing they'd as soon I sing the old stuff. Anything to dance and drink by.

But everytime break come, our manager would start in meddling again: "Smart bunch like this didn't come to hear none of that sanging-troubadour crap."

I didn't say nothing, but when we went on after the last break, I passed Little Noah his guitar and told everybody he was going to do Elvis: wake him up like my daddy did me when I was about that age, bad to moon and make people wonder if I could sing or not. Little Noah looked like a hog with his throat cut, but he sang, and it was bad. I knew I'd done him a disservice, but he didn't know no other songs good, and I'd seen him imitating Bo Dink's Elvis and I couldn't just let the youngun stand there on the stage mouthing chorus.

Our manager kept grinning—the crowd didn't seem to pay no mind—the later it got, the more tanked up and tolerant they got—but when we got done for the night he blowed up at me.

"I told you that Elvis crap is out of style." He poked out his lips with his belly and toddled off, one foot sliding and snagging, circled and come back to where I stood by myself along the wall.

"That was Bo Dink done it last time." Arms crossed, I

looked him right in the eyes.

The boys had gone to get them a drink. Everybody else was clearing out the front.

"Don't matter." He quietened down. "Ok, Merdie," he said, lifting his chin till all I could see was his bushy beard, "we gone have to let that boy go."

"Little Noah?"

He nodded.

"Forget it." I started to walk off toward the open side door where cigarette smoke boiled out like the building was on fire.

He headed me off. "Listen here, you know he can't sang worth a shit. You know it." He was all pumped up, stomach working with his breathing.

"I don't know no such athing." I stepped around him and out the door and leaned against the rough wall of the building. I did know. "Let me work with him."

"How come he can't just stand there and pick his guitar?" He leaned beside me and lit a cigarette.

"Because he wants to sing," I said, stepping away to look at him. "He's the only one of the bunch wants to go to Nashville."

He dragged on his cigarette, squinting, and studied over what I'd said. "Yeah, ok, just see he don't sang no more of that Elvis crap, and train him good before next Friday night. I got two gigs lined up for y'all."

"Two?"

"Friday night, here, Saturday night over yonder at Top Twenty on 84."

Katy Land must have died. "Don't know if we can get off on Saturdays." I looked through the door for the boys, all hanging around the bar. Israel had some gal cornered.

"How come?"

"We just can't," I said, going on before he could ask. "We live way out yonder in the Swanoochee County flatwoods."

"Here's a little extra for the gas." He pulled out a wad of cash and counted off four tens in my hand. "Go up 84, out of town on the left. You can't miss it: they's a big sign says 'Top Twenty.' Green canopy sticking out from a gray brick building. You got any falsies?"

"What?"

"You know?" He cupped his hands on his chest, puffed them out with his cheeks.

"Nope."

"Well, I'll get you some. I got a red sequin dress I got off a old gal sings for me. Big boobs, but about your size. I want you to wear that dress next Saturday night. And put your hair up high. Got to get you looking fancy."

Before I could answer, the boys trailed through the door, lugging their guitars. I wasn't fixing to fuss about the falsies, because, like Hamp, the boys might get mad about some man mentioning my bosom.

I balled the money in my fist and walked behind them to the car. I'd give them ten apiece and keep the extra ten to pay Jeanette for setting with the revenuer. Still didn't add up. I'd need ten more for the next week.

On the way home I had my little talk with Bo Dink about the sheriff. Everything come out wrong. I used Israel as a example of how somebody could turn out, how somebody could get into bootlegging and get stuck—"Like dope," I said. (I wasn't ready just yet to come right out and ask or accuse.)

Israel blowed up, then sulled like he did when he'd failed trying to fly. He was about nine then, and somehow he'd come up with the idea to make a pair of wings from chicken feathers, said he just knew he could fly. *If my chest and back and arms is strong enough to swim, I can fly. All I gotta do, Mama, is get the wings right.* I made the mistake of telling him that he could do anything he set his mind to—what I always said. I hadn't been paying good attention's what it was. So, everyday he'd set out on the back porch in a circle of feathers collected from the shedding chickens and mend them by pressing the split fringe along the curved feather boning. Then he haywired them together, layering feather over feather, till finally he had a pair of limber wings. Next, he wired a wing to each arm and practiced bailing off the porch, flapping like a clipped chicken. At first, the wings turned under, but he kept rewiring till he got them tight, then headed out for the sawdust pile.

When I heard him crying and cussing, I set out running in a cold sweat, expecting to find my biggest boy-baby sinking and smothering under a cave-in of hot, rotted sawdust. But there he laid, sprawled at the bottom of the tall orange hill, sawdust from head to toe, like he'd been mealed for frying. Broke feathers scattered from the peak of the pile, on the sliding trail down, to the bottom, some still hanging bent from his corded arms.

Now, I was beginning to think I was better at making Israel see where he went wrong than where he could go wrong, maybe save my least boys. Or maybe I was just looking for some way to cut them all loose and leave me free. Then I wouldn't hurt so bad when they did what it looked like they were going to do anyhow.

Bo Dink said he didn't care what I said, I wasn't fixing to ruin his chances of making a little on the side from the sheriff. Besides, he said, puffing hard in the back, thanks to me we now had a revenuer on our hands and the sheriff would turn us in if he didn't haul voters.

Maybe that was the truth, but no maybe to it, Bo Dink was itching to drive that sheriff car. I got mad with him and Israel, took Bo Dink's ten back, glad that at least I'd have enough to pay Jeanette next week. Then I jumped right in with the news: "Next week, we've got to sing on Friday *and* Saturday night; got a new gig over at Top Twenty, someplace off 84."

Then Israel and Bo Dink really put in to rearing.

Saturday nights, Israel always ran shine for the sheriff, from Macclenny, Florida, to Thomasville, across the state line, a longer run with faster cars and fancier rigs; the big Chrysler he picked up in Moniac had a shine tank built in from behind the front seat to the cooter hull. Doing right at 145 mph, when he got to Thomasville, he'd make the switch—keys in one place, cars in another—and make another long, fast haul back to Macclenny, without seeing a single soul all night. The law on both sides would give him the all-clear, without ever showing theirselves, or let him know if the revenuers were on the lookout. He'd make a smooth hundred dollars, always did, which beat the hell out of ten for singing.

Bo Dink said he wasn't fixing to sing in some new place. And poor Little Noah just set there, fat, dumb and happy, the only one willing to sing where I said but not able.

When we got home and I started down the hallway, I could hear Hamp snoring in our bedroom and Jeanette talking to the revenuer in the sideroom. The door was open a crack and the light from the lamp streaked across the floor boards.

"I told my first old man he could set-tail at the house and starve if he wanted to," she said, "but I was going out to work. Gone get me a job where I can feed my younguns. That's when I got on at the telephone office. Course it's changed a sight now. Used to, operators got to talk back and to with callers. Now, we just set there..."

I tipped to the door and peeped in at Jeanette, setting with her legs sprawled in the chair by the bed. The revenuer was asleep, breathing rough through his mouth. Splotchy-red cheeked and white around the gills.

"He's sawing logs," she said when she saw me. Got up and stretched, yawning.

I went over and placed my hand on his forehead; hot and dry as fire under glass. "Israel's out waiting in the car to drive you home." I gave her one of the tens in my fist.

She took it, mouth open and chin up, gazing down at me. I thought she was fixing to tell me she was doing it for free.

Huh uh, I wasn't about to buddy with her, have her under my

frocktail everytime I turned around. This was business. "Next weekend we got to be gone Friday *and* Saturday." But if I wasn't a little nice, I could lose her. "Reckon you can come over and set again?"

"Lord help, Merdie, I don't know." She stumbled around, going to the door. "I might have to work night shift, and besides, J.B.'s rearing, ready to fight me everytime I come in. Thinks I'm having things to do with that poor ole revenuer." She shook her head.

I handed her the other ten and brushed past her, headed for the kitchen to get him some aspirins. She followed me and stood looking over my shoulder while I got the bottle of tablets from the window sill. I started to turn around to get a glass for some water and bumped her with my elbow, but she still stood there. Hoping she'd get the message she was in my way, I slid along the edge of the sink to where a row of glasses was turned upside-down on a towel.

Her onion breath was strong on my neck. "Merdie, I don't hardly know how to tell you this but... Well, looks like J.B.'s got it in for you too. You know, for you getting on to him about the revenuer."

I turned, trying to look calm but almost dropped the glass.

"Yeah," she said, flinching like I might hit her. "Somebody—weren't me—told J.B. about you sanging with the boys."

I didn't even know she knew I sang. Thought everybody but my mama figured I just went with the boys. "He better not tell."

"He would," she said, "he'd tell in a heartbeat. Ain't nothing J.B. wouldn't do and him mad, he can't help it..."

"I don't want to hear it, Jeanette, don't start." I waved her off and walked to the hallway.

She followed me like a kitten. "He about got the story from somebody from church, that's where I got it from."

"Just tell me if you can come again next week or not." I stood at the sideroom door, my back to her. "Ten everytime you make it."

"Well, I'll see you then." She waddled off down the hall, taking her coat from the nail on the wall by the porch. "Looks like the revenuer's suffering from headcold to me. You got any Benadryl?"

When I went in the sideroom again, his eyes were wide open, and he was sucking cold up in his head. "I can't take any more of Hamp and Jeanette," he said. "They've argued and hollered, all but came to blows. And her talking...God!" He threw his head back, coughed. "Even gave me a math lesson; told me how ugly both she and her first husband are, said that's why her children are so ugly." He laughed. "Aught plus aught makes aught, she said."

I got a clean handkerchief off the chest and held it while he blew his nose. Then I picked up his head, and when I placed the aspirins on his tongue, his hot scabby lips touched my fingers.

"Are you really going both nights?" His head stayed sprung when I let go.

"I've got to." In light of the new threat from J.B., I really did; it's called making hay while the sun shines.

He closed his eyes and groaned; his hands were lapped on his chest, pink flannel casings black with Ithmaol ointment.

I covered him up to the chin and put a extra quilt on top. He was shaking bad. I switched off the lamp, went out and closed the door.

The boys didn't guard no more since the revenuer's arms and all had got so raw; he'd learned the more he yanked, the rawer they got, and I reckon he figured if he got loose wasn't nobody but the gators and a bunch of bootleggers and deer hunters out there. And from what he'd said that evening, he was looking for one of them to lay him low.

I went on in my bedroom and put on my pink nightgown— it came up above my cold ankles without the ruffle—and laid down, listening to Hamp snore. Wide awake and cold, I thought about Little Noah and the manager, Bo Dink and the sheriff, me and Israel, this new business with J.B. setting solid on my stomach like something bad I ate for supper. The sheets were cold and stiff, rattled if I wiggled my toes. Felt like they'd been starched and froze on the clothesline. But even the cold couldn't take my mind off my troubles. Finally, it came to me that if I would lay off J.B., he wouldn't tell because he couldn't risk me telling Hamp about the dope. He knew I'd tell, too. So, shifting a new frame in my mind, I checked back over all the old worries, trying hard not to think of the revenuer and what went on when I took him to be-excused. But that's all I could really think about, that and his shivering with fever, his eyes begging me for more than not leaving him next weekend.

Hamp had built a fire before he laid down, and now it burned low and cold, casting orange butterflies over the mound of his body.

I thought about how crazy I'd been about him, wild and strong, when we got married, how I loved him now like one of the boys, like Israel when he got hurt bailing off the sawdust pile. No, I didn't never want Hamp to go to the pen and him crazy. It'd be the easy way out for me—it would—but shut up, he'd die. I was glad I didn't have no money to send him to some asylum, I'd have been tempted. Besides, if he got caught for bootlegging, the boys would get sent with him. Everlast one of them might get sent off for dope. If we didn't kill one another first. I felt like I might cry, though I never did, never had, didn't like women who did. Women like Jean Stover and me and my mama kept the flatwoods children from starving, we also kept the flatwoods in children.

I got up and tipped out of the fire-spotted room to the dark hall, hearing the tv fizz in the boys' room. I eased on in the sideroom—my bare feet freezing so that the soles were like walking on cardboard—and closed the door. What I had in mind, or thought I had in mind, was cutting through the sideroom to get to the middle room, but the old body must've had different notions.

I could hear the revenuer breathing slow, like he was waiting, and I knew he was awake, maybe listening for me to come back.

I slid under the covers and pressed against his side, smelling the rope and feeling it rough between my breasts, his arm hot through my gown. He moaned and wiggled over for me to lay down.

"Hamp," he whispered. "Where's Hamp?"

"Sleeping."

"The others?"

"Watching tv, shh! I come through here all the time on my way to the middle room to sleep."

"What's to keep them from short-cutting through there?"

"Junk in the middle room and you in the sideroom. Them scared you might ask for something. Besides, the door between their room and the middle room is latched." I placed my arm across him and pulled close, and he moaned again.

"Go to sleep," I whispered. "One peep and I'll be in the next room before you know it."

Then, he rolled his face to mine, breathing quick, warm and wet. "Merdie," he said. A song.

VII

fter that night, I went in every night and slept with the revenuer, me knowing I'd be going before I went: back and to regular, checking the latch on the middle room door, spotting the squeaky rotten boards among the solid ones on the hall floor; and then when I got to the revenuer's bed, staying awake to listen for Hamp and the boys till the rooster crowed at the corner of the watershelf and sideroom wall. Then I'd get up, ease out to my own bed, and lay down to sleep till good sunup. I'd have a fire in my belly the livelong day—something torturing, something sweet.

On the second night, the revenuer, shivering cold and scared, set in to begging me to cut the ropes anyhow, to take off his clothes anyhow. I didn't and I didn't touch him down there except to take him to be-excused. He didn't never ask me to hold it again, but I wanted to. I wanted to bad. I wasn't dried up like I thought and knowing that must have made me a little happy, that and knowing that I could make a man want me again. But I felt guilty thinking that too, and silly. What man wouldn't want a woman, no matter what she looked like, being she was the only woman he could get to? Animals ain't picky neither.

I got mad with myself, and all day long while I minded him, I'd tell myself I wasn't interested in no revenuer, wasn't going to sleep with him no more. But I did, and I got to where I was looking in the mirror, fixing my stringy hair, even took to parting it on the side or pinning it up one.

Tuesday rolled around and Bo Dink went with the sheriff, and I must have been waiting for something to make me glad enough or mad enough to do what I done.

I waited till the boys got bedded down good, watching the tv, then paraded through the fizzy blue light in my nightgown, like a sleepwalker, and yanked on the nail knob of the door that went to the middle room, fussing low because it was latched from the other side, and then I passed back through, with them ducking to see the tv around me, and marched straight down the hall to the sideroom.

And that was the night I went in to the revenuer, thinking about Hagar going in to Abraham, and while standing over him on the bed, I picked out the knots of the ropes on his ankles, him still and breathing against me, the kind of breathing a man does wanting a woman bad, or maybe just wanting a piece. I couldn't wait, and yet all the time I was picking out the knots in the dark, I was looking for Hamp or the boys to bust in and catch me, waiting for the revenuer to hightail it out the door. I wasn't scared of him though. All of those feelings mixed together just made me want him more, something hot in my head streaking to my groin. I got his feet undone and laid the rope by the bed like you would a pair of socks. He pulled his knees up, then set on the edge of the bed, breathing hard and on hold, while I worked at the rough knot that drawed his elbows back. He still didn't say nothing, just went to breathing even like he was too scared to breathe hard the way he'd been doing. One time I thought I heard a rotten floorboard squeak and stopped, waiting, and we both held our breath, staring off in the dark. I started to put the ropes back on while I could, started to make a dash for the middle room bed. He seemed to read my mind.

"Nobody's coming, Merdie." He strained to me, breath sweet as dew on my face.

I felt Hagar's fire in my head, Abraham's pull in his loins. I undid the knot holding his wrists together, and he jerked his arms around front, went to rubbing them and breathing quick and happy, scared to be too happy, to hope. I felt like a fool, just stood there over the bed. Blue-black spangles going off behind my eyes. Now he could get up and go or reach out for me. His choice.

He set there, his leg touching mine, like he was trying to figure which too.

"Go on," I said.

He stood up, his body not two inches from mine, heat shaping his form in the dark. "Merdie." Sounded like he was fixing to say I'm sorry.

"Just go," I whispered.

He shuffled to the door, the way he did when he'd been roped, rattled the knob, and come shuffling back. Then he put out his hand and touched me on the chest, feeling up for my shoulder. Both arms went around me; he pulled me close and like a man hungry, kissed me. I kissed him too, my ears ringing like locusts. He rubbed my back, his body molding to mine like cooling wax, then melting hot in the cold room. Something shutting out all but us, one. I was lost in him—that's all I know. Maybe I was a little lost in him because it had been so long since anybody had loved me, and never like that, but I felt in love, in-love like I always sang about but never felt. And there's a big difference.

Later, I expected him to get up and go but he didn't. He made love to me two more times during the night, us both straining our ears to pick among the ordinary sounds for anything out of the ordinary, straining our eyes for light brightening the gray seams of the door, and straining to hold one another like one shift of light or sound might break us. *Us.*

And still later, I expected him to go; I could tell he expected to go too. He kept setting up, laying down, rolling to me, and everytime whispering "Merdie" and kissing me like he couldn't stand the cold on his lips. And if you don't think fear makes you hot, try it. We laid clutching each other against the coming light and racket, just around the corner of the next blood-tingling peak. His body was little like mine, and fit to where it felt like we were paperdolls cut overlapped. No matter what else I thought that night, no matter what else I doubted, I never doubted that he wanted me as bad as I wanted him, and I've never felt guiltier because if he hadn't he'd have gone then.

Maybe he thought he'd go the next night, sure there would be a next and a next.

I got up when the rooster crowed, raw as a virgin, and put the ropes back on just like they were, and neither one of us didn't say a word.

That day I learned something important about men and women and loving, how come the world to go on, people to go on having more babies, despite sin and starvation. One more thing I now knew—I couldn't claim ignorance like Jean Stover and them. Loving that good, you'd think we'd have been satisfied, but all that morning we both were in an air pocket of wanting. When we went out to milk the cow and hang clothes, and when I cooked dinner, it was there around us, a craving on air, drawing us together, him at the woodstove, me at the cookstove, the radio running and the songs a background for our wanting. I didn't touch him except to take him to be-excused, and every time he was hard, wanting me and making me feel more a woman and more sure he wouldn't try to get away, no matter if I untied him and left him walking around loose. A trap. A good-feeling trap, like bogging in a feather bed. Everybody else seemed way off.

Bo Dink thought I was mad with him, the other boys didn't notice, neither did Hamp. And it seemed to me for sure that everybody could tell, but they just walked around our pocket of air. I even forgot to worry about moonshine, dope, singing, and what baby was due when.

The revenuer's eyes never went off me, and for the first time since I turned old I wished I was young, felt bad about my sun-tough face, my sapped body. But my breasts felt full as they had with milk after my babies were born; I tingled all over.

My mama come up after dinner, and me and the revenuer went with her to Pineland to make a sick call on Injun Gal's old man. Me scared to death mama could tell. But there I set in the backseat with the revenuer, our knees touching hot.

What I'd done to throw Hamp and the boys off was pick another fight about who had to mind the revenuer. I wasn't fixing to take him with me, I said, and Hamp hit the woods and the boys hit the hardroad. Well, I wasn't fixing to leave him with them neither, they'd said, and them doing their dead-level best to tend to business.

If the revenuer was hoping to run up on somebody to help him, like at Jean Stover's, I couldn't tell it. His knee kept pressing mine all the way up the hardroad to Fargo.

About halfway there, we passed the silver fire tower, spearing the blue sky, sun striking like matches on the shiny corners of the room at the top.

My mama rolled down the window, wind beating at her fuzzy red hair. She waved at the tower keeper, then rolled the window up again, gazing in the mirror. "If you looking for somebody up there to help you out, boy," she said to the revenuer, "don't get your hopes up. Emmacee Mae keeps the fire tower, looks out for revenuers same as fire. Guess she missed you, huh?" Mama cackled out. "Ain't all that smart, but Emmacee can shore spot a woods fire. Good state job. Course if they knowed she was half-albino, they'd get shed of her. See good as you and me, when she wants to. Loves a fire good as she loves to talk. I helped her get the job so she could feed her girl. Helps keep her from burning up people's barns and all, you know." Her eyes in the mirror switched to me. "Her baby's due long about next week, Merdie. If I ain't home, you go on without me, you hear?"

"Yes 'um, but what if I'm gone?"

"Don't be."

The revenuer bumped my knee twice.

I figured Mama'd pull something on me, make me go to deliver Emmacee Mae's baby myself. She'd been building up to making me deliver, where generally I just went with her, handed her things, cleaned up, and let the women hold to me. "Mama, I..."

"Don't sass back, missy."

The revenuer kept his knee pressed to mine as we turned left at Fargo and bumped over the railroad tracks, past the filling station and the cafe, a few scattered trucks and cars pulling out or into the road-front yards, then on apiece and left down the woodsroad to Pineland.

Mama kept talking in the mirror, driving fast and cackling out, talking mostly to the revenuer like a tour guide in the Okefenoke State Park, other side of Fargo. Up the dirt road apiece, she had to slow for two pickups parked on either side, a drive-through space between them. Hunters in orange vests were perched on dog boxes on back of the pickups, scanning the pine woods, with rifle stocks clamped under their arms. Mama waved and one threw up his hand.

"See them woods out there, boy?" Mama kept calling the revenuer boy, driving crooked up the straight road. "Used to be a shine still ever ten miles or so. Now, dope's taking over. You know that?"

"Yes ma'am." He looked straight ahead, knee to mine, eyes clear green in the sun glare.

"Not all that much for a revenuer to do," Mama said. "Ain't you getting short of work?"

"Yes ma'am."

"If it weren't for us, you'd be out of a job."

He nodded.

"Used to, before the no-fence law, Bluejohn cattle grazed these woods. Weren't none of these planted pines in rows. Pines used to grow in clumps all about, around ponds and bays. Early spring, my daddy and the boys would buy matches and go out on horseback, striking and tossing them to the dead grass, letting fire blaze across the flatwoods. In two weeks' time the grass would come back green, and the short, scrub Bluejohns would graze unbound. When they come up on another herd, they'd turn back. We trusted one another back then not to steal one another's cows. One more way we had of testing a man's mettle. Bet you done knowed all that, didn't you?"

"No ma'am." The revenuer seemed ready with the same answer anytime she took a break.

She started again. "Way back the gover'munt took a notion to make us dip our cattle for ticks in vats they built, and I can't say we liked it. Took all day on mule and horseback just to round up a little drove of cows. Some was knowed in these parts to dynamite a dip vat. Course the gover'munt made 'em built 'em back. If they found out about it. Sometimes a gover'munt man got blowed up in the vat and nobody wouldn't never know it. I bet being a gover'munt man yourself, you heared about that."

The revenuer shook his head.

Mama slowed and turned right on another road just like the last—same tall straight pines and bunchy fanned palmettoes—

while she kept talking in the same tone.

"You ever seen a man with the blind staggers?" She set up, grabbing the steering wheel in both hands as the car hit a rut. "Say?"

"No ma'am." He jolted around, our knees fell away, drew together like flames.

"Encephalitis," I explained, afraid she was getting suspicious of my quiet. "Injun Gal's husband come down with it spring before last."

He nodded, staring out the window at the green light shedding off the pinewoods.

I wondered what he was thinking.

My mama turned down another road; the woods looked the same coming and going, all over Pineland where Injun Gal lived. Once a big turpentine camp, now nothing left but the memorized spot and the name.

Mama's eyes popped up in the mirror again. "Bet you didn't know we got Indians around here?"

"No Ma'am," he said.

"Well we do." She drove on along the straight dirt road, talking loud as the car got louder, faster, tail pipe framming under the car as it bucked over bumps. "My girl Merdie there's part Indian, but no blood kin to the ones we going to see. Plum pitiful, these Indians. Come down here from Florida, looking to make a living in the pulpwoods. Huh! Too many gover'munt regulations in a honest living, to my notion." She waited for the revenuer to say something.

He just set there.

"Yeah, my dead husband's great-grandpappy was full-blooded Indian, they say. Called him Billy Bowlegs." She scrunched her neck. "About 150 years ago, he got caught by a bunch of white Christians over on the Alapaha River. They let him loose in the Okefenoke, what the Creek Indians come to call *Land of the Trembling Earth*, and what you'd call Okefenokee. Right?"

"Right."

"Well, Mr. Know-it-all," she piped, "bet you didn't know that Okefenokee started out with a "i" stead of a "e" in the middle. Course, the gover'munt changed that too." She gloated a minute, then picked up where she left off with the story of Billy Bowlegs. "Anyhow, where they caught old Billy, they built a church name of Macedonia, at Mayday. Still there." She veered left, then swerved to the center of the road.

Leaning, the revenuer almost smiled for the first time.

"Hold it between the ditches, Mama." I smiled at him.

Her eyes in the mirror were on me solid now. "Where you from, boy?"

"The Ozarks, ma'am."

"Huh"—she drove on, gazing ahead—"you ain't no town boy yourself. Bet they love you back there."

"No ma'am." He laughed low, hung his head.

"How'd you get mixed up in revenuing, anyhow?"

"Well, I..."

"I can't hear you, speak up."

He set up and gazed at the back of her head, at her wrung eyes in the mirror. "I landed the job while I was a student..."

"School, huh?"

"Yes ma'am." He set back. "U.T."

"U.T.?"

"University of Tennessee."

"That anywhere close to the Grand Ole Opry?"

"Same state," he said.

"Family? You got family?"

"Yes, ma'am. A mama still living, two boys who stay with her."

He'd lied to me about having just one boy: he could have been lying about Tennessee too. I moved my knee and his followed.

Mama cut down a logging-tram road, taking the ruts hard, and slung the revenuer into me.

"Merdie's crazy bout Tennessee, wants the boys to go to Nashville someday," she said. "Can't go herself cause she's got to take up delivering babies here when I leave off." She didn't never say die, sounded like she was going on some trip.

"Is that a fact?" He pressed his shoulder to mine.

Fire streaked through my body.

"She can some sang"—Mama took a left curve—"but she knows all in all it's a bunch of foolishness. Folks needs her around here. Don't they, Merdie?"

"Yes ma'am." I wouldn't get into that with her now; I might not never talk to her about it again. Somehow nothing seemed important but the revenuer, who Mama was talking to now like he was one of us, and who she'd raised me to hate with a purple passion.

"Woods used to be full of hogs, now if you can catch a mess of fish you doing good..." Mama talked on, no lesson in it now.

The car screwed on into the woods where the sun shined weak through the thick pines, where split deer tracks cut into double paths lined with wiregrass, and didn't slow down till the gray shack showed in the clearing ahead.

You could tell Injun Gal and her younguns had been hearing the car from away off, because there they stood, open-faced and waiting in the flaring shade of a giant magnolia. To the left, the unpainted shack looked like a hog pen next to the tree.

Five fice dogs dashed lickety-split from the shade to meet the car, brown and white spotted coats hugging their ribs. They barked at the tires and then backed off, eyes crossed from turning with the wheels. Mama pulled up in front of the shingled-roof shack and stopped quick to keep from running over the dogs. Under the edge of the porch floor, one of Hamp's jimmy-john jugs laid broke in two like a big split bubble.

Injun Gal stood there a minute under the magnolia, grinning and swaying, then come walking up, flat-footed. A old gray sack frock hiked on her stocky body. Solid and round but not fat. Even her cheeks were round, her arms and calves, plump swells of muscle.

My mama got out, nodding to Injun Gal, whose hide-like skin looked smoked beneath the eyes and the set-in seams of her nose and mouth. She grinned, black eyes so worried they didn't fit in her grin-pooched face.

Mama waved at the boys with false-healthy faces, and they went on circling the car. "You boys there, come help me tote in this sugar and mash."

Me and the revenuer got out of the car while Mama hurried around and flipped the lid on the cooter hull, then started handing out ten-pound sacks of sugar to the boys. As they passed either side of the car, stepping heavy on flat bare feet, they glanced sidelong at the revenuer.

"I raise honey bees," Mama said to the revenuer and laughed. "That's how come me to order so much sugar."

Scattered under the magnolia, like a mechanic's junk, was the shine still me and Mama helped Injun Gal rig after her old man took sick. Two blue-black, fifty-five gallon drums stood next to the square brick well, one for working off the buck— fermented sugar and mash, corn or berries—the other for cooking it. Black glazed sticks of wood from the last cooking had burned down around the brick bats under the cooking drum. Set off against the green of the wide waxy leaves, a copper tube coiled from the cooking drum to a wood hog trough full of rainwater. Hamp's five-gallon jugs were strung from the dark circle of shade to the bright strip of dirt where the yard ran to woods.

Everytime we come, we had to set up the still again and start over. In summer, it took just two to three days for the buck to work; winter, it took more like a couple of weeks. Then, we'd dip the soured berries, corn or mash, and sugar—whatever come cheapest, whatever we could lay hands on—from the buck drum to the cooking drum and heat the buck, steam cooling through the copper tube in the trough of water and running clear and sparkling to the jugs.

To solder the copper tube to the drum, we used a iron I got off Hamp, the old kind with a chisel end you had to heat over the fire. To seal the cap on the cooking drum, we made a flour paste. Flour snuck out from my house too.

It was my idea to set up the still under the magnolia, so the revenuers couldn't spot smoke from a helicopter; we weren't worried about them driving up and spotting it if we set it up in the open, because strangers couldn't find their way back in them woods. Mama said that setting up under the magnolia was a good idea on my part. First time ever I knew more than my mama.

Last summer, before we set up the still, Mama'd heard about a market in Jasper, Florida, that bought palmetto berries, so she put the Indians to picking the giant pods from the throats of the clustered fronds throughout the woods. Next, it was passion flowers. Hairy-petaled, purple flowers growing every yard or so from miles of vines that hooked by sticky tendrils to the bays and pines.

Me and Mama would haul the berries and flowers ten long miles through the woods to the warehouse, then tote in the croker sacks of solid marbled barries and fluffy purple flowers, piles of them done shriveled and rotting on the musty wood floor. Smelled like puke. The man there would weigh them and give us maybe five or ten dollars to start with, then drop the price next time. "Getting too many," he'd say, "you under-stand."

Last time we went, I asked him what was made from the berries and flowers. "Pain killers and nerve pills," he said. Legal dope. So, we went back and set up the still. Bootlegging kept the Indians in groceries.

Dogs circled us all, wrapping our legs and yapping. "Berries gone, berries gone," said Injun Gal, now checking out the revenuer.

"What berries?" Mama said.

Injun Gal pointed to the still, then to the woods.

"Oh, briarberries, you mean, for the shine." Mama stared into her warm round face. "Berries come back in the summer. Soon as it gets hot."

She wheeled around and spoke to the revenuer. "Ain't nothing the matter with Injun Gal." Then she lifted a ten-pound sack of sugar and shoved past us. "She just can't talk our talk. Injun talk."

"Boys," she hollered, "put them sacks inside, out of the wet." She hobbled on toward the sagging porch.

Just ahead, the boys stomped through the sprung-wide screen door, into the house, and dropped the sacks, rattling the two windows over the porch. The dogs yapped, backing as we walked ahead; me and the revenuer following Mama, while Injun Gal creeped behind, crying, "Berries gone, berries gone."

Looked like she was following the revenuer, asking him for berries. Like him being a man he could get them back. He kept glancing at me. "This is incredible," he said. "Your mother's incredible, you're incredible." And I figured he hadn't never laid eyes on no poor people before.

"Honey, listen," I said, dropping back to take Injun Gal's arm—that racket was getting on my nerves. I talked in her face like Mama did. "We brung some mash to make buck from, don't need berries."

The revenuer went up on the low V-ceiled porch and stood waiting, while the boys, coming out again, stepped around him with black eyes down and hopped off the porch.

"Berries gone," Injun Gal said right in my face.

"Honey, listen," I said, "you can use mash to ferment for shine just as good. Better, don't have to pick no briarberries. See?"

"Berries gone." Injun Gal still grinned, tears in her set-in eyes. Then she walked around me, stepped up on the porch, and went to saying it to the revenuer.

He shrugged.

"Me and Mama learned her how to make briarberry shine,"

I said.

"Berries," Injun Gal nodded, twisting her big smoked hands.

"Merdie," Mama hollered, "get on in here. I think I know how come Injun Gal's carrying on so."

I rushed in, the revenuer right behind me. The room was nearly dark except for the smeary light through the two windows over the porch, and a runner of gray light cast from the dirt through the open front and back doors. Centered on the runner, was a square eating table with a black iron pot and a gnawed deer shank bone covered in green blowflies. A old wood cookstove set off to the right of the back door. Two beds with rusty iron steads stood along the left wall, stained mattresses and clothes strowed from one side to the other.

The house stunk of lard and piss, raw deer and dead varmints. Not that the house was ever clean, and there was something almost worse than the dead smells in the air, something ignorant to the point of evil. One time when we come, the boys were out in the back yard throwing knives at a softshell cooter, its head snaking in and out of its checkered brown shell, but not quick enough to miss the knives. One knife pinned its flat head to the packed dirt and they all whooped and darted the other knives, blades stuck up on the shell like a wood block. The old man, setting on a gum stump, went to laughing and slapping his knees. Said that was how he learned his boys to kill cooters to eat, how he learned them to look out for theirselves in case they ever had to go to school.

The boys and the dogs now blocked off the dim aisle between beds, gaping at the revenuer, while Mama stared at Injun Gal's husband. He was shrunk and old, with gray skin that carried to his fine patchy hair, milky no-color eyes rolled up to the ceiling.

"Mama," I said, "he don't even look like the same man. My God, we just saw him..." The last time we come he'd been tied to the magnolia, drooling, a rope about his waist to keep him from wandering off in the woods. But straining against the rope, he'd looked strong, his sleeping spell spent.

"Berries gone, berries gone." Ingun Gal stood right behind the revenuer, who hung close to me.

Dogs wrapped around our legs, steady barking, loud in the house.

In the right front corner, weak light shed through the window over the porch on a pile of dried deer tongue scattered from a heap like cured tobacco, the smell powdery and swelling in the stifling room. That summer Injun Gal and the boys had picked it wild in the woods to sell for snuff tobacco, but Mama's car was the only way they had of taking it off, and we couldn't keep up with when the man that bought it would be stopping off in Homerville.

"Is he dead?" I said, leaning over the old man with Mama.

"Got a blood-pulse, but it ain't much." Mama talked low, then loud. "Injun Gal, he's holding his own."

"Berries gone." Injun Gal said it to Mama this time, not even glancing at the man on the bed. Then she started in on the revenuer again.

"Thinks a man can fix everything," Mama said to the revenuer, handling his shoulders to pass.

He stuck his face in Injun Gal's face, speaking up. "We're going to make you some shine out of mash. Understand?"

"Berries gone." She grinned and swayed, thick arms clasped behind.

"Mama, let's take the old man to the hospital in Homerville," I said.

"Can't help him now; he's lived longer than they said he would anyhow. Besides, do it look to you like Injun Gal can afford it?"

"Welfare..." I started.

"Hush your mouth!" Mama waved her arms and wagged her head as she plowed through boys and dogs. "Shoo! Shut up, Injun Gal, and come on." She walked on toward the back door and stepped down to the overcast dirt.

We made a line out behind Mama, just like we come in, Injun Gal huddling close to the revenuer and babbling.

Out the door, where the stink got stronger, a dead possum laid on its side, baby possums like rats wiggling from the pouch of her bloated belly. Her legs stuck straight out.

Feet trampled behind me.

"One of you boys," I said, standing to the side and grabbing a big healthy-looking boy by the arm. "You! You go bury that possum." I made digging signs with my hands, started with a shoveling motion, then with my fingers.

The dogs sniffed the Mama possum, yapped at the squirming babies, then backed off as the boy picked it up by the hard curled tail and walked off across the yard toward the woods.

Injun Gal clung to the revenuer's arm now, still babbling, and yanked at the rope across his back as he turned in circles on the yard.

Mama hollered from the shine still out front, "Injun Gal, get out here."

"Don't bury the littluns alive," I shouted, running in behind the boy, watching one of the little possums drop and a dog snatch it up between his teeth. "Git! Git!" I kicked the dog under the belly and it yelped, then slunk off with the squeaky pink possum in its mouth, gazing back with droopy accused eyes.

Another baby possum wiggled from the pouch, and the addled boy dropped the mama possum with a thud looked at me and grinned.

"Git! Git!" I hollered, chasing the other dogs from the scattering scraps of flesh.

"Merdie! Injun Gal!" Mama called. "Y'all get out here. I ain't got all day."

One of the dogs kept barking at the revenuer, while the others barked at the possums, while Injun Gal worked at the knot on the revenuer's back, singing, "Berries gone, berries gone."

"Merdie, look out!" Mama yelled around the side of the house. "She's turning your revenuer loose."

"Let her," I said, kicking a snarling dog away from one of the hairless pink possums. "He ain't going nowhere."

I stopped and looked right at him. He peeped around Injun Gal and the boys and the barking dogs. His hands fell low as the rope at his elbows dropped to the dirt. Injun Gal now gouged at the knot on his wrists.

One of the boys dashed up and snatched a baby possum before the spotted hound could and ran around the house.

"You can't take care of him," I hollered after the boy. "How long can you keep him before he dies from being shut up." I still stared at the revenuer. "Can't live like that. Besides you have to feed him and what-all."

As the final rope fell away from the revenuers feet and curled on the dirt like a snake, Injun Gal dropped to her knees saying "Berries gone" like she was worshipping him.

I started to cry.

The revenuer, free now, stood rubbing his arms, feet planted on the tracked dirt, looking long at me while Injun Gal yanked his arm and headed in the direction of the house. She stopped yanking when he didn't move and kissed his hand. "Berries gone."

Mama finally got everybody rounded up under the big magnolia and had one of the boys drawing water from the well with the squeaking teakle, dumping buckets full into the buck drum, while two more toted out sacks of sugar and mash. Another one cut open the sacks and dumped them sliding dry into the gurgling mix in the drum.

Just beyond the shifting shade of the magnolia, where the yard met the road, the revenuer stood chopping firewood from a sprawled pecan tree. Injun Gal grinned and swayed, just clear of the axe swing, while her least boy toted armloads of split wood to the cooking drum.

Every now and then, the revenuer would stop chopping and look off at me, at the car, at the road through the woods.

A buck crossed the logging road and the boys took out whooping after him, dogs barking and running with them. Injun Gal let out a squeaky laugh.

I felt like a fool for crying earlier.

Mama hadn't said a word to me, just went on setting up the buck barrel like my crying weren't no different than Injun Gal's laughing, than the man's death rattle in the house. She kept dumping sugar and mash, trying to get Injun Gal's attention to show her what to do when the mash got done working.

Injun Gal turned and nodded to Mama, her smoked brown cheeks welted from the pressure of her grin, and then watched the revenuer, love in her eyes.

A spotted sow and eight pigs waddled up snorting and sniffed high at the buck barrel. Mama chased them off into the woods, then come back to me at the well, brushing her hands on her plaid flannel shirt. "How you reckon we gone get the revenuer back to the house?" she said, biting her nails.

I didn't know if she meant how would we get him away from Injun Gal or how would we make him go. I shook my head.

"He could stay here," she said, "but I reckon Hamp'd have your hide."

"I'll take my chances." I'd done made up my mind to leave the revenuer, to let him go free.

"You can stay with me; Hamp ain't fixing to come messing with me." Her scrubbed, shiny face turned tough, white-blazed around the nose and mouth.

"I got the boys." I took a bucket of water from the scabby cement ledge of the well, hobbled over and dumped it into the buck barrel, a powder of mash and sugar drifting up to my face, the damp mix in the drum churning inside-over.

"Merdie," Mama said, "it's about time you face up to the fact that them boys can come and go as they please. They old enough. Around these parts boys is men right after they're babies. Hamp ain't got the mind to stop 'em, he don't care."

"It's deeper than that, Mama." I set the bucket on the fine humped roots of the magnolia. "They wouldn't leave, wouldn't do nothing but set there without me to make them. I got things going now with our singing, won't be long before we'll get out. Together."

"Well," Mama said, "you stood it this long, you can stand it awhile longer, but if you bound and determined to face Hamp without the revenuer, I'm going with you." She screwed the lid on the buck drum, then went to waving and yelling at Injun Gal. "Get over here so I can show you what to do when the buck gets done working. I ain't got all day."

Injun Gal turned and grinned, then again watched the revenuer chopping a stringy pecan limb with the dull axe.

"She ain't studying me." Mama walked off to the car, yelling at the boys, now trotting back through the woods, hassling with the dogs. "You boys go get them jugs of shine and put 'em in the back of my car."

They stopped out of a fast trot and stared, then walked toward her. "Show 'em, Merdie," Mama said, "will you?"

I crossed to the well and lifted a jug of shine from our last running and lugged it to the cooter hull.

In a minute, the boys come toting up jugs behind me, setting them in till the car set down in the back.

Injun Gal kept her eyes on the revenuer, who'd dropped the axe and was walking off around the house, then glided behind him.

Mama shook her head and went around to the front seat and took a fruit jar of eggnog and one of boiled beef likker and walked into the house.

I closed the trunk lid, and when I looked again the revenuer was coming around the house, walking slow and carrying his ropes, with Injun Gal grinning on his heels.

"You staying or going?" Mama said, coming out the door in

time to meet him at the edge of the porch.

He didn't answer, just walked on toward the car and got in the back beside me, while Injun Gal stood off and watched.

Mama got in, slammed the door. "Injun Gal, we'll come back in two or three weeks and help you run off a batch. See you don't let them boys take off the lid, possums'll fall in."

Mama cranked up and framed her eyes in the mirror. "If y'all see the law, lay low," she said, backed out and tore up the road, the backend of the car scratching wiregrass.

VIII

hat night I slept deep, dreaming I was awake, watching for day and holding tight to the revenuer—the room dark and warm and smelling of us, curled front to back on the bed. Something woke me, and I opened my eyes to a gray streak stretching around the sideroom door. That old strain of getting caught seeped through my skin and laid hold to my heart. I laid there, stiff, blood pumping cold at my temples.

The revenuer opened the door a little wider and stood in the frame of gray, then closed it with a whisper of air and eased back to bed, rocking as he set, first on edge, then laid down beside me. He'd put on his clothes, and they felt cold and rough as he scrunched to my back, breathing in my hair. I smiled at the thought of him not leaving while he could, but felt the same raw sad feeling rise in my gut as at Injun Gal's. He was free! And sleepy as I was, I kept my dry eyes wide till I had to get up and put the ropes on again and sneak out to Hamp's room.

While I milked that morning, the revenuer stood studying me from the shadowy corner of the stall.

"Move around," I said to Filly, pushing at her tick-tight belly. Her rearend twisted toward me. She shifted, stomping one polished brown hoof and then the other, and swiped at me with her tail. She couldn't get used to the revenuer; her filmy swole eyes got wild with him around. Sometimes she wouldn't let her milk down till he went out and waited in the lot. I hated to ask him to go, hated the thought of him out in the cold. Hated being without him for even one minute.

"Merdie," he hissed, peeping at the house through a crack in the barn wall, "come go with me."

I looked back, hoping he meant out, maybe to be-excused, knowing deep-down it was more.

"My pickup's just out there in the woods, keys and all," he said. "Let's go now. Please."

"Why didn't you leave last night?" Squeezing on two pale pied udders, I smiled, sly as a calf after cream. I knew the answer now.

The cow shifted, chewed her cud.

He leaned against the wall, still peeping through the crack, and switched feet in the rattley hay. "He'd kill you, wouldn't he?"

"Probably not." I stood with my bucket of milk and crossed to set it on the shelf in his corner. "What about your wife?"

"I don't have one."

"You said you have a boy."

"I lied, I'm sorry. Guess I figured you and your mama might take pity on me if I had children. But I did have a wife, we're divorced." He moved close, cold and stiff and roped. "Why did you marry Hamp?"

"Cause he asked me." My hand was still on the chilled bucket handle.

"Are you staying because of your mother, because people here need you?"

"No."

"The boys?"

"Yes."

In a band of sun, his eyes looked like cracked green glass. "Let's go."

"I can't."

He stood there studying my face while I studied his, like now we'd learned each other's outsides we couldn't wait to plunder each other's insides. Who was he? Where did he come from? "You own land?" I asked.

"What?"

"You own land?"

"Do I own land?"

"Yeah—what are you, some kind of English teacher?" I leaned against the wall, watching for Hamp and the boys.

"I started to be," he said and laughed. "I started to be a lawyer, I started to be lots of things. But I met Ruth, my ex, and got sidetracked."

"Ruth?"

"Yes."

"Was she worth it?"

"No."

I waited for more about "Ruth"—more important right then than the land because she was a living threat. She'd laid with this very man and could for all I knew lay with him again.

"Why would you want to know if I own land?" he asked.

"Do you?"

"No, and I don't expect to."

"Why not?"

"My daddy owned land, 800 acres of cattle ranch, and it drained him. He never left Clarksville, claimed to be happy where he was. How could he know if he never made comparisons?" He scratched his chin with his shoulder.

"Sounds like he's dead."

"Five or six years ago. Heart attack."

"What happened to his land?"

"My mother sold it after he died and split the money with me."

Even his mother seemed like a threat—he'd want to go back to her, just like I would to my mama. "What about her? Where is she?"

"In a rehabilitation center for alcoholics, last I heard."

"I hate that." I really did and hated myself because of what I'd thought. "My daddy wouldn't have let me look at you twice, you know that?"

"Because I'm a whiskey revenuer?"

"That too, but even if you wasn't, he'd have called you a loafer. No land."

"What about your mother?"

"Her neither." I thought about it. "I don't know, she might figure now, after Hamp and me, all I've been through, a drifter ain't no more risk."

"Let's not ask her, what do you say? Let's just go."

"I can't." I led the cow out to the lot, smiling at the bluing morning. A half moon hung in the east like a thin potato slice. Now I knew he really was free. Wasn't the gators or the bootleggers keeping him there. Wasn't the ropes. If he stayed, he'd stay because he loved me.

From the kitchen I could hear Little Noah talking to the revenuer in the sideroom. His voice was fast and girly thin, like he'd talk when telling stories. Running stuff in the ground. Home from school sick—ha!—he had him somebody cornered that would listen for a change.

Well, let him talk: wasn't hurting nobody and it would do him good; I could get some cooking done without him under foot. Generally on sick days, he'd watch tv till he got hungry— staying in his room just long enough to look good and laid up— then hang around the kitchen, pestering me about how much longer before we'd eat.

Every now and then, he'd get quiet and, out of habit, I'd listen, try to figure what he was up to. He'd go back to talking again and the revenuer would mumble something, one word to every ten of Little Noah's.

I was just taking the cornbread out of the oven, when here comes Little Noah, walking flatfoot across the hall and into the kitchen. He come up behind me and I could hear paper rattling at the back of my head. When I turned around, a sheet of notebook paper was stuck in my face.

"Oh, so you been drawing, I see." I didn't want to get him started again, really. He'd about quit drawing and I was glad not to have to tack his pictures on all the walls, glad he was maybe growing up and might amount to something, might take his singing serious. But I'd missed those pictures, too. I took the drawing and carried it to the window over the sink to better see it in the light.

He stood still with his hands behind, belly bowed and grinning. "Ain't all that good," he said, "not real-looking."

"Yeah, it is," I said. "A real likeness to the revenuer, I'd say."

Swinging his head, he walked over and looked too. "Yeah?"

"Yeah." I gazed at the pencil drawing of the revenuer: laid back with his hands behind his head, a sprig of hair sticking up like it'd do. He was grinning big—not like him. "You did good on this one, Little Noah."

"Naw," he said and twisted, his head so close I could smell his sleepy-baby smell. "You notice anything especial about him?" His blue eyes met mine.

"Well," I said, shaking the paper bad because you couldn't never tell what Little Noah, slow as he was, might have picked up on.

"See, Ma," he said, poking the paper with his finger, "he ain't tied up no more."

Late that night, after Hamp got to snoring good, I looked in on the boys, sleeping before the blank fizzing tv, and went in to the revenuer. I didn't get the sideroom door shut good behind me before he started snickering.

"What's so funny?" I whispered, feeling for the bed in the dark.

"I've got a surprise for you."

I laughed too. "What?" I patted the foot of the bed.

"You won't believe it."

"What?" I touched his toes, patting up his britches leg, along his sharp shinbone.

He was tickled good now; so was I. We'd giggle awhile, then stop to listen for Hamp and the boys.

I felt for the edge of the bed, found it, and slid in beside him. "Shh!" I was laughing louder than he was. I snuggled close; he reached over and hugged me tight, laughing in my face like he was drunk. "What?" I said. "What?"

He was laughing so hard now, he was shaking. He rolled on top of me, tucking me good beneath him.

"Wait a minute," I said, drying up. "How'd you get loose?"

He rolled off and set up. "Little Noah," he said, laughing still.

I set up too. "You mean he...?"

"Yes"—he slapped his knees—"he came in here right after you went to bed and took off the ropes."

"No!" My first thought was, where's the ropes?

"Yes," the revenuer said. "He told me about an old bird dog Hamp tied up one time because it wouldn't point quail. Said he—Little Noah—let the dog go too. Then he just nodded, backing from the room."

"Where's the ropes?" I said.

"Right here." The revenuer gathered them from under his pillow and placed them across my lap.

I thought about the old bird dog Little Noah had let go, about how he swore it had gnawed the knot free. "Thank God he left the ropes," I said, clutching them.

"Yeah," the revenuer said, no longer laughing. "But now that I'm loose, how do I get caught again?"

Early the next morning, I took Little Noah out with me to do the milking and told him how sweet he was for letting the revenuer go, but how his daddy would blame me, and we all could go to jail if the revenuer went to the law and told. "We're kidnappers now," I said. "Understand?"

"Yes 'um," he said, hugging hisself and toeing the hay and shit on the dirt. Looked like he was primping up to cry.

I hugged him. He was soft. Softer than a grown boy oughta been. "Honey, you're so sweet," I said. I felt sick of myself, of the revenuer, of us all up against his innocence.

"I ain't sweet," he said, voice cracking, "I just got carried away. Stuff gets in my head and I can't get it out. I'm messed up. Different."

"No, sugar"—I looked into his eyes, new-blue as the day—"the rest of the world's different."

Got to where soon as the boys got off to school or wherever, and Hamp and J.B. cleared out of the house between meals, I'd take the ropes off the revenuer; his wrists and elbows were healed good now that he'd quit yanking.

Close to dinnertime that day, I put the ropes back on, and he set by the woodstove with his hands folded like he was praying while I put on a pot of vegetable soup.

"I've come to a decision," he said.

I went on prying lids from Mason jars of soup mix I'd put up that summer, thinking, *Don't think, Merdie, don't even try to guess*.

"I've decided to reason with Hamp."

143

"You what?" I dumped a gurgling jar of okra, tomato, and corn mix in the soup pot and turned around.

"Yeah, that's what I should have done in the first place—I'm a real believer in reason." He laughed low.

I heard a roaring way off and looked out the window over the sink. I could hear Hamp flamming around at the still beyond the border of blackgums, the roar just a background racket bruising the still blue sky.

"And if reasoning don't work, I'll punch the sonofabitch's lights out."

I was half-listening to the roar, getting closer, half-listening to the revenuer. "You're crazy. How you fixing to do that?"

"Wait until I'm untied—that's where you come in—then walk up and sock him in the gut and..."

"Hold it!" I turned around and held up both hands. "The reasoning part, how you plan to do that with a man like Hamp?"

"The same way I'd reason with anybody else."

"Hamp ain't just anybody else, unless it's anybody else in the flatwoods."

"Just wait," Mac said, fanning his fingers and standing up. "Now, when he comes in for lunch, I'm going to..."

A creaking of floor boards on the hall picked up with the way-off roar and Hamp pushed open the kitchen door and stood staring at the revenuer, who stared back with his mouth open. "Hamp," he said, "I want to talk to you, see if we can negotiate some sort of..."

Hamp took three, four quick steps across the kitchen and drew back a fist like a litard knot and punched the revenuer in the face. The revenuer landed in the chair, skittering to the wall behind the woodstove, and a blue-gray lump rose on his left cheek like his bones were chunks of granite and a punch in any place would make the chunks shine through.

Hamp turned around and marched out, closing the door behind him, and shuffled down the hall to the yard, me watching out the window for him to show. Off the doorsteps he stomped, shinning his teeth, and gazed up with one hand shielding the sun from his eyes. Oh, Lord! Had he heard us talking? What was going on?

"Well, if I hadn't been tied up..." the revenuer said, scraping his chair around. "He's left me no other choice but..." He stopped jabbering and listened with me to what sounded like a train had jumped the tracks and was rumbling across the woods for the house, getting closer and closer.

In a minute, helicopter blades went to beating over the yards and then the house. I turned down the fire under the pot of soup and looked out the window again, spotting Hamp as he scooted from shadow to shadow of the blackgums, gazing up.

The revenuer was gazing up too, like he could see through the ceiling. His face was all swole. He said something I couldn't hear for the racket of the helicopters—every window in the house rattled like a giant was shaking it.

When I looked out again, I couldn't locate Hamp; next thing I knew, he was standing in the kitchen door again, gazing at the revenuer like he'd gazed at the helicopters, with wonder and dread mixed. Like he hadn't seen him in a long time.

His thick lips moved, words falling dead under the steady drubbing over the house. But by then he'd said it so many times, I could read his lips: *I oughta gone on and knocked the revenuer in the head.*

The revenuer set still, staring at Hamp, and listened out. Then the helicopters moved off the house and went to circling the woods out back. Rifle shots blasted off in the woods—two, three times—and I couldn't tell if it was the law or the deer hunters, who'd been all morning after a buck in the brake behind the house, or maybe after J.B. and Hamp for killing their dogs, which they're said to love better than their own families.

My heart was whipping in my throat. I don't know what worried me most: Hamp hearing us talking, or the law finding the still—an old worry wrought from habit—or maybe the dope, or about them finding the revenuer. Maybe I was worried most about them not finding him. But the longer I watched Hamp's wild, glittery eyes on the revenuer, words forming in the room, I decided I wished the law would come.

The lid on the soup pot went *ba-ba-bap*, picking up where the helicopters left off. And Hamp, easing closer to the woodstove, backed up to warm, studying the revenuer. His mad fits didn't scare me half as much as this quiet, brooding study. "Reckon you know how come them buzzards to be out?" He spoke to the revenuer, who just set there, hands folded like he was praying. In the shallow light through the kitchen window, his face around the lumpy bruise showed white.

"I shore hate to do it." Hamp turned, facing the woodstove, and spread his stiff scratched hands to warm. "Looks like I ain't got no choice."

"Hamp," I said, the *ba-ba-bap* of the pot lid beating with my heart.

He made like I wasn't on the place. "Reckon me and you'll be going for a walk soon as they get done snooping." Hamp cut his eyes up, his hands were shaking.

I knew he'd made up his mind now, and that was how come him to look so sane. Hands behind his back, he stood listening to the helicopters with his eyes and stepped to the stove again. The wild beating over the house started to fade out, and when we couldn't hear it no more, Hamp went to talking like he was talking to hisself, like he hadn't never quit, just picked up where he left off. "Me and you's about due for a little walk in the woods." He said it looking at me, then said, "Woman, go get my shotgun." He nodded toward the wall that divided the kitchen from his bedroom.

I stood there by the cookstove, feeling the soup steam rise to my face. "Hamp, you kill this man, you'll go to the pen."

"Shut up!" He watched the revenuer, whose arms fell slack against the sling of ropes on his elbows.

I tipped out, closing the door behind me. I didn't know if I'd go back and hand Hamp the shotgun to shoot the revenuer with, or if I'd shoot Hamp, but I'd do one or the other. But killing Hamp would be like killing some poor old mad dog. I hadn't never shot so much as a possum after my chickens.

I eased up the hall, my feet stepping off one beat to every two of my heart. In the cold bedroom, I went to Hamp's bed. When I leaned to get the shotgun, propped against the mantelpiece, I could smell his salty sweat and sweet hair oil on the pillow.

The barrel felt cold in my hands as I grabbed it and placed the stock under my arm, then braced it against my shoulder, shaking. I knew it was loaded, and I knew I had to decide what to do before I opened that kitchen door. I'd have about a second to lay Hamp low or get laid low. My mouth was dry, my tongue felt rough as wet wool.

I tried to hate him, walking slow from the bed, tried thinking of all the reasons why I should, backing up time, easing ahead, recollecting how, for a fact, Hamp had loved me, how he'd daddied everlast one of my babies, their faces rising up in his face to haunt me. I couldn't recollect a single thing right then to make me mad enough to shoot him—he'd almost hit me that once, true, but the scared feeling didn't come clear enough to mind for me to pull the trigger my finger was on. But I knew he meant to kill the revenuer, knew it in my soul—he wasn't fooling—and I braced myself, went to walking through the bedroom door, hearing the helicopters way out over the swamp now, and nothing else on the place but a *pck pck pck* that could have been my rooster's claws on the front porch.

"Merdie?"

I dropped the barrel of the gun and swung round to see the sheriff standing in the yard, fist raised to rap again on the front porch floor. He grinned, his close-set blue eyes casting out at the lot, then at me, at the shotgun.

"Sheriff!" I said, for the first time smiling at that sonofagun. "Come on in."

He dropped his head and stepped up on the porch.

147

"Come on in." I leaned the shotgun against the door facing. "I got a big pot of soup on. Hamp's in the kitchen."

He brushed his feet and walked quick along the hall, hair oil sharp as creosote on hot crossties.

I went on ahead, hearing the helicopters double back, their rudders setting off every glass in the house rattling. I opened the kitchen door and let him step through ahead of me. He just stood there, blocking the doorway. I shoved around him and tipped to the cookstove. While I stirred the soup, watching the swirl of peas, okra, tomatoes and corn, I watched all three men out of the corner of my eyes, a sweet taste of relief on my tongue.

Nobody said a word till the helicopters cleared the house and went hawking over the east woods.

"Well, Hamp," said the sheriff, "I do declare, you got you a passel of trouble."

Hamp rocked on his toes, still backed to the stove, with his hands locked behind.

The sheriff stared at the banged-up revenuer. "They onto you, Hamp." He nodded to where the helicopters faded off in the woods. "Weren't me sicked 'em on you." He held up both hands, grinning. "I been holding 'em off."

"They after him or my shine still?" Hamp turned to face the woodstove, spreading his hands.

"Could be both." The sheriff strutted to the eating table and pulled out a chair, set and crossed his legs. "Miss Merdie, you got any coffee left from breakfast?"

Miss Merdie! A side to the sheriff I hadn't never seen, put-on manners in a woman's kitchen. I turned on the eye under the coffee pot and listened to it sing, the helicopters gone now, and even the chickens clucking under the house sounded loud.

"What y'all aiming to do?" The sheriff's eyes roved from Hamp to me and landed on the revenuer.

"Don't rightly know." Hamp faced the scorched V-ceiling behind the stove flue.

"You weren't fixing to shoot him, was you?" The sheriff tee-heed, then quit. "I'd of thought you would've done away with that fellow awhile back."

Hamp stared with the sheriff at the revenuer.

"Course I ain't you, but I wouldn't run no risk of him getting loose and turning me in. You get it?"

"I shore reckon I ain't dumb."

I tiptoed over and set a cup of mud-off-the-morning-coffee before Sheriff Crosby.

"I'll take some sugar with that, Miss Merdie." He slid the cup and saucer over on the table, then pulled it to him, and took the sugar dish I handed him in both stubby hands.

"You can't hold 'em off?" Hamp nodded at the revenuer. "How long?"

The sheriff swigged the sweetened coffee.

"Till I can get shed of him."

The sheriff swigged again, screwed his potato face. "It'll cost you."

"How much?"

"Upwards of, say, five hundred."

"Five hundred!"

"For starters." The sheriff set the cup in the saucer, sloshing coffee on my white tablecloth.

Hamp stood straight, looking at the sheriff like he could eat him. "Run go get my money bag, woman."

I rushed out and up the hall, snatching the shotgun on the way, and on into the bedroom, sliding it quick under my bed, then snugged the throw-rug around it.

Damned that sheriff! I'd half-expected him to sidetrack Hamp from killing the revenuer. Well, I wouldn't make it easy. I dashed over to Hamp's bed and dropped to my knees, feeling around at the head for the flour sack of money. He always kept it right under the side where he slept, but this time it was over near the wall, and I had to lay on my belly and reach way under to grab hold of it. When I hooked the draw string on one finger, dragging the bag, I got up and brushed the dust off my shirt and lit out for the hall, and didn't slow down till I hit the heat of the kitchen.

I didn't look at the revenuer, couldn't, because I knew they'd see the relief in my eyes, that and something else. I would have shot Hamp. I would have.

Hamp turned to the off-side of the woodstove, away from the sheriff and the revenuer, fiddling with the bag, then in a minute turned with a handful of dollar bills. Bag tucked under his arm, he handed the money to Sheriff Crosby.

He counted the bills, poked out his short legs, and stuffed it deep in his britches pocket. "I tell you what, Hamp. While you got that moneybag out, you bout as well go on and count out another hundred for me to keep hush-mouthed about J.B. and Colin's pot patch."

"Pot patch!" Hamp's parched forehead wrinkled.

"Dope."

"I don't know what you talking about."

"I hear you." The sheriff tee-heed into the cup, swigged long, head tilted to drain the sugar. "Little independents like that think they can get away with murder."

"Them boys ain't never growed no dope."

I held my breath, the lid on the soup pot going *ba-ba-bap*, like the helicopters were coming back.

"Could be the feds is done picked up on it out yonder in Al Hammock. Could be on their way to see me right now."

Hamp went to breathing hard and shuffled again to the space between the woodstove and cookstove, counting again. He turned around, reached way out to hand the money to the sheriff. "They ain't worth it," he said, a note of grudging and begrudging in his voice.

And I knew we were still in for trouble around the house, but it seemed like nothing up against Hamp shooting the revenuer. He was safe for now, but I could tell by his pale set face he didn't know it, that he'd do his dead-level best to get away soon as I undid the ropes, and I'd let him. I'd let him.

That night, cold air streaming through cracks in the sideroom walls, I untied the revenuer's ropes for what I thought was the last time. I guess he thought so too. He didn't say nothing, just held me close and rubbed my shoulders and sides like I'd been hurt. All the time kissing me deep, his tongue pushing against my throat, then sucking mine back. He rubbed my legs and then my stomach, one hand streaking to my breast and cupping it warm. He seemed to have to stop kissing me, to have to think deep and breathe, while he gripped himself, holding me tight around the waist, aimed and held and slipped inside me. Then he went to kissing me again, pumping his hips and breathing through his nose, holding me tight like I might slip away.

Afterwards, we laid in the dark, face to face, warm in the cold room. We didn't sleep and we didn't talk. We just touched bodies, stretched out, our toes wiggling against each other's like we were playing and time was free.

When I was little and couldn't tell time and didn't have no clock or watch to tell time by nohow, I'd play a whole day, sunup to sundown, and days were long and time was nothing and life was full. And that's how it felt that night with the revenuer.

I got up before daybreak and didn't put the ropes back on, and I went out in the hall, lit by the cold moon, satisfied I wouldn't never see the revenuer again. I felt lonesome already, and hurt, but a good hurt, knowing he'd get away and now Hamp wouldn't shoot him, knowing I wouldn't have to shoot Hamp or even make up my mind to leave the boys and my mama forever. That's the truth. One thing was about as bad as the other, to my way of thinking. But you can't have everything, I'd learned that a long time ago.

I checked on the boys, Bo Dink and Little Noah sleeping two to a bed, and Israel dead to the world in the bed under the front porch window. Good, they wouldn't hear when the revenuer left. For once, the tv was off, and in the moonlight coming through all four windows, I could make out Israel's white leg crooked over the dark quilt. Of a sudden, it dawned on me that moonlight don't bring out much color, just shapes and shadows. My pink gown looked white. The patchwork quilt on Little Noah and Bo Dink's bed looked black and white checked—a quilt top I'd pieced together from scraps of their old colored shirts. The whole room was a drained white with black shadows. Sad looking. But saddest and scariest of all was going through the whole house in my mind and finding no color. I hadn't never give a thought to color. Never even planted a flower.

I closed the door and tiptoed in to where Hamp was snoring heavy. A log smoked on the fireplace. I rolled it back with the poker and got in bed, listening for the revenuer to tip out. I knew every squeaking board in the house, could hear when he got up, when he crossed the doorway, the last board telling on the back porch in front of my washing machine. I heard the old dog's tail thump on the porch floor and smiled because even he'd got used to the revenuer. I don't know when my smiling turned to crying, and I didn't cry out loud or even hard, just slow hot tears that formed cold on my cheeks. I closed my eyes, picturing the revenuer in the dark woods, feeling his hands on my face, the way he'd held it to kiss me for the last time. I really did love him, and I knew he loved me, and that's how come him not to beg no more for me to go. I figured he knew I had things to do since me and Mama took him to Injun Gal's. And besides, he'd come in a wan of getting us both killed that day and it was eating him up.

I didn't get up at my usual time. I waited, watching the sun stencil twenty-four windowpane patterns across Hamp's bed. I listened to the birds singing off in the woods, a empty sweet sound, and later to Hamp and J.B. quarreling in the kitchen. And even that seemed ok. The early morning rattle of spoons on cups, the coffee smell, made everything seem gelled and sunny-cold, so sad, so same, but right. I couldn't have gone, I couldn't have left here.

One time, J.B. jumped up and slammed a chair against the wall and bellered at Hamp, and it seemed far away, didn't matter. Even my singing didn't matter, and generally on Friday mornings I went to thrilling about that night. And memories are sweet, something to hold against the sameness of days, against a wall of loneliness. I felt like I'd plugged back into my world the way it was before the revenuer come. I started thinking like I used to, about trying to get the boys out and away from there, to Nashville, and didn't even picture myself going with them, just staying on to take care of Hamp. Where I was in the beginning, seemed like, nothing out there for me. Because it was too late, too late. I was old again.

Generally, when I didn't get right up, Hamp would knock on the wall. He didn't that morning, so I waited while him and J.B. stomped out back, still quarreling, shaking all twenty-four windowpanes.

A quiver of sunlight settled over the room with the bitter smell of cold smut. The leftover fire made a ticking sound, smoke rising up the smut-feathered chimney. I watched the melting log as I listened to their quarreling fade out to the woods. Then I folded my hands under the pillow and closed my eyes, sleepy now, sleepier than I'd been since I was a girl going to school. Up at the break of day to catch the bus, then standing sleepy-eyed out front to wait. The woods pine-tart and waking with birds and squirrels while all I wanted to do was sleep. And later, in the school room, I'd come alive only to doze during one of the teacher's talks. A lot of the girls had best buddies; they'd hold hands up and down the hall. I didn't want one. The quickest way to make a close enemy is to make a close friend. The quickest way to get hurt...

Just about the time I dozed off, I heard one of the boys easing barefoot up the hall, like they'd been waiting for J.B. and Hamp to clear out. I let go of the sound and fell deep into sleep, like dropping down a well, with my stomach streaking fire, then snapped awake to lips on my forehead.

The revenuer stood over me, holding out his dirty pink-flannel ropes, smelling of black Ithmaol. His smiling face was scratched, his green eyes sunk in his head. "Keep me awhile longer," he whispered.

I buried my face in the pillow, feeling the end of a feather stick my lip. "Go away, go on."

He laid a hand on my shoulder. "Not without you. He's crazy. He'd kill you."

"No, he would not." I didn't look up.

He turned me over on my back; I kept my eyes closed, dark behind the lids.

"He could," he said. "I can't risk it. I can't go back without you."

"Then I'll go with you." I stayed there, still and shaking.

He laid beside me, sideways to keep from falling off the edge. "Merdie, don't cry, don't cry."

My bed was full.

IX

was beginning to know a sadness I'd never known before, a film settling over my eyes. I'd known fear and I'd known pain, but not all that much, because if I couldn't fix it, Mama could.

At the Legion that night, I sang "Wall of Tears" with as much feeling as K.T. Oslin, but in my own voice, my own style— Merdie Lee, toe-tapping and all—not so worried about Hamp killing the revenuer as my promise to go. It ate at me from the inside-out, and strange too, I felt somehow I'd let down the daddy of my babies.

Standing up there singing my heart out, with everybody for once cold-listening, I thought about Bo Dink, who'd got out downtown at the pawn shop. Now that he had a little cash to call his own, he couldn't wait to spend it, probably on a knife or some shotgun shells. Didn't give a flip about singing no more.

Just last week, I'd made him sing in the school talent show, for experience, and it went bad as you can imagine. One or two of 'em laughed at him, made him mad, made me sorry I'd pushed him. Course he won—nobody else couldn't sing. So in his estimation he hadn't done a thing but run a risk of not being popular. But it was for his own good, I kept saying to myself. For his own good. How many mamas say that when really it's for their own good? And now I felt sad, knowing I could be leaving, though I didn't never believe I would.

My eyes were tearing up; my voice cracked. I even felt guilty for showing such sadness, for that film settling over my eyes. I thought about Israel, picking his guitar behind me, and I knew he'd come just to haul a load of shine. Not to sing. And then when I thought about Little Noah, I missed a whole string of words in the second verse. He couldn't sing. He really couldn't. He sounded like a tobacco auctioneer. My baby, my baby that I could up and leave for some stranger! My baby, I pure hated to hear sing! What he loved was to draw and I didn't even want to look at his pictures no more. And what if he was touched in the head and nobody else wouldn't take up even the little bit of time I took with him? To get through the song, I had to think mean about all of them, how they'd let me down. And when I did get through, the crowd clapped and whooped, then went on with their drinking.

During break, Old J.J. the manager, grinning and raking his beard down, set in for me to sing "Two Hearts" by K.T. Oslin. I told him I didn't know that one, but I did. Got to where I could lie and look him straight in the eye.

That night, seemed like everybody loved the serious, sad stuff, didn't care a bit for the old half-joking love songs about broken hearts that wouldn't mend but did.

I was shaking cold and couldn't keep my mind on the old stand-bys me and the boys sang together. Sometimes I made up words, and I'd catch sight of J.J. shaking his head. I didn't care.

When we'd get done with one song, somebody'd pop up again with a request for "Wall of Tears," and I'd put them off long as I could, till I knew if we kept drag-assing on the old stuff, we'd get kicked out. I don't know why I didn't want to sing Oslin; I could sing her so easy without having to think— get on with my worrying—cause she said *fanger, thang, thank, sang,* the same way I'd been raised to think those words.

A man with long legs and a spotty black beard yelled, "Hey, Merdie, stop shitting around and sing 'Wall of Tears.'"

I did it again, backtracking over old worries like they went with the song.

When we got done singing the last set, I went to the door to wait for the boys to get a beer, and the manager come up and stood beside me. I figured he'd go to hammering on me making up words to tunes, or on Little Noah, and I was fixing to tell him off.

"Merdie," he said, "you keep sanging like you done tonight and pretty soon you and the boys'll be ready for Nashville."

I shot him a look.

His eyes set on the parking lot where the cars was frosted over in the white lights. "Yep," he said, smoking, one boot propped against the building, "I got connections I ain't told you about."

The moon was up good, almost full, like a bubble in the wind. I watched it, waiting for the thrill I'd come to expect, and it didn't come. But something stirred inside me—hope. "Little Noah too?"

"Shore." He drew on the cigarette and flipped it out, the orange glow fading on the white cement.

"But I thought you said he couldn't sing."

"I did," he said, poking his hands in his pockets, "but tonight he sounded better."

I knew he was lying.

"Round up Bo Dink tomorrow night." He started back inside. "I got a drummer and a steel guitar lined up to play with y'all at Top Twenty. Even got a keyboard. See you learn 'Two Hearts' before then."

We picked up Bo Dink downtown at the corner of Ashley and West Hill. He was setting on a bench by the street, tapping his toes and gazing off at the corner store where night lights burned in the windows around squares of for-sale signs.

On the way home, I put in like I was real excited about singing at Top Twenty, all the time listening to Bo Dink flicking his new switchblade in the back seat and Little Noah begging to hold it. Israel turned on the radio, and K.T. Oslin was belting out "Wall of Tears."

I'd about had a bait of her and that clicking switch blade. "Turn off that shit!" I yapped at Israel, then half-turned to where the other two gentlemen could see my face. "And if I hear tell of a one of y'all dealing dope, I'll beat the hell out of you." When I'd opened my mouth, I hadn't had no idea what would come out.

They set up straight then. They hadn't never heard me cuss before. And I knew they'd go to Top Twenty tomorrow night without a word out of the way.

One thing didn't let up before another one come down. I'd checked the latch on the middle room door, checked Hamp through different stages of snoring, checked the boys settled in, watching the tv, before I went in to sleep with the revenuer.

Me low like I was, he set in to bring me out of myself, doing stuff we hadn't never done, stuff nobody in the flatwoods hadn't never heard tell of. We quit, listening to a keen spray of water on the dirt, other side of the wall. "What's that?" he whispered.

"One of the boys peeing off the porch." I held my breath, setting back and astride the revenuer's chest.

A floor board squeaked on the porch, another on the hall, steps coming to a halt at the sideroom door.

I went to lunge off the revenuer and got tangled in the quilt, jerked forward, and the cot legs folded under the head—

eeeeeeiyeek-wa-wop—tilting him down to the wall and pitching me to the floor, where I crawled like a scared turtle to the middle room door, got up, opened it, closed it, and dove on the bed, yanking the rough homespun sheet over my nakedness.

The sideroom door off the hall swung wide with a curious creak. "What you up to in there, man?" Bo Dink. His scared voice.

"My bed fell," the revenuer answered. "You want to get over here and fix this thing?"

"Not specially," Bo Dink said, getting closer.

The revenuer said in a strain, "How am I supposed to sleep on my head?"

Oh, no, I thought, the ropes, the ropes are off. In my head I was set to yell out, but kept so still that red squiggles rose before my eyes. What was the revenuer doing?

"I'm sleepy, man," Bo Dink said, in the room good now. "Sides, it's cold. Ma'll fix it in the morning."

"What do you mean *Ma'll fix it in the morning?* Prisoners of war have better accommodations."

What in the world? I thought.

Bo Dink opened the door to the middle room, a little gray light shedding from the open door to the hall. "Fuck yourself, man," he said to the revenuer. He passed through the room, keeping to the trail between Hamp's mama's old Victrola, her treadle-foot Singer, and a black wood bureau with a mirror that thank the Lord hid the bed.

"You little brat," the revenuer said, "get back here!"

What *was* he doing, and what was Bo Dink doing talking such a way?

He unhooked the latch on the door to the boys' room and tried to close the door twice, cursing the nail knob. "Don't nothing work in this G.D. house. Fuck it!" He kicked the door and it flapped to, then swung wide, and the bedsprings squeaked as Bo Dink laid down. His and Little Noah's head on the other side of the wall from where mine was. Pure sweat was freezing on my back.

"Move over, fatso," he said, and Little Noah smacked and rolled.

Now, what would I do? With the door swinging to and fro, I couldn't get up and rope the revenuer again. But if I waited till morning, Hamp or the boys one would for sure find him untied. I laid there, my chest stinging so I thought I was having a heart attack. I could hear the revenuer breathing, not twenty feet away, but he'd quit yammering at Bo Dink. Then I figured out that he'd ordered Bo Dink around, betting against him doing what he was told. I thought about that, how the revenuer could have laid there and not said nothing and Bo Dink would of switched on the light and found the ropes by the bed and the revenuer buck-naked and then he might have seen me too, woke Hamp and the boys and... Lord God in heaven! What have I been up to? Hamp would kill us both for sure, this time. I still didn't know if he'd overheard us talking the day the helicopters come. And the boys, my boys... I hadn't never done a thing to make them think bad of me. And my mama...she would know. And my daddy would roll over in his grave. I tried thinking about Mary Madgalene and Jesus and how he got around that crowd fixing to chunk stones at her—*Let he who is without sin cast the first stone*. And I knew my whole bunch would chunk stones at the Lord hisself.

How was I going to tie up the revenuer again?

A breeze picked up and flapped the door to the boys' room. It swung a little and swung back, a regular racket. And with each fresh squeak of the hinges my heart leaped, teeth tearing at my bottom lip.

"Shit!" Bo Dink jumped up and kicked the door to with a shrill *eeeeeiek-ba-bap*, then dragged a chair across the floor and propped it shut.

I just laid there. Thank you, Jesus, thank you. I could feel the revenuer thinking it too. I thought about how much worse off he was than me with blood rushing to his skull. Had to be. He hadn't moved a hair since the head of the cot went down. Still I didn't get up. I just laid there. Till I could hear the old house settling on the blocks, a faint ticking, till I could feel my boys sleeping good, the way a mama'll do. There ain't no mistaking a youngun awake and a youngun asleep, and they ain't no way of explaining it to somebody ain't never been a mama.

Must have been around four o'clock, when night gets darkest, that I eased up, hanging between the bureau and the Singer like a hog in coldstorage. A gray glow on the square mirror the only light in the room, like a blank tv screen in the dark. I tipped slow to the sideroom, pending air between each step, breathing easy cause there weren't no use in giving myself a stroke—what would happen now, would. And I must have been light on my feet, cause the revenuer flinched when I touched his face.

"Merdic?" he whispered.

"Hush." I bent low and felt along the cold floor boards, my fingers feeling for the brittle ropes, finding them, and then feeling for his head, still tilted down—he was scared to move for fear the whole cot would drop. Him lifting up much as he dared, I run the rope through one elbow and under his back, threading it through the other one, and tying the knot on the side closest to me. Took what seemed like thirty minutes. A little light was making in the hall where it sounded like the dark was humming as it thinned. Next, I tied his wrists, knowing how in the dark, I'd done it so much, like changing a baby diaper, and then I went to feeling down his cold hairy leg under the quilt that draped from his hips to the floor.

"Oh, Lordy!" I hissed. "We forgot to put your clothes on first."

"Hell, now what!"

"You gotta stand up."

"I can't; if I do, the bottom legs of the cot might fold too."

I was already undoing the knot at his elbow and my fingers felt raw from picking at the thorny threads. I got it loose and stood there, neither one of us saying a word. The frame of gray light from the open door was getting sharper, so sharp I could make out the joints of V-ceil on the hall wall, then the kitchen door. What time was it? What if Hamp got up?

"Listen, Merdie, listen," said the revenuer.

"To what?" I froze listening.

"No, I mean listen to me." He breathed the words. "Get under the bed and brace the standing legs with your feet and lift up on the center of the mattress. I'm going to get up. Take your time, don't panic."

It must have took another five or ten minutes for me to scoot under and down and brace my feet on the cold metal legs, then lift up on the thin grate that held the mattress, steadying the whole cot while he got up. I felt a little give and spring to the mattress and waited for a loud bump or squeak, and was still gritting my teeth and pressing up, freezing my naked hiney off, when I saw—yes, saw!—his slender white feet on the floor, his britches rise from a heap and glide up one leg and then the other, like a reverse slow-motion movie of a man dropping his pants.

The rooster crowed on the backporch, *Herca-herca-hoo*!

"Hurry," I said low.

"Come on out, I'm dressed." He reached under and grabbed my hand, and I walked on my butt, picking up splinters, a cold burning. Me froze from my teeth to my toes. But I sprung up like a ballerina dancer and took the ropes he handed me. Threading again, through his elbows and following the groove to make a knot.

"Hurry!" he said.

The floor joists under Hamp's room sounded like they cracked and split end to end of the house; he cleared his throat and I could picture him from old habit and fear dumping sand and what could be a blackwidow spider from one brogan and then the other, could hear him grunt as he tugged on the right, set it down and tied the laces, and grunt again as he tugged on the left and laced it, standing and springing the irritated floor like he was trying out a new pair of shoes.

The rooster crowed again, this time right in front of the sideroom door where we could see him solid black like a stamp on the hall wall, his tail and wing feathers spiked like he'd been in a fight.

I tied the knot on Mac's wrists and then his feet and slid back under the bed and braced both feet on the standing metal rung, lifting up on the mattress with all my might. And as Hamp come out of his bedroom and ambled up the hall, clearing his throat and belching, Mac laid down, praying the bed wouldn't fall, and I slid out, scooped up my nightgown, and dove to the middle room bed, praying, period.

Thirty minutes later, Hamp was out and gone to the still and the cot was set level, and thirty minutes later, the revenuer and the boys was squared off around the eating table, having breakfast. I kept my place at the cookstove, scraping the grits pot, wood spoon shaking in my hand.

I was waiting for Bo Dink to speak, but he just set there sulling over his eggs—out of Sugar Pops. They were too quiet; what did that mean? Bo Dink ordered me to bring the salt, and the revenuer eyed him, got up, and shuffled to the woodstove and set down in his same old chair.

"Next time you go to bouncing around on your bed," Bo Dink said to the revenuer, "think about it."

"Next time that excuse-for-a-bed falls in the middle of the night, you think about it before you leave me lying there upside down."

"Don't see as you're in no shape to do nothing about it," Bo Dink snorted.

The revenuer got louder. "Well, your mother will; your mother who by-God is not your maid."

At first I figured he was trying to throw everybody off by talking over the cot business with Bo Dink, but then I caught on that he was jumping at the chance to make a point. To stand up for me, Lord help! "The bed's fixed, no harm done, now let it go." I started toward the table with the box of salt, checking the round of sleepy faces for suspicious looks. How much did they know? How much did they guess?

"Well, I tell you what, Ma," Bo Dink popped up, "if ery one of us'd tore down a bed, you'd a wore us out."

No problem with Bo Dink, he was homing in on his jealous self. But Israel was cutting his black eyes from me to the revenuer, like what he didn't know, he'd guessed.

All Saturday morning, Hamp fussed about J.B. and Colin, their dope doings, getting off on the revenuer. Back to old talk of getting shed of him. And the revenuer was some edgy, not just about the night before. Where he'd been just fine and dandy about me going off on Friday night, about Jeanette setting with him, he put in to begging me not to go Saturday night, for let's me and him to go on and leave while we could.

Mama come by that evening and we drove out to the fire tower, close to Fargo, to check on Emmacee Mae.

I hadn't tried to pick a fight with Hamp and the boys about who was going to mind the revenuer and me gone, I just decided to take him on with me, because I might as well—what was the use in trying to throw them off track? What was set in Israel's head was set. And I was too wore out and sleepy to be messed with. The revenuer was ill as a hornet too, said it was a mystery to him how come I didn't make the boys treat me with respect. Said it right out in front of them! And I come in a wan of jumping on him, right in front of them.

First thing, when Mama saw the revenuer, she went to prying into how he come up with a knot on his cheek—it was healing a sick green—and he jumped down her throat too. We'd about been better off not to go to the fire tower, better off if I'd left him at the house, but I still couldn't tell if Hamp had overheard us talking—sometimes he'd wait till you forgot and then remind you—couldn't tell what he would and wouldn't do if the mood struck him. So, I made up my mind to be civil to the revenuer—he had his moods too, I was finding out—and go on about business. Much more of that yaa-yaaing and we were fixing to have everybody suspicioning us.

During winter, when the woods were dry and prime for fire, Emmacee Mae set watch practically every day. After first frost, when the rains let up and the sap went down, pine straw bedded at the base of green slash pines. The broomsage would turn brown and brittle, a handy torch for the straw and the scabbed-over pinetar, and the least spark mixed with wind would send a sweeping blaze tree to tree across the snoozing Okefenoke.

We climbed up the fire tower stairs, Mama first, the high dry wind flapping our shirts and britches, whipping harder the closer we got to the top. The silver sun, glancing off the patch of billowing sage below, looked like it might bust into fire as it inched west.

Of course, the revenuer was untied, stepping up behind me, while Emmacee's crazy cackle carried down like she was throwing her voice.

"She's touched," Mama called back, stopping me and the revenuer on one of the zig-zag metal landings.

Emmacee Mae laughed out again, probably talking to somebody on the tower radio.

"Ain't never been married." Mama stopped again to rest. "No man won't have her. Shore ain't a bit above using her, though." Her bow legs shook on the landing above, where she held to the sun-streaked rails. Red hair fanning against the high blue sky, she looked like a perched tilly hawk.

She was scared of high places—the only thing she was ever scared of, to my beknowest. I knew she'd stopped to talk till she could get the guts to climb the last set of beat-metal rungs, shadowed by the bottom of the tower room.

When we got to the top, Mama pushed through the square metal hatch, and me and the revenuer went in behind her.

Emmacee Mae was setting on a stool at a stand in the middle of the room, talking into the mike of a two-way radio on the shelf below. A glass dome over a plate of numbers, like degrees on a compass, was bolted to the top of the stand, with what looked like a little cannon aimed at the north woods. Her big belly set on her lap, snugged round by a dingy white t-shirt with a blue arrow pointing down to her skinny long legs. The word "Baby," in the same faded blue as the arrow, bagged on her bosom. She looked girlish with her tender pink skin and straight body, but like myself, was no spring chicken.

"I got company, Ella Faye, I'll call you back." She laughed—sounded like she needed to spit—and the shrill racket filled the glassed-in room. She kept her pinkish-green eyes on the revenuer.

Me and him stood stacked up against one another in the space on the other side of the stand, while Mama sidled around and bent down to check Emmacee Mae's ankles.

"You must be the revenuer everybody's talking about?" Emmacee ignored Mama, hopped off the stool and stood still.

Mama set back on her heels, eyeballing Emmacee's low, hard belly under the hiked top. "Baby's done dropped."

Emmacee's long face was set off by frizzy blonde ringlets, drab in the brightness.

"How you holding up?" Mama asked.

"Back's a-killing me." Emmacee grabbed her back and cackled, spit spraying in the hazy light. "I ain't never seen no revenuer before."

The revenuer looked at me, his face waxy in the glare of glass. "How'd you hear about me?" he asked her over my shoulder—"just curious."

"Why, everybody in these parts knows you took up at Hamp and Merdie's."

Mama listened to Emmacee Mae's belly through the stethoscope. "Had any labor pains yet?"

Emmacee looked down at Mama. "Uh uh, not yet."

"Can you operate that apparatus?" The revenuer nodded to the dome glass on the stand.

"That thang?" Emmacee nodded too. "Some. Mostly I just holler for help when I see smoke." She held up the mike.

"How far does that radio transmit?" the revenuer asked.

Emmacee looked puzzled, skin gathering on her high white forehead.

"This radio..." Reaching out, the revenuer took the mike. "How far does a message travel?"

"Clear out yonder to Cornerville, next tower." She pointed west out the window over the weed-like trees where a few tin roofs glinted in the sunhaze. "Far enough to get word to the forest crew if they's a fire."

Mama peeped over the smeary glass dome at the revenuer as she folded the stethoscope and placed it in her bag on the floor. "Son, don't go getting your hopes up, ain't a soul around on your side." She shook her head. "A crying shame."

I thought maybe she meant it was a crying shame that he was a revenuer, then she went on. "Swanoochee County's a world to itself—we don't get much hearing from out there." She waved her hand, as she stood up and gazed out. "They don't get *none* from us."

"Y'all see them helicopters yesterday morning?" Emmacee Mae's weak eyes lit up, her scoggin neck stretched. "Like to run clean into the tower. Racket come in a wan of blowing out the winders. I thought the world was coming to a end; sun turnt just as *dark* with big shaders falling everywhere. I got down on my knees and covered up my head, just a-hollering. Hope they didn't mark the baby."

"Did you talk to any of them?" The revenuer held out the mike, clicked the button to static, let go.

"Who me?" Emmacee cackled out. "I ain't fixing to, not with them aiming for the tower, me in it."

Dau2

= 2

Janice Daugharty

I looked at the map of Swanoochee County hanging on the west wall, at the graph lines that to me stood for nothing, then out over the woods at the tops of trees I'd never seen, except cut and laying broadside. Sandy roads marked the woods in picture puzzle pieces, trees an even green in the still haze. Planted pine saplings in rows of square clear-cuts, no seed trees left to seed a natural, interesting and cheap forest. I could see the black ribbon of Tom's Creek in the east and the Swanoochee, a little west, which ran in the same direction, thinning out to a brown thread across the green woods. And I wondered if maybe the flatwoods was really all that different from anywhere else, say, Nashville for instance, if we weren't doing about the same things they did—thinking alike even—if life wasn't the same all over the world, just living. But it still seemed better and busier out there in the big world, more to pick from. More what? And what if *out there* was just somewhere I thought I oughta want to be?

Looking southwest at the dirt roads parting the woods, I could make out the bright red, green and blue pickups of deer hunters, colored dots on the roads, like stick pins on a map. And I thought about the time I'd happened up on a bunch of them in Al Hammock. One of the hunters, standing at the let-down tailgate of a pickup, pumped up and back in a rhythm, holding fast to the rump of a dead doe deer. Her cloudy-brown eyes gazed out from her sharp lolling head, the coat of her neck sliding loose on the truck bed. The others, huddled around, cheered the man on. Directly, the man shuddered and groaned like he was hurt or cold, seized up, then backed off and zipped his pants. Another man come up to take his place, flushed and wall-eyed—they all were. And even with them crowded round, their backs to me, I knew what they were doing. And deer hunting, how it used to be, was tainted forever after. I hated them for that, and I was scared, cause if they'd do that to a doe, I figured they wouldn't be none too choosy about what they'd do to a woman. And maybe, just maybe, the world out there was

168

just as nasty, people were.

"Emmacee," Mama said, "you send somebody running when you feel the first pains. Don't wait for your water to break. Best of my recollection, your babies don't mess around when they start coming." She lifted the hatch, started wobbly down, and called back. "And don't raise your arms up to hang out clothes, cord might wrap around the baby's neck."

The revenuer stepped down behind her and stopped to wait, me still in the tower.

Mama called up, "If your girl don't find me at home, tell her to go on to Merdie's."

Emmacee cackled and set on the stool, holding the mike. "Tell Hamp and the boys I said hey."

When we got back to the house, Hamp was still gone. From where me and the revenuer set on the back porch settee—him hog-tied again—we could hear him knocking around at the still. I set close to the revenuer, feeding him sips of hot coffee while we watched the sun set low behind the trees and the full moon rise in the east. Rose and silver light mingling halfway the hall.

I listened for the train whistle, hoping to keep from getting into it with him over the boys, over me going to sing. I fed him another sip, cupping my hand under his beardy chin—in all the commotion that day, I hadn't had the chance to bathe or shave him, had got use to him doing it hisself, but the only time he'd been loose was to go to the fire tower. Saturdays, the boys were in and out.

"Don't go tonight." He looked me right in the eye.

"I got to." I stood up, peeping off the edge of the porch for Hamp. I could hear him talking to J.B. or maybe Colin. Somebody'd said Colin was back from Florida. Then I heard Israel's car crank up at the old sawmill, done loaded up.

"Listen," I said, setting beside the revenuer, "I *have* to go

169

tonight. Last night our manager said he might be able to hook up with somebody to get the boys to Nashville."

The revenuer leaned forward for me to feed him some more coffee, then set back. "I don't mean to sound as though I think you're stupid—understand? But this *manager* might be a con man, out to take your money."

"He pays *us*, paid us good last night."

"Well, I'd look out." He wiggled around on the wood settee, staring off the end of the porch where Hamp and J.B.'s fussing carried to the yard. "Pretty faces and good voices are a dime a dozen in Nashville."

"You just saying that cause you want us to leave tonight." I could feel myself getting mad. Why did I always have to battle to get to sing?

"No, I'm not. It's just that sometimes you're a bit...naive."

"Naive?"

"Yeah, unworldly, unsophisticated."

I held up one hand; the cup shook on the saucer. "I know what *naive* means, and I know you think I'm ignorant."

"Innocent."

"Same thing."

"No, it's not."

We were talking too loud; I spoke louder. "Makes me wonder how come you to have anything to do with me."

He threw his head back and laughed.

"You better go on to your room before Hamp comes in; don't want to tempt him." I got up and went around the corner to the kitchen and set the cup and saucer on the table.

"Merdie." The revenuer toddled to the doorway. "I'm in more danger than you know. Let's go."

"No." I shoved around him and started up the hall. "I ain't going nowhere with you. Tonight I'm turning you loose. Go by yourself."

"I'm sorry I laughed, it was just funny. I didn't mean I wouldn't have picked you, given the choice. I *do* have a choice.

Remember?"

"No." I felt raw inside, blistered. "You're just like Hamp and J.B., the rest of them—needing to come."

"That's a lie!" He hobbled behind me to my bedroom, poked his head through the half-shut door. "And I'm sick of being called the revenuer, *woman*."

That evening, on the way to Top Twenty on 84, I didn't say nothing to the boys. I didn't say let's sing, I didn't say let's don't. I wasn't begging Mr. Nobody. And they must have thought I was mad for sure; that's how I got their attention since I'd quit switching their legs.

I didn't say nothing to our manager neither. When we got to that fancy-dancy place—nearlybout as big as the city auditorium—I just followed him down the gray brick hall to a dressing room, walled in the same gray bricks, mirrors on all four sides—for me by myself! Him blabbing in his tight-lipped way about how he wanted me to snap my *fangers* and tap one toe and not two, said he wanted me to take the mike and walk out in the audience and *sang* to the crowd. Then he handed me a plastic bag with a pair of six-inch red heels inside.

He stood outside the door and smoked while I went on in and stripped down and put on the red sparkly sequin dress he got off the old gal used to sing for him. Waist wasn't big around as a doll's. When I got it on and got it zipped, the snug, heavy skirt reached to the floor, and the top bagged to the waist from the skin-colored mesh neck where a row of sequins picked up above what was supposed to be the bustline. The mirrors, ahead and behind, shot back the reflection of my brown nipples, withered hibiscus, draped in mesh.

When Little Noah was born, I took the mastitis and Mama had to bind my breasts with a diaper. A month later, when the binding come off, they was shriveled and flat as scalded flowers, like the diaper had mashed the air out. How had I let the revenuer touch them—I covered them up with my hands—and what if I was wallowed-out down there too? Little Noah was every bit of twelve pounds, and I'd tore bad when his shoulders come out. For a long time, I'd lived in a dread, remembering what my mama had said to Aunt Teat the beggar woman after one of her crippled babies was born. She'd told the old woman not to worry if she heard a farting sound from her tee-hiney; it was just air from getting so tore up and wallowed-out. I'd been safe as long as no man messed with me—safe from knowing for sure—because on the outside it didn't show.

I was fixing to take the dress off when I thought about something. Falsies. What had the manager said about falsies? Rummaging around in the bag on a chair, I come across a compact of pancake makeup, some blue eyeshadow, a bunch of colored pencils, a stick of black mascara, and some candy-apple red lipstick—God, I hadn't never wore makeup in my life, never wore color of no kind. I wore white blouses and skirts, either dark green, navy, or brown, and shoes I could walk in, either loafers or ballerinas. Something in the bag snagged my nails and I peeped in at two white styrofoam balls, the kind you decorate with for Christmas. Huh uh. Lord, he couldn't mean for me... My titties might be flat, but they still had feeling.

I put the balls in anyhow, feeling the sandpapery grate on my nipples, but they stuck to the sequin material like it was made for styrofoam balls. I looked sideways in the mirror and saw them sticking out hard and round; wouldn't fool nobody, not even in the dark. But that was ok—even my own boys wouldn't recognize me in this get-up—and if I didn't move around too much, I could stand the pain.

"Don't be sparing with the makeup." Our manager knocked twice on the door. "And don't forget to tease that hair up, high."

Tease. Uh huh, that's what I looked like, a tease. I didn't answer, could hear drums throbbing up front like somebody's bad heart through a stethoscope.

Finally, I got my hair up high and tight, pulled a few bangs loose, and put on the sticky pancake, the same stocking color as the mesh chest of the dress. I looked like the corpse of a holy-roller—oh, Lord! But when I got done with the eyeshadow, the lipstick, and the mascara—I didn't try the pencils, figured I couldn't fit another mark on my tiny face—I at least looked alive.

"Merdie," our manager yelled, "get a move on. Time to go."

Now, I didn't know if I could walk out there or not in such a get-up. Felt like my face was on fire. I turned around to set down and put on the shoes and stepped on the tail of the dress, it drawing like a corset on my rump. The shoes were a good size too big, so I got some wiping paper from the toilet and stuffed the toes. When I stood up again, I leaned like the wind was blowing at my back. I took a step and felt the split in the tail of the dress rip a little higher. Now, I *knew* I couldn't walk out there.

I toddled to the door, one foot crossed over the other, and opened it a crack, just to where I could see our manager's green-plaid shirt stretched across his belly. "I can't walk in these shoes," I whispered.

He tried to peep through the crack. "Shore you can," he said, grinning. He threw his cigarette down on the cement and ground it with his boot toe. "I want you to do what I said, walk around with the mike and sang to the crowd."

"I can't walk, *period*."

He shoved the door open and caught one of my sharp shoe toes. "Let me look at you. Yeah, you need a little more lipstick." He went on past me, got the lipstick off the gray counter under the mirror and come back, parting his lips, that gash in his beard, and smeared it around the natural line of my lips.

I didn't want to look. Oh, Lord, what would the boys say when they saw me?

"That's it." He stood off, holding up the long red lipstick, it flashing in all four mirrors like a dog's ding-dong. "Yeah, just how I like my girls—miniature figgers of a tall woman. We gone make a star out of you, babe."

Well, so what if the boys thought I looked funny. I went back to thinking like I had when I got there; I didn't owe nobody nothing, was doing the best I could. So was J.J.

By taking short, quick steps I made it down the long hall to the door of the main room, where J.J. made me stand while he went in to introduce me, pumping me up to be somebody. When the crowd went to clapping, I tipped on in, smiling like a clown, a spotlight searching out and slamming me. I didn't look at the boys, but I could tell, as I stepped up on the stage, that there were at least four more fellows with them, loose and waiting in the near-dark.

I didn't say nothing. I just went to singing "Two Hearts" like the manager'd said, the band blasting and blurring out my boys. For all I knew, they could be gone. All I could see was smoke and flashes of faces either side of the hazy beam of the spotlight. When I got done with that song, I didn't let my tongue cool before I lit in on another number—everlast one of K.T. Oslin's—stuff I didn't know I knew. I got real comfortable singing Oslin's music, till we ran out of her songs. Then I yodeled, picking a guitar passed from the back, and made up words to tunes chose by the band like my daddy learned me, like I'd learned my boys. *Just cause you can't catch the words on the radio*, Daddy'd say, *don't mean you can't sang to the tune*.

I had everybody eyeing me, eyeing the boys, the back-up steel, the drums, and the electric guitar making us sound like we were something. The keyboard, played hard and fast and wild by some pimple-faced boy wearing a Grateful Dead t-shirt, sounded like two bands in one, alive like the radio. The bright whang of the steel made my hair pull tighter, my raw breasts shrink.

During break, the boys loafed off, looked like they didn't

even notice the dress nor nothing—well, well. I didn't dare try
to step off the stage or set on the high stool brung up for me to
sing from. Once I'd tried to set on it while singing and it scooted
back and I almost went with it. I just stood off to the side and
talked to J.J., my feet killing me. Again, he put in for me to walk
out in the crowd while I sang. I didn't say nothing. Deep down,
I was scared not to do what he said—uptight anyhow, now I
knew we were close to getting to Nashville—scared not to give
it my all while I had the chance.

When I went back on, I hit 'em with two made-up songs—
a real risk. I couldn't tell if they were good, tunes and songs
kept in my head. Felt like I was showing the crowd my flat
breasts. I picked a guitar by myself, the band standing loose-
handed and dumb behind me. First, I sang "I Can't Go Back
Without You," and then "Sam Plus Sue Minus You." Stuff I'd
dreamed up at home. I didn't know if the songs worked or not,
but I sang 'em like I meant it. And I figured K.T. Oslin, flesh
and blood just like me, probably did the same thing and that's
how she got there. Maybe mad. Mad at every man ever crossed
her.

J.J., standing off against the wall, looked like he was God
and he'd made me. He clapped hard with the crowd, letting off
when it looked like the stained glass windows couldn't take no
more.

Break time come and I gave the boys a few minutes, then I
went back on and asked for requests. Both of my own songs got
hollered out, and I knew I was in business. If I could handle
men at the house like I handled men at Top Twenty, I'd have
it made. Be bossy, you got 'em eating out of your hand.

> *I started our poor*
> *and I can go right back*
> *where I could count the chickens*
> *on the yard through a crack*

I can give up the car,
I can give up the house,
I can give up the gold
and the fifty-dollar blouse

But I can't,
no, I can't go back without you

When I went on the road
I had a dollar and a dime,
I had a broke-down Chevy
and a yen for cheap wine

I had a twenty-dollar watch
and a yearning to climb,
come up on my future
with the past on my mind

and I can go back,
I just can't go back without you...

When I got done singing for the night, when everybody went to clearing out from around me—people wanting my autograph—J.J. shuffled up grinning. I saw his teeth for the first time through that shaggy beard. Those styrofoam balls were eating up my nipples.

"Well, well, well," he said, set down on one of the round tables and tucked his hands under his armpits.

I looked him dead in the eye. "Good, huh?"

He laughed, shook his head. He crossed his legs and swung them. "Makes K.T. Oslin sound like crap."

The boys come up to the table, grinning and slugging beer. Neither Israel nor Bo Dink even looked at me, at my skin-tight dress; Little Noah kept gazing like he wondered what I cost.

"Well then," I said to J.J., "how bout you giving us the cash tonight, you keep ten, this time?" If money was what it took to make the boys sing, I'd get it.

J.J. held up both hands and uncrossed his legs. "Hold on there a minute. If you ever hope to sang outside Valdosta, we gotta use the two hundred I took in tonight towards what it takes."

"Nashville?" I said.

"Yes ma'am." He got down, turned around, and placed both hands flat on the table, talking through his teeth like he was telling some secret. "Way I see it, you got your own songs. Nobody can't fault your sanging." He stood up and stretched back a finger with each new thing he thought up. "Look passable geared up in that dress. Got your own back-up here, home-born and raised. But what you ain't got, Merdie, is the cash money for a demo."

"A record?" I said.

"Yep," he said. "Cost a good grand, plus money for the trip there."

I started to dun him again; he held up both hands again. The boys were standing, listening, like they were ready to pick up and head out to Nashville anytime. What more could I want?

J.J. cut his green bubble eyes around the room, now emptying drunks and their smoke, pulled out his wallet and went to counting hundred-dollar bills, slapping them on the table. "I got five here, need another five big'uns to go with it."

"Well," I said, "if we sing a few more like tonight, we'll have it." A good lesson for the boys—work for what you get, save till you get enough. Don't mess with dope and bootlegging for a quick buck.

J.J. shook his head. "Nope. Don't work like that. I got a good buddy in Nashville owns his own recording studio. He owes me a favor. Giving me a bargain if I can get y'all there right after Thanksgiving while business is slow."

Israel stepped up, sway-backed with his white shirttail out. "We ain't got no money, man."

Bo Dink and Little Noah set down at the table, drinking RCs out of the bottle.

"Aw, y'all can't tell me you can't come up with five measly hundred." J.J. slapped Israel on the shoulder.

"I am telling you, man." Israel stood earnest-eyed and pale before him. "We ain't got the money."

Little Noah set up, hands locked around the RC bottle. "I know where some's at, under Pa's..."

Bo Dink elbowed Little Noah, both of their faces blistering. "We ain't got go money," he said.

"Borry it—I don't care," said J.J. "I got big plans for your mammy here." He winked at me. "Gone swing by the Blue Bird Cafe, *the* place to sell a song in Nashville. Woman owns the place does the judging, got pull, decides who gets to sang, what songs gets sold, and she's gone love your mammy." He nodded at me, a prime hog bound for the sale. "See, demo tapes get sent to big record companies; they always looking for good sangers and new songs, good songs like your mammy's. Songs about things right around you, songs about suffering and happy crap." He clicked his tongue and made to walk off. "None of them little independent record companies for our gal, no siree. And we ain't gone stop with the record business, boys: soon as we make your mammy a big star, we gone send her off on the road to tour, us picking up the cash." He rubbed his thumb and finger together, an oily grin on his face. "Get the money and be back here"—he jigged in place—"next Friday night. They want us regular."

"Let's go," Israel said, grabbing up his guitar from the stage. "Ma, we'll wait in the car till you get done changing and washing up. You look like a wore-out whore."

When we got home a slow drizzle was coming down, like it wasn't raining nowhere else in the world but the flatwoods.

I didn't care what Israel thought, none of them, long as I

could keep them headed in the right direction. One week till Thanksgiving; I'd get the money.

Inside, Jeanette was walking the floor and wringing her hands because she'd had to fight Hamp to keep him off the revenuer. A big pecan-stain bruise stood out on her moley white arm. Plopping on the edge of the bed, right at the revenuer's feet, she went on about how J.B. had been by, drinking, and accused her of having things to do with "Merdie's pet." Then him and Hamp had got into it over where the still oughta be set up.

So, I thought, Hamp did hear me and the revenuer talking in the kitchen the day the helicopters come—who knew what else he'd heard, maybe seen! Blood tingled in my face, a red I could see. But how could he have heard around the racket of the helicopters outside?

The rain beat harder on the tin roof, picking up the leftover beat of drums in my head.

I told Jeanette not to worry, and that I'd pay her next week, and she said she was leaving J.B. and wouldn't be back. "Well," I said, "I'll look you up and pay you. Besides, I won't be needing you no more."

The revenuer laid still, watching me, his hands up like he was begging.

Soon as she left for Israel to take her home, I made sure Hamp was hard asleep and Bo Dink and Little Noah was in their room watching tv. Then I went to undoing the ropes, gouging at places where the braid had wore grooves.

The rain was coming down loud and I figured it was ok to talk out. "Wait till Israel gets back, then go." I kept my eyes down.

"Merdie," he said, "please go with me."

"No." I finished picking the ropes on his ankles and started on his wrists.

He raised his face to mine. "I can't leave without you. Please go. I've lived the emptiest life on the road, didn't even know it."

"Strange, I thought you knew everything."

"Merdie, really, this is ridiculous!"

"I've heard that word before."

"Why must we backtrack over...over everything?"

"Go," I said through my teeth, "me and you don't have nothing in common."

"My word!" He yanked the knot out of my hands. "If we don't, who does?"

"I mean like family...music...stuff?" I started working on the knot again on his lap—ok, his crotch.

"We do, we do!" He laughed, like now we were getting close to getting back together. Together. "Hear this," he said in my face, "when I was a boy, I used to go out to my mother's big Buick, parked in the lane, and listen to the car radio. A radio in the house wouldn't go with her decor."

"You blame other people for everything."

"I don't. Why do you say that?"

"Well, you blame your mother for not having no radio."

"My word, Merdie! Forget it. Let's just go."

"No." I kept working at the knots I'd tied that evening.

"Merdie, if I leave you here, Hamp'll kill you for setting me free." He breathed hard in my face.

"He won't." I finished that rope, chunked it at the wall where it slid down under the cot. "Set up."

He set up, staring at the door. "Merdie, he's crazy..."

"No crazier than most." I picked at the knot that had slid over half-way his back.

"I'm not going without you." He sighed, his shoulders went slack, arms falling as the rope fell.

I slung the rope at the wall and watched one end hang on the bed, then crawled across to free it. "If you stay, what happens ain't my fault."

"Merdie." He caught me from behind, pulled me to him and kissed my neck. "Merdie, please, I didn't mean to insult you."

"You didn't." I jerked free, my body tingling all over.

He slumped, rubbing his wrists. "If I go, Merdie," he said, "I'll come back with a warrant."

"I expected you would."

"No"—he looked up—"nothing to do with the shine operation. I don't care about that... I'm coming back to free you."

"From what?"

"From Hamp and J.B."

"They ain't done nothing to me."

"They have, Merdie."

"I did it to myself."

"Well"—he stood up—"they damned sure kept me a prisoner."

"So did I." I heard the rain beat harder, water gushing off the eaves and splattering in the mudhole under the watershelf.

He wiped his face like trouble was dirt.

"Don't worry bout me." I turned to walk out. "I'm leaving anyhow right after Thanksgiving." One last look—he was wringing his wrists, staring at me.

The rain was coming down so hard it was spraying along the hallway, wind sweeping through. I was thirsty, wanted to go to the kitchen for a drink of water, but I didn't. I went in Hamp's room, shut the door, and stood in the dark till I heard Israel come back and go to his bedroom. I still held to the cold door knob, listening around the rain beating on tin for sounds of the revenuer leaving, listening around Hamp's snoring, and the room was dark and still, the way a room is still with more racket outside than in. I felt dizzy, my throat on fire from singing and thirst. I tried to swallow and my tongue was too swole.

I waited another fifteen, twenty minutes, maybe longer. Time goes fast in the dark, where in moonlight it moves slow. *Dark of the moon* come to mind. What did it mean? I'd heard all my life that dark of the moon is when gravity pulls and things weigh more and people eat more, when the moon is straight under. I thought about the moon under my world of swamp and trees, a world I loved and hated, a world needing me, drawing me all the time. And how gravity pulls more than just planets, pulls people together too—is fate. I knew the moon was hanging there above the clouds.

When I figured the revenuer'd had time to be gone, I creeped straight to Hamp's bed. I couldn't see my hands before my face; I couldn't hear my own feet, no squeaking floorboards, no snoring, just the rain on tin, rain on the window panes.

Soon as I laid hands on the foot of Hamp's cold iron bedstead, I got on my knees and crawled toward the head, guided by my shoulder brushing along the bedspring edge. One knee went down on his rough brogans, set each night so he could step right into them when he woke in the morning. I reached under the bed, holding my breath, and felt for the money bag. I hadn't never touched it before except to run it back and to to Hamp. Never needed to touch it. Dragging it to me, the cloth felt sharp as a razor.

I smelled Hamp's face turn to mine, his warm whiskey breath, before he spoke. "You aiming to half it up with your revenuer?"—his young voice.

I dropped the bag, froze, and waited for him to rise up, for what would come next. My left hip was jam up against the fireplace bricks, the shotgun there against the mantelpiece. I couldn't feel it, I could see the barrel shimmery-blue before my eyes, like it was lit up, like the moon was coming strong through the paint-black windows. My ears felt stopped up, the rain way off. I smelled wet smut, felt cold rain drops splattering off the fireplace.

I don't know how long I set there, but when nothing happened, when Hamp didn't get up, when the ringing in my ears leveled off to hearing just rain, my eyes changing back to seeing black, I wondered if maybe he'd been talking in his sleep. I told myself that over and over. Sometimes he did that. But it didn't matter, he knew.

X

laid in my bed, still as death, till the rain let up and the cold, thick as the dark, come seeping through the old walls, till I could hear Hamp snoring. I was thirsty, I was cold, I was scared. And I could feel in my soul that the revenuer hadn't left.

So, I got up and tipped out to the moonlit hall, staying close to the wall, and stopped facing the sideroom. When I crossed the hall, stepping high over bad boards, my shadow streaked halfway to the front porch. In the east a little light was breaking over the woods, the full moon shining low in the west through trees that cracked cold, icing over.

I'd lost track of time, didn't know if I was getting up too close to Hamp's waking time or not. But it had to be getting on toward morning.

I opened the door and heard the revenuer's even breathing, and it sounded like Hamp's between snores. When I got to the bed, I shook his leg. He didn't move but quit breathing.

"Get up," I whispered, "you've got to go. He knows."

He just laid there like he was studying.

"Hamp caught me trying to steal some money, asked if I was getting it to half up with you."

He raised up. "Where is he?"

"Asleep."

The revenuer sucked in and laid back.

I felt for his arm, yanked it. "Get up and go."

"No." His arm swung up and hooked around my neck, pulling me down.

"Please go." I felt like I was sinking, the way you do sick when you close your eyes.

He kissed me, his mouth soft, cool and moist, like well water on the lip of a metal dipper. His skin felt shrunk and dry from the cold. He whispered in my ear. "I'm staying till you decide to go."

"I've decided," I whispered, breathing quick as he pulled up my frocktail and rubbed my leg, then my hip. He kissed my neck, my cheeks, my eyes, cold tracing his lips. "I've made up my mind and that's how come me to go after the money. I've got to get five hundred for a demo record."

He stopped. "Did your manager ask for it?"

"Yes." I kissed him, felt him hard against my belly. "Let's wait, don't! I ain't checked the middle room latch, I ain't even looked in on the boys, what if Hamp...?" But we couldn't have stopped if Hamp'd stuck the shotgun to our heads. Could be, since the cot had fell and we'd got by, we were brave, sure luck was on our side. Maybe like me, the revenuer halfway believed that despite the sheriff's prodding, Hamp wouldn't have the heart to kill neither one of us. But if we hadn't believed it...

"Sometimes...ahh..." The revenuer sounded addled as he slid inside me.

I went to moaning with him, rocking the bed, fire streaking from my toes to my face. The ringing in my ears sounded like it was raining again.

"Merdie, you don't know...ahh... You don't know how these music people operate."

"You don't want me to sing." I set back, ramming him deeper.

"I do...ahh... I do..." He held my hips, moved me up and down, up and down. "You're too good not to, I'll help you."

"Shut up." I kissed him, my tongue searching out his as he searched inside my womb.

A bar of moonlight from a crack in the wall cut his face in half. "Trade places, so I can see you in the moonlight," he said.

I laughed. "Moonlight, sleeping in it, will give you heart dropsy."

He laughed, then groaned, rocking. "Could you do one thing for me?"

"What?"

"Call me Mac."

By midday on Monday, the weather had changed to warm, dry and still. Crickets keened in the bushes bordering the yard. Deer rifles cracked way off in the woods. But that was all that had changed.

Hamp had moped all Sunday, no more puffed up than usual. I decided he must have been talking in his sleep, didn't have a clue to me and Mac. Him or the boys.

Mac now—the revenuer was gone from my head. And I loved him, I knew I loved him. I didn't know what I'd do with that love when the time come, and maybe we'd wind up like lovers do in love songs, pining away, never to be together. And yes, he loved me too; taking that as fact was as important as saying it, as giving love...

What else hadn't changed? Bo Dink got sent home from school for talking back to the teacher. I didn't ask for more details, didn't want to spoil such a fair day. I was used to all of them home on Mondays anyhow.

I went up the hall to set Mac in the sun, and Israel shoved around us, went in his room and shut the door. Scared I might ask him to help out with the revenuer, I supposed. I swear the boys didn't hardly notice him no more, and it all got funny, was to Mac too, because the way it turned out—the boys and Hamp trying to dodge housework—me and Mac had time to ourselves. But the only time we touched and stuff was out in the milking stall or at night. Days seemed to stretch between nights after our blow-up on Saturday.

Oh, yes, two more things had changed: One, I followed J.B.'s example and made it a point from then on, starting with Sunday night, to string clear sewing thread from nail to nail, already driven in the hall walls, across Hamp's door—might not slow him down none, or tell us when he was coming, but at least we'd know if he'd been. And two, me and Mac put our heads together and come up with the idea to tie slipknots on his wrists, ankles and elbows—just in case Hamp took a notion to carry out his threats, or J.B., or whoever might be in with the sheriff, come calling and me gone. Enough shotguns and rifles in the boys' room to start a war, I told Mac, just a hop and a skip through the middle room.

Mac set on the top doorstep, getting on about dinnertime, and I set on the front porch above him, rocking and gazing out over the woods where the sky was clear and blue.

Little Noah woke up and ambled flatfooted down the hall to the kitchen. He'd eat breakfast, and I'd be cleaning out the grits pot while I cooked dinner. That used to burn me up. Now, I didn't care. I could picture him getting up early, someday, like I wanted him to, making hisself useful. I couldn't picture how.

When there was no more noise in the house, no squeaking of floorboards, no voices, Mac turned around and smiled at me. Then he patted the doorstep, motioning for me to come set beside him.

I shook my head, smiling, and went on rocking, satisfied. Satisfied that the man I loved was thinking what I was thinking—a harmony of minds—wanting only what I wanted. And, thinking too of the first time I saw Mac, who he'd been then in my mind, who he was now. I had a feeling of running up on something that made my eyes and mind open wide. Would you ever have thought it, me and the revenuer!

The mailman drove up in his gray pickup, stopped at the mailbox behind one of the big oaks, and Mac leaned with his head behind a porch post like he didn't want to be recognized. Guess he figured that since Hamp hadn't killed him yet, he could look for somebody else to try. The mailman waved as he drove away. I waved, rocking.

The way it felt, setting there, was like nothing would ever go wrong, nothing would change, and we'd go on, all of us, the way we were. Nothing would happen to Mac. I wouldn't have to leave Hamp, with him crazy and needing me. The boys would go on, us singing Friday nights at the sinspots, Sundays at church, the sun would shine, would go on shining, the mailman would come and go, leaving nothing but sale papers, and I'd go with Mama on calls, getting by with her doing the biggest part of the work. Just like Little Noah did me.

Course, things didn't turn out that way. They never do. And you can bet on things going the direct opposite from what you expect and try to expect yourself around it.

I saw Emmacee Mae's girl, Bobbie Jean, come walking up the road, not in no big hurry. She looked just like Emmacee from away off, same drab blonde ringlets and long straight body. All legs. She stopped to pick something out of her foot, then moseyed on toward the house.

"Who is that?" Mac mumbled.

All at once, I got hot all over. I jumped up and went to the edge of the porch. "Bobbie Jean," I hollered, "go on to my mama's."

She stopped in the road, just off the patchy oak shade, and gazed dumb at the house. "I done been there. She ain't home."

"Dern!" I said low, and tramped down the doorsteps, past

Mac, and met her under the oaks. "What you mean, she ain't home?"

"She's gone in her car." Bobbie Jean rolled her hands in her thin print shirt, her faded green eyes pinning the revenuer.

"Well, then," I said, "I hope your mama ain't in no big hurry to have that baby."

Bobbie Jean squinted at me. "She is, she's done down. Told me to run for the grannie woman quick as I could."

I was fuming. "And I reckon you been running quick as you could ever since."

"Yes 'um." Bobbie Jean watched the revenuer, who still set on the sunny doorsteps.

I couldn't untie Mac with Hamp and the boys around, and I couldn't wait for him to hobble along behind me, a mile or so through the woods, to make it look good.

Addled, I called, "Mac, run tell Israel to mind you till I get back. I got to go deliver Emmacee Mae's baby." I walked off with Bobbie Jean up the bright sand road.

Then it hit me. I'd called the revenuer Mac out in the open, and the name revenuer never come to mind.

On the way to Emmacee Mae's, we got held up a good five to ten minutes, hiding in the bushes for a deer hunter's truck to pass. A woman ran some risk of getting raped by a regular man out in those woods, but a deer hunter, after what I'd seen them do to that doe, was a sure-nuf danger. As the truck slung a long curve in the road, it sounded like it stopped, the raw scold of the engine flattening over the woods. So I made Bobbie Jean lay low while I sneaked out to check, keeping close to the edge of the road beyond the curve. Nothing. The tire tracks went on. Finally, I figured the man must have pulled down one of the three-path roads to search for deer tracks. They'd about quit messing around the house since Hamp and J.B. had killed their dogs. Besides, Hamp'd took to walking over deer tracks, leaving his own big shoe prints and no deer trail to follow.

Before we got to Emmacee Mae's little lopsided house

trailer in the pines, I could hear the tv running wide open on some game show and Emmacee howling like a hurt dog. A wheel was grinding on the tv with everybody hollering, "Come on! come on!"

I ran up the doorsteps and through the open door, and there she laid, naked as a Jay bird, on a mattress. She was holding to a yellow tabby cat, sweat pouring off her face, green from the tint of the tv. Her knees were sticking up, her blonde tee-hiney hair shining. Her stomach looked like a blue-streaked balloon, like it didn't belong on such a skinny body.

The cat was curled, purring on her chest, yellow glass eyes squinting light, rising and falling with Emmacee's breathing.

Clothes were strung and strowed till you couldn't tell where the mattress started and stopped.

Of a sudden, Emmacee quit howling and her pinkish-green eyes rolled like she was having a fit.

"Oh God," I said, thinking over all I knew of her case history, as my mama called it. She had epilepsy, she was almost albino, she was retarded, hadn't never been married, was supposed to be one of a blue-dozen younguns daddied by a man called Pappy Ocain—tomcat of the flatwoods, thirty-odd years ago. All of that business had nothing to do with her *case history,* but I couldn't separate it, and as I tried to think above the racket, while trying to decide whether to poke a spoon in her mouth to keep her from swallowing her tongue or check the baby, I forgot everything my mama'd learned me about birthing. Oh God, I didn't know one thing.

"Mama, how could you do this to me?" I stumbled over junk between the living room and kitchen and started pilfering in the tiny sink of greasy, crumby dishes for a spoon. Through the peephole window, I could see Bobbie Jean rambling along the road out front. I found a spoon, turned on the water to rinse it off, and a rusty trickle ran on the grits-coated metal. "Bobbie Jean," I hollered out the window, "run back over and see if my mama's home yet. And duck down in the bushes if you see any deer hunters. You hear?"

Squinting into the sun, she set off walking the way we had come.

"Poor lil ole youngun." As I watched her disappear around the front of the trailer, I recollected that Emmacee Mae'd had two babies born dead, one deformed, before Bobbie Jean come born with a double veil—which, according to my mama, meant she would have a special gift—and everything jumbled in my mind with the hollering on the tv and Emmacee's rattling howls.

I took off to the mattress, got on my knees, and lifted her head. The light from the tv made her drab hair look green. Damp ringlets wrapped around my fingers like worms. Her eyes were rolled up like she was looking out the set of windows behind, and her pink, slick mouth was wide, tongue flat out— low moaning now. I poked the spoon in... well, what was I supposed to do?

Emmacee's eyes shot low, leveled, bored me square in the eye. She spit the spoon out and jerked her head from my hands. "What the hell you think you doing?" she said.

"I thought you were having a fit."

"Well, I ain't," she said, "I'm having a baby." A pain must have hit her because she doubled up, howling in that spit-thick voice, and tumbled the cat to the mattress, where one pale nipple set like a crossed eye. "Where's Grannie?"

"My mama ain't home." I set on my heels. "Bobbie Jean's gone to try and get her." I felt so dumb, even with dumb Emmacee Mae. "I don't generally come by myself."

"Well, she don't do nothing nohow." She howled, then puffed hard and fast with her eyes closed. Directly, she gazed up at me again. "It's me does all the work."

I felt madder than dumb then, because that's how her and all the others acted to my mama to keep from being obliged.

"I can go then." I got to my feet. I knew I wouldn't go, no more than my mama ever did.

Emmacee went to hollering and taking on, raising her sharp white butt off the mattress.

I dropped to my knees at her feet on a pair of old britches. So, her water's done broke, I thought, noticing a pinkish pool on the black-and-white striped bed ticking.

Her knees drawed together tight, but I pried them apart, gazing at her wet gaping tee-hiney. She kicked at me; I dodged, let go of her knees, then grabbed them again and pried them open, and I swear I saw a little white heel pop out from the matted hair.

"Emmacee, listen," I hollered above her howling and the tv. "I want you to take deep breaths. Even, real even. Try not to think about nothing else but breathing."

She didn't hear me.

I glanced over at the tv, at the people shouting "Come on! come on!" while the green wheel whirled round. One fat woman was jumping up and down, looked like she was how come the picture to roll. Spokes of green fell on Emmacee's wasted legs, on my hands, making me swimmy-headed.

Of a sudden, Emmacee kicked me hard in the stomach, and I felt a thick hot gout rise in my throat and what breath was left, going with a grunt. Then she twisted on her side, coiling around the cat curled close on the mattress, and gazed first at me, then at her stomach, like she was trying to see the pain. The yellow cat looked too, then dropped its head like it had lost interest.

"Emmacee," I said, easing to her legs. "Listen, I've got to deliver the baby breech. Lay back and breathe. You hear me?"

"Ooo...eee...eee," she screamed, the people on the tv screaming with her. A gong sounded, the fat woman jumped up and down, the picture rolled.

"Oh my God!" I sneaked to where Emmacee's feet were jigging, her legs spraddled good this time, but she covered her groin with both hands.

The minute I touched the insides of her hot damp thighs, she kicked me in the head. I landed on my side at the open door, glimpsing green pine needles, then crawled back to the mattress in the fake-green light, picking up a jump rope as I went. Walking on my knees to the head of the mattress, I looked down at Emmacee Mae's devilish face, all screwed up in pain. The cords of her neck was tight all the way to her side-slung, jiggling breasts where her arms crossed over to cap her groin.

"Emmacee, listen," I yelled, "I gotta tie you up, so you won't hurt the baby."

She jerked toward me with her mouth open and snapped at my hand with sharp yellow teeth. Talon-like fingers clawed at my face. I reared and dove on her chest, pinning her wrists overhead. Her head jerked again, teeth snapping in my face, but I ducked and wound the rope around one wrist and then the other, thinking about tying and untying Mac. At least I knew how to do something. My heart ached. I hated her, that mouth snapping at me, but hadn't never felt so sorry for a living soul. All the pain of birthing, far back as it was, come to me, a terrible tearing in my very groin. Then she bit my shoulder, the burning pressure of her teeth making me hate her good. I brought my shoulder up quick and rammed her under the chin, and she howled louder, organ music wild on the tv, the wheel grinding, that dern bunch hollering, "Come on! come on!"

Even roped together her hands were free to work up and down like a sludge hammer on my head, as I dodged between her knees, those long-toed feet raking and kicking. She rolled over, trying to get up, and knocked the cat sidewinding. It yowled and tipped back with its spine arched.

"This won't do," I said through my teeth. One thing I knew about birthing: a breech baby had to be delivered quick to keep the cord from tangling and wrapping around its neck. "Lord, what business does Emmacee Mae have having a baby at her age!" I said.

I checked around for something to tie her legs apart with and snatched up the britches, wrapping one ankle and tying a knot, while the other steady kicked. My shoulder and chest were aching, my scratched face on fire. Now what would I do to anchor the feet? While I held tight to the waist of the britches, she gave me one good swift kick in the forehead, slamming me backwards to the tv. I let go of the britches, the room rolling good now with bars of green light.

Then the tv went to static, like it had signed off at midnight; Emmacee got still, like she was dead; the room filled with sunshine from the facing double windows. I crawled back and felt for a blood pulse on her thin-skinned throat, watching her face stretch long, up in the sun, her pinkish-green eyes walling like sun on water. I found the pulse, good and strong—she'd just passed out—and started to get up. Then I remembered that albinos can't take the sun, so I covered her face and chest with a ratty green dress and took off quick between her knees, ready to pull the baby like a calf. I'd done that. I could be too late already if, like I thought, the baby was breech. But I had to try, and I had to hurry before Emmacee Mae come to.

Her scrawny legs had folded back, limp and wilted, and the dark crown of the baby's scummy head poked out of the eye-shaped gap. I blew out, relieved, and went to breathing deep and even for Emmacee, for myself, how I'd done with my own babies, how I'd seen other women do, but there was nothing else in the world but me and that baby, face sideways and turning down, sliding up and out, shoulders squeezing through the pink opening. Nothing else but me and that baby. "Bear down, Emmacee," I said, more to myself than her, "bear down."

After the oozing of the baby's head and shoulders, light striking its face for the first time, it stopped, arms pinned at the sides. It didn't look in pain, it didn't look at peace, but like it didn't yet know the difference in stuck and free, could hang there forever between life outside and life in the womb.

"Emmacee, bear down," I said again, up close between her legs with my hands spread around the slimy, warm-pulsing head—not pulling because I was scared I'd hurt it or maybe stop what little bit of movement there was. Maybe I thought if I pulled, it might back up and come breech. So, I thought, this is birth and this is death, and the first time I go by myself, Mama, I kill one. I wanted to cry but didn't, because to cry would be too selfish, to admit I quit.

All at once, Emmacee's britches-wrapped foot shot up and a metal snap caught me in the eye, a quick yellow light. I fell back, slamming my head against the door frame, my eye burning like potash, my nose running, my ears ringing like Mama's bee bell. Emmacee Mae went to hollering and twisting round, beating her tied wrists on the floor.

I scooted to the foot of the mattress, and with all my might pulled her knees apart. The baby was out, curling on the striped bed ticking in the pool of bloody water. Not all that different from the baby possums at Injun Gal's. Arm crooked, head turned, face screwed. One hand made a fist. "It's over, Emmacee, it's over." How dumb—of course she knew that—but I kept on saying it and laughing.

She laughed too, her spit-thick laugh somehow worse than her howls, but she laid there with her legs spraddled like she was waiting on some man to come and start over.

I put the baby on Emmacee's stomach—her still sprawled and cackling and gazing up—and then finished, somehow remembering everything my mama had learned me, cutting the navel cord with a boiled knife. Somehow I got Emmacee to take the baby to her breast and somehow got her cleaned up and back to normal—normal for Emmacee Mae. I even made soup, gave her water, straightened up the room. Her just as nice as could be, like I was from the church or the welfare office, just dropping by to help.

Picking a good spot on the yard from the window, I went out to bury the afterbirth, wrapped like chicken guts in the green dress. Between two pines, I dug a hole, hacking roots clean, and dropped the bundle in, and covered it up, packing with my feet, while the cool air dried my sweaty shirt. Then I went inside again.

I had no idea what time it was, but when I got done, the sun had switched to the west windows, a lazy swath of light creeping up the foot of Emmacee's mattress to the baby boy at her breast. He laid where the yellow cat had curled, in the same curve.

I kneeled to check the baby again, its tiny scrunched mouth working at the blistered tit, its dark-fuzz head rocking, skin ten shades darker than Emmacee Mae's. "Emmacee," I said, "now, don't you lay out here in the sun tomorrow morning, you hear? I'll be back. Bobbie Jean oughta be in soon to take over."

"I ain't." She laughed and peered down at the baby, her slack chin folding on her pink chest.

"He's cute as pie." I held his tawny hand, felt his tiny fingers clinch. Little milk bumps ran along the flat bridge of his nose.

"What you gone name him?" I got up.

"Israel." She gazed up at me and cackled.

I almost went to my knees again. "How come?"

She pried open a tiny fist. "How come you think?"

I felt tired, so tired. I crossed to the door and stood, staring up the patchy shade road for Bobbie Jean. Every place I'd been bit or kicked went to paining. Then I stepped out to the welcome woozy evening light. Smoke was settling over the woods in the northeast, streaked layers above the green pines. Either somebody's house had burned, or the woods had caught fire. I didn't care. Deer hunters were shooting close by, and I didn't care. Ant mounds were building high instead of flat— rain. I didn't care.

"Tell Israel I said hey," Emmacee called out, "and tell him he's got hisself a boy."

When I got home, two squirrels set under the liveoaks, nibbling acorns. Spying me, they chased up a tree and wound into the leaves, sucking air through their teeth. A mama squirrel's been known to castrate her boy babies at birth, and I wondered if it was really because they were too plentiful or because maybe she'd seen how mean they could be.

I stood there a minute, watching the sun glance around the rust patches on the tin housetop and haze down the sides, pushing the oak shadows toward the east woods. Bright yard shimmery and still, a make-like peace. My feet were blistered, my bones ached—a burning, drained tired that started with my eyes, heavy and drawing. My hands felt numb, too big, like a man's stiff tarry work gloves.

I eased on to the porch, smelling the sunned wood, then down the hall, where the sun fell in lazy slants, dust curls drifting to the set-back shadows of the ceiling. I stopped where the sun started, at Israel's door, not knowing if he'd be there or not. I turned the knob and kicked it to the wall, jarring the windows.

He was laying face down across the unmade bed, and when he heard the door hit, his head jerked up, eyes wide and staring.

"Emmacee Mae said to tell you hey and you got yourself a baby boy." I reached out and grabbed the knob and slammed the door shut. Then I dragged on up the hall, sun striking my eyes, to the next door.

Mac was laying on the bed, head sprung, just like Israel's.

I went in and closed the door and stood there. "I won't be leaving now. I got me a grandbaby that'll starve if I do. My no-count son just used a crazy gal, old enough to be his mama. Neither one of 'em ain't fit to raise a baby."

He set up, still and staring. "Come here."

I stood there, numb. "All I did, I did for him, for them. I didn't really think I was going nowhere, I didn't believe I would. I just didn't want my boys trapped. Trapped."

"Come here." He stood up, shuffling toward me.

"I'm trapped."

He leaned close and put his face next to mine, and I felt my tears wet on his cheek.

XI

The trap got tighter.

When it looked like the long day would go—the sun might—dusk closing slow over the still woods, Tinion Culpepper come by to tell us Mama was dead. They'd found where her car had hit a tree, didn't know if she died from a lick to the head or what. She was all swole up. Said he figured she probably got bee stung and was going for help.

Bees! Mama! Why did you always have to dare God? tempt fate? Why couldn't you be like everybody else and run from death?

She'd nearly died from a bee sting a few years ago, had stopped breathing, then joked and told the doctor in Homerville, who'd charged her ten dollars, that next time she'd spit a little tobacco juice on the sting to draw the poison. Maybe she didn't believe in her own death no more than she did in her quack medicine, or maybe she believed as much in her quack medicine as her own death.

Going on two years, she'd been searching for some answer to how come so many of the beekeepers' wives become allergic to stings, when for so long a sting weren't no more than a needle prick. Didn't have nothing to do with how many times they got stung, the buildup of bee poison, had to be something to do with pollen, what they'd been breathing in, she claimed. So she went to making up pollen capsules and giving them out to build up resistance.

Mama, I swear! Did you know Emmacee Mae's baby was Israel's? Did you trick me into delivering my own grandbaby, knowing I'd never leave the flatwoods once I saw him? Maybe you weren't beestung—maybe you loafed off on purpose and happened to hit that tree? Did you suffer, my mama?

Questions kept popping to my head. Did she die while I was cussing her for making me deliver Emmacee's baby? Did anybody care that she was dead? Did anybody even notice all she'd done, all she'd give up for them?

My answer to the last question come when people started showing up that night from all over the flatwoods. Bringing in banana puddings and pots of venison stew and plain yellow cakes that smelled warm and eggy.

A steady stream kept coming through the front and back, brushing their feet and mumbling, sidestepping along the hall. A whole bunch done setting out on the front porch, rocking and swapping notions about how Mama might have died. Younguns were out and in, bapping doors and whooping, chasing my chickens off their roost. Every light in the house burning, even the yellow bug lights on the porches, every room in the house buzzing, every bed full of pocketbooks and babies. Even Mac's bed.

I didn't try to hide him, neither did he try to hide. While I saw to the food and talked to the women rattling dishes, he set in the hall by the kitchen door for anybody passing through to gape at. They'd all heard he was there. You could tell by the way they looked right over him, ropes and all.

Hamp didn't run Mac back to his room neither. He come up to me once, pushing through the crowd, long arms hanging like a ape's. "The widow woman had her ways, but she done good," he said and shambled out, not even noticing Mac.

Two gussied-up ladies from the church wandered into the kitchen, gazing past Mac, who'd been almost sideswiped by their triangle-shaped pocketbooks. They put their foil-tented bowls on the table and crossed to the sink to hug my neck. "She was loved by all," one said, holding me off to stare with turtle-like eyes.

"Lord, yes," the other one said, hugging me, "umm umm."

Ethel Henderson, one of my mama's old patients, turned from the icebox where she'd been trying to fit a bowl of wobbly red Jello between rusty-topped jars of hot pepper sauce and blackberry jam. "Last night I dreamed about fresh meat, and I told Nate this morning, we could look out for a death." She'd lost the pointer finger of her left hand from where she'd got finned by a catfish and caught blood poisoning, and now the thumb and middle finger met to where you couldn't hardly tell.

Jeanette come puffing in, black bangs hanging in her worried eyes. Both arms were loaded with papersacks of donuts and coffee and froze pot pies. "Merdie, I come soon as I heared—just got off work. Bless your heart." She set the sacks on the middle of the stove, come over to hug me, and Ethel went to plundering through the sacks and trying to squeeze pot pies into the iced-up freezer of the icebox. Just enough room between the walls of frost for the two blue ice trays.

"If there's anything we can do..." said one of the church ladies, now rubbing my hand.

"I reckon you done made all the arrangements," Jeanette said, tugging her white shirttail over her hips.

"Mr. Tinion called the funeral home in Jasper," I said. "They come right on."

"When I got to the road and seen all them car tracks, I

figgered..." Jeanette looked back at the door where Mac set like a deaf man left to wait by the side of the road.

And that went on till we went to bed, me in mine all night, out of respect, Mac stiff in his ropes for what would go on two days.

Then the next morning the neighbors piled in again, along with the preacher, a tall bald man with pinched lips, and the sheriff, all saying howdy-do to one another and to Mac—the revenuer most of them had heard about but never seen, the revenuer like a mad dog rumored to be wandering the woods.

Out of respect for mama—and me I guessed, since I'd be taking over her doctoring—they mostly wandered past his chair in the hall to the kitchen and fixed their plates, then headed for the front porch again. But now and then, I'd spy a huddle of men, mumbling and eyeing him. Mac, not up on our customs yet and edgy as a dog with mange, didn't know it but he could rest easy for a couple of days: even the sheriff, who no doubt was taking advantage of the wake to check on Hamp's progress, would be behaving like a Christian. Same as on Sundays.

I wanted to be by myself with Mac, and I wanted to go to Mama's, to set at her little house and think, to let go and cry. And I wanted Mac with me. All wishes I couldn't have—*Spit in one hand and wish in the other and see which gets full first,* Mama'd say. Dozens of people kept ambling in, loading the table with food, women taking over my kitchen, fanning me, and handing over their handkerchiefs. I knew everybody by name, but hadn't never toted them up to so many, had seen them before in my mind as scattered out and about the flatwoods, in what seemed like a few little houses.

Bo Dink and Little Noah brought chairs for everybody, looking sidelong at me like I might cry and they wouldn't know what to do. They were quiet and using the manners I'd learned them, the same way they did when I got mad or when I threatened to dose them with castor oil. Now and then, they'd slip off and be gone for a long time, then come back, red-eyed. They loved my mama. They hadn't never done a thing for her, but they loved her.

One time when they were little, she'd took Israel to Bible school at Bony Bluff. I knew it cost her in pride because she hadn't never made no bones about how she felt about *man-made religion*—that's what she called it. She read her Bible, lived right by it—by what she took it to mean. But at Bible school somebody must've got on her toes about not going to church, because she come home, hot-eyed—Israel, a big bull yearling at six, draped asleep over her shoulder—with all kinds of cake slices and cookies wrapped up in soggy napkins for the other two at home who wouldn't go.

I reckon I went to church, she said, *now I can go back home and go to being a Christian again, doing good to get back good.*

Mama, I cried inside, while the church ladies worked around me in my kitchen. *Mama, I'm not you, I'm not even good.*

But at least Mama's dying got my mind off the dope, off Israel and Emmacee Mae, off the baby, for a little bit. And I might have killed Israel otherwise, I was so mad. He stayed out of my way, and I did his.

With Mama gone now, you might say I was free from having to take over her birthing business: I could sing, I could leave— Hamp really wasn't what kept me in the flatwoods. He probably wouldn't even notice I was gone. And I'd give up believing he knew about me and Mac. The thread I looped across his door at night hadn't never been touched, no sags nor breaks, and if Hamp had suspicioned me and Mac, he wouldn't have let dark catch him in his bed. No, Hamp wouldn't never miss me.

But my grandbaby was a different story. Him and Emmacee Mae. Both now stood for every woman and baby in the flatwoods. What would come of them without me? And Mama's being gone now—not dead, I couldn't think dead, in keeping with her wishes—in the same way it freed me, trapped me.

The day of Mama's funeral, the day before Thanksgiving, rain fell cold and slow over the woods, the kind of rain that goes on, seems to go on forever, to hook days to nights, to stop people from doing what they generally do to be happy or just survive.

Hamp didn't go to the funeral; I didn't expect him to, never asked. Mac couldn't go and I felt he should, that somehow he was close to Mama, her to him, and whether or not it was true, I found some ease in thinking so. I believe even now that she knew about us, me and Mac, and in her heart no longer thought of him as the revenuer, though she never called him by name.

In the little board churchhouse up the road, where me and the boys sang most Sunday nights, the tall, bald preacher preached Mama's funeral around how good she was—he never said saved because that might've been a lie—even though the church full of Hardshell Baptists didn't believe that good was good enough to get you to heaven.

Everybody, wet and scrunched into the double rows of straight pews, or lined along the unceiled walls, nodded while the preacher brought up all Mama had done good, and I thought about what Mac had said about her having more power than the Georgia governor in the flatwoods.

While the rain tapped on the tin roof and spit at the tall wavy window panes, the preacher read from Solomon, the song about a virtuous woman who goes out each dawn to gather food for her family, and how my mama's family was the whole flatwoods. He called her Grannie and the word flared up inside, was so familiar; the name said in strange surroundings made me feel how important the title was. Not just a name.

Since I didn't want no singing—the usual funeral songs

"Rock of Ages" and "In the Sweet By and By" were sung to make people cry—the preacher had to preach longer, while the rain buzzed over the pines, a no-light gray lasting from dawn to dusk.

Injun Gal stood near the open door, smiling and swaying, her face oily in the rainy light, and stared down the row of people along the wall. I didn't want to know how her old man was doing. I figured he hadn't died—I'd have heard—unless she'd buried him out in the woods next to the possum and hadn't never told nobody.

Jean Stover's baby, a row over from me and the boys, sucked at her tit, wailing out when she switched him to the other one, and I thought about birth and death, how alike they are, how my mama's going linked to my grandbaby's coming, and I knew she'd been right about the cycles and seasons, the moons and tides she went by, the signs in the head or neck or loins, what she used to explain pains and problems when her bag ran low of bottled miracles.

But walking out behind the casket in the rain, to the dug grave covered with fake grass, I could hear behind me the rasping of human legs going to the graves of their babies, and I thought about how sad life was, about the difference my mama made, and it didn't seem like she'd changed nothing much. We all would die.

I looked out over the green pine woods, singing with rain, and in a blinding light like Paul's in the Bible, it come to me that you spend your whole life trying to become a whole person only to die.

That evening, after the neighbors left, just before what would have been sundown without the clouds, I slipped off with Mac, him hobbling behind till the woods hid us good from the house. Then I helped him undo the slipknots. The sky was gray and flat with unrepented rain, the bark on the trees dark, wet and spongy. No sign of sun.

Deer hunters were shooting off in Al Hammock, rifles cracking like water-sogged limbs. Hamp and the boys were laying down in the house, resting up from company, leaving me where I wanted to be—minding the revenuer.

Soon as the rope dropped from his wrists, he gathered me close, rain falling soft on our hot bodies. He didn't say a word. I leaned against him and shuddered; I didn't cry, though I knew I could now. With Mac. I straightened up and we walked on together, holding hands.

He didn't ask where we were going; maybe he thought we were at last leaving. But I think, like mine, his wanting to go was on hold, the rain a bond of days and not-doing. Not doing nothing. Time like it was when I was little, a clock just a ticking on the mantelpiece, a slow time that wasn't time but timelessness. And I was going back, Mac's warm hand in mine, taking him with me, like I could start over. Me and him growing up from there.

What I'd set out to do was feed Mama's cat, maybe clean out her icebox. Seemed like there was always something needed doing, where what I'd really like to have done was set and cry. All at once, I didn't want to cry, and what needed doing seemed not so important, would have to be done over tomorrow and tomorrow and tomorrow...

Stepping from the woods to the clearing, seeing the little house on the right, wet-wood gray, and the closed store on the left, off the sideyard, I thought about Daddy. Only then did I really miss him; before, my mama had took his place, meant we could go on, our family could, me still the child with somebody older over me.

"That's the house where I was born and raised," I said, pointing to the empty house with the dead windows mirroring the gray splotchy light. "And right yonder's my daddy's store." I walked toward it.

The creosote-treated boards of the old store, running up and down, reeked like rancy tonic in the damp, the same muddy red-brown shade. Built one-room square, the store set flat on the dirt, the cold drink box out front rusting bottom, up.

Mac walked beside me along the wet dirt road. The stretch of sideyard grass, between the house and the store, had blanched blonde as the hair of a child and gave off a queer yellow light in the hovering dusk. Everything looked sharper in the rain, though mist swagged like spider webs along the road and over the woods. Woods loud with frogs, the only sound, like the summertime frenzy of turpentine hacks.

At the front of the store, I stood a minute, then stepped under the sagging porch where four raw creosote poles had been reset to shore up the tin watershed. I opened the door, and the grainy cave-brown light seemed to speak, to draw me inside where my daddy used to set by the hour on a stool behind the whittled-on mahogany counter. Stacked in the middle of the room were crates of old soda water bottles, milky green, and cardboard boxes, a couple of mildewed white bee soupers, and a spalling crock lard jar. Odd in the dateless, colorless void of the room, a 1986 Coca Cola calendar hung on the wall behind the counter, tacked back to the month of December, with a picture of a smiling girl in a red Santy Claus outfit. The month and year Daddy died from a heart attack. So young, everybody said, and I knew him as old, my mama too, because they were older than me.

I nodded to the shelves along the walls. "Used to be stocked with sardines and soda crackers and potted meat, what all." I didn't turn to Mac, but felt him warm and damp-breathing behind me, heard the rain ticking from the eaves. My voice went off like a harmonica. "Sugar—he bought lots of sugar for his bees. In the honey business. And sometimes the revenue men would come to check him out for ordering so much. Figured he was a bootlegger."

"Thought you'd never seen a revenuer before me." He held me from the rear, kissed my neck.

"Not like you—they'd come out in the open. A revenuer like you sneaks around." I laughed, feeling my stocky, thick-necked Daddy watching from the stool, watching the revenuer he'd probably hate kissing his little girl's neck.

"He never bootlegged?" Mac wandered along the walls of empty, dust-cankered shelves and picked up an aqua, dome-glass electric insulator saved from the old-timey light poles.

"He never bootlegged," I said, pacing along the other wall to meet him. "He used to send the money home from the store with me every evening in a sackful of candy so nobody wouldn't know when it left the store and try to rob him. He wasn't scared exactly—wasn't scared of nothing as I know of. But I was. I'd walk stiff-legged to the house and when I got there, I'd hand over the money to Mama. I'd be eat so much candy, I couldn't eat supper, and I'd lay awake praying no coloreds wouldn't break in and kill us. Always stories about colored turpentine hands breaking in and killing you with a axe. But what coloreds worked the boxes in the turpentine woods made it a point to be out of the flatwoods by sundown. Knew people didn't want them here. Daddy could've been suspicious of the very bootleggers he protected from the law. He was a fox hunter, kept a pen full of foxhounds, didn't care enough about getting rich—the way Hamp used to—to make shine."

"Did he get along with Hamp?" Mac said, walking the line of shelves toward me.

"No, but they were close kin, and kin looks out for kin here."

"Your mama said that you're part-Indian," he said. "Guess that explains why Hamp and the boys look Indian too."

"Hamp and my daddy had the same grandpa, full-bloodied Indian, according to Mama." I could hear her vowel-laden voice in mine, smothering the dead space like the must smell. I picked up a fishing bait left in one corner of a shelf. He'd whittled the beetle-shaped body out of wood and glued a bird feather on the end. "My daddy made this, Mac, made all kinds of fishing bait. Once he made a little gator out of the tongue of a old shoe."

"Daddy loved to fish, huh?" Mac said, hooking his arm around my shoulder.

"Mama too." I twirled the bait, watching the dusty gray feather spin. "Used to, they'd go off fishing on Billy's Island, be gone the whole day, and when they caught a mess, they'd feed the rest to any gators come nosing round. You fish?"

"Yes." He seemed to be waiting, waiting for me to tell him about the swamp, what I knew. What Mama knew.

"Back in 1932 there was a big drought and wildfire broke out," I started. "Even the dried-up bays burned—covered the better part of 750 miles of the Okefenoke. And everyday people around here would go out to fight fire, trying to save the timber and houses. Mama's Uncle Basil—they were Irish—ordered a bunch of puff water guns to fight fire with. Course, most of it they beat out with pine saplings. According to mama, weren't hardly enough water to drink, much less fight fire with. Late evenings, they'd go out to watch the Bluejohn cattle and wild hogs come up to drink from Tom's Creek, dried up to a trickle."

"Sounds bad," he said with feeling.

I laid the bait on the shelf. "Well, right after that fire, they say the big swamp come back better than ever. Lakes of open black water so pure you could drink it from your hands. All the fish a body could tote out. Course the government got into it, built a big dam where the Suwannee River runs from the swamp to keep the water level up. Going to do away with fires. Cypress won't hardly burn nohow; their tops are too high, feed roots and tap roots both are under water. The government didn't know that. Anyhow, like most things the gover'munt's got a hand in, as Mama would say, they messed up the swamp. Maiden Cane and myrtle bushes are taking over, leaving little sloughs of water a boat can't hardly get through. They're talking about whether or not to let the swamp go on and grow up or set fire and burn it off again." I could hear Mama saying *Fools!* then turning on the revenuer, saying, *You have anything to do with that, boy?*

"Your mama certainly didn't have much use for government intervention." Mac laughed.

I knew he meant me too, and I didn't. Till now. Till Mac.

We eased out and closed the door, a light whoosh in the tapping of rain, like the closing of a casket. I might not be back, I thought, and went cold.

We walked across the sideyard, the dead grass still glowing in the thickening dusk, and stopped at two shed pear trees with bent branches forking from straight shoots of switches like they'd warped from the weight of the pears. One pear still hung, withered brown and sapless as a old woman's tit, and I wondered out loud what possessed my mama to let the fruit go to seed.

Mac shrugged, and we wandered on to a post at the end of a rail fence section where a Mason jar full of water set with a green cocoaler bottle stuck neck-down in the jar.

"This is...was...how Mama and Daddy could tell when the fishing was good off in the swamp." I lifted the empty bottle, watching the water level go down on the jar. "When the water sucks up in the bottle, that means high tide. When it drains, like this, that means low tide."

"Which means good fishing?"

"Can't remember." I walked up on the porch where my mama's canvas shoes set apart like her feet on a rag mat above the doorsteps. No sign of her cat. "I don't want to go in, yet." I already was—opening the front door with its rattly double panes that rendered waverly images of me, of Mac behind on the doorsteps.

"Why not wait then?" he said.

"Because Mama wouldn't have her house turned into a shrine. Cause her old Tom will come back from prowling and need food." Need or want, Merdie? Why food, why death?

208

Why life? I could feel a burr of grief in my throat as I crossed the low yellowish living room with its cold smut hearth, through the curtain partition, to the square kitchen: so neat, so practical, so Mama. But her icebox inside was a confusion of leftovers in bowls covered with plates, saucers topped with saucers. A dab of oatmeal. A spoonful of greens. She never wasted nothing.

I set out a white butcher-paper wrapped bundle of smoked sausages to take home, links so dry and sagey they seemed more for smelling than eating, then dumped all the peas and grits and greens into one big bowl and carried it out back, raking out enough for her old tom in his milk-filmed dish on the back porch where her khaki pants hung from the line between posts. The rest of the food I carried across the yard to her sawdust fishing-worm bed, and while I raked it out, I looked at the store, sinking into fog. I didn't know what I'd do with her place yet, but I wouldn't leave it a shrine.

After washing all the dishes, I decided to turn off the hot water heater in the bathroom and drain the pipes in case of a freeze when the rain let up.

I needed to get home, but at least I didn't have to worry about cooking supper.

Going into the living room, I looked for Mac on the doorsteps through the open front door and he was gone. "Mac," I called.

"In here," he said and knocked on the wall to my left where the bathroom separated the two bedrooms.

I opened the bathroom door to rolling watery light and steam and there he laid sprawled in her giant claw-foot tub with a skin of rust-tinged water wrinkling around his chin.

"Thought I might as well make use of her facility while I waited." He set up, shaking his wet head and water rilled over his shoulders to his waist. "Room right here for one more," he laughed and swirled the water between his legs.

And then I cried.

He stood reaching for me. "Merdie, I'm sorry." He pulled me close, him wet and steamy warm. "I didn't mean to be irreverent, I didn't. I just wanted to make us feel alive, alone, free."

"It's not that, Mac, I know." Already I was shedding my clothes—shoes, sweater, skirt. Then I stepped into the tub behind, sliding with him, skin to skin, along the slope. Hot water lifting us, my pain, all thoughts of food, so oddly associated with death.

XII

ays and nights still seeming to connect in the rain, I slept again with Mac, leaving him free to hold me, to snuggle deep and dry against the wet outside, against the dark of my mama's dying.

I'd gone to extra lengths that night to set up my security system: sewing thread strung as usual across Hamp's bedroom door, latch hooked as usual on the middle room door; I even jammed the top of a chair under the side room door knob, which I knew would look mighty suspicious if somebody tried the door, and probably wouldn't stop them nohow, but at least it might slow them down and give me some time, and in my head I could lay there without watching for that gray seam around the door to grow. I even went so far as to order Bo Dink and them not to sleep with the tv on—to go against my wishes, they'd watch it all night. All well and good, but this time I rigged up a kind of alarm in Hamp's room: I dropped a handful

of pennies in one of his brogans, knowing he'd dump each
before putting them on.

"Won't Hamp get suspicious finding pennies in his shoe?"
Mac asked when I told him.

"No," I said, "stuff's forever spilling out of his pockets
when he drops his britches at night—pocket knives and bottle
caps and change. Old nails and rocks."

"You, Missy, have no conscience."

"Yeah, I do, Mac. Sometimes I feel bad for Hamp—most
times I do. He's pitiful and I don't know if you've noticed but
he's getting more...you know, like he's drawing up inside
hisself."

"I have noticed, but don't expect me to sympathize with
him. The way I see it, if a man like Hamp never got old and
feeble and forgetful, he'd end up with too much power. Like
King David and those other jokers in the Old Testament, who
would have you done away with in a minute. I know you and
your boys would have been beheaded a couple of times since
I got here."

"He still might try." I laughed.

"All the more reason for us to go now."

"I didn't aim to start that."

"Sorry, that started when I came through that door." He
waved his hand before the gray streak of light.

"Tell me how you found us," I said, wedging the backs of
my knees to his bony kneecaps, "how you followed us home
that night."

"I can only give out my name, rank and serial number."

"What?"

"Just teasing, Missy. If you got captured in Nam, that's all
the information you should give the enemy."

"You got drafted and went to Vietnam?"

"Volunteered. Stayed four years."

"Did you get captured?"

"Yes." Mac tightened his grip on me, got stiff.

"Was it bad as they say?"

"Not as bad as being Merdie Lee's prisoner." He laughed and I knew he didn't want to talk about it, and I hurt for him, for that body close and safe, hurt worse picturing how he could still get hurt, how lightning can strike twice.

"How did you follow us home that night?" I asked, changing the subject.

"Actually, I'd been staked out here for a couple of months, watching all of you. Collecting evidence. My partner and I had been on assignment in South Florida; I'd got wind of some racket in South Georgia and North Florida; so on one of our rounds from Atlanta to Miami, I had him leave me in Valdosta, rented a truck—redneck style—and camped out here in the flatwoods."

"So your partner did come looking for you, just like the sheriff said first time he come?"

"What else did he say?"

"Said he'd sent him on to North Florida—you know how he goes on and on."

"Yeah. Apparently, they've been delayed finding me by having to search South Georgia and North Florida—all these woods. No tellings how many J.B.s and Hamps they've run into who gave them bum clues. Who knows? Maybe they've given me up for dead." He laughed. "I'm just joshing: seems they've intensified the search since it's for a body now."

"Well, they got close. With the helicopters, I mean."

"Merdie," he said, "I need to tell you something else—the truth about myself. Eventually, you'd find out anyway."

I rolled over and sucked in. "Ruth, you're still married to Ruth?"

"No, hush, this is more pertinent to us, to you and me..."

"Then how bout using words I know, huh." I laughed, trying to keep what I could feel was dead serious from coming out too quick.

"Merdie, I'm no whiskey revenuer." He stayed on his side,

facing me. "I'm a drug agent. Never was after Hamp's shine operation. I'm with the FBI. You all assumed I was a revenuer."

"You wasn't after us for bootlegging?" I was caught between taking a deep breath and letting one go.

"No ma'am." He shook me, laughing. "Bootlegging is obsolete; compared to drugs, nothing, a joke. Old Robert Mitchum movie stuff."

"My God, and all this time..."

"Yeah. I got caught for being curious, wondering how the hell you folks are still in operation, who buys bootleg whiskey these days. Hamp's still is ingenious. Did he invent that condenser?"

"I guess so." I felt like a fool. "How come you to follow us to Valdosta and back that night?"

"I figured Hamp's operation had to be a cover for drugs, that's why. I mean, otherwise why would you haul a load of shine to Valdosta, leave it sitting right out in the open? I thought maybe the Mafia was involved till I found out you were so desperate to sing that you'd risk the whole operation."

"Why didn't you just come right out and say you were after drugs?"

"Ha!" He laughed. "J.B. would've killed me for sure. Much safer posing as a revenuer. I didn't know whether I could trust you for so long, since your boys..."

"Are they dealing dope?" My tongue stabbed against my gritted teeth.

"I don't know, I really don't know. I suspect that Israel runs dope on Saturday nights from Macclenny to Thomasville."

My chest, my whole body, felt like I'd stuck my finger in a light socket.

"Dobbie Stover is definitely growing pot, trying to make big connections," he said. "That's why he was laughing so the night his wife was having a baby. Thinks of revenuers as horseshit. J.B. does too."

"Would you turn my boys in?"

"I don't know. That's one reason I didn't leave...only one reason...the night I said if I left I'd come back."

All at once, I felt sorry, really sorry, for Hamp. "Poor Hamp."

"Yeah, man thinks he's some big threat to the law." He buried his face in my neck. "Even your sheriff knows better; he made the switch a long time ago, but he still bilks innocents like Hamp, as well as the little drug dealers and growers. It was to his advantage to keep Hamp believing I'm a revenuer, so he'd kill me. Either him or J.B." He laughed. "And who'd get the blame when the body was found? The sheriff and his gang's who I've really been after, them and some of the deer hunters."

I laid there trying to rethink everything I'd ever thought, what I'd took for truth.

"But I have to admit he's slick, the sheriff is, the way he pumped Hamp for money to make it look good. I'll just bet he's hired somebody to do what Hamp either hasn't got around to doing or doesn't have the heart to do."

"Like who?"

"Maybe somebody right here."

"In the flatwoods?"

"Or in this house."

"Mac!" I could sense the truth in that but I lied. "Not one of my boys, not that. They wouldn't dare."

"Well. Well, could be this Colin-fellow then, but I doubt it. My guess is he and J.B. are on the outs with the sheriff. He said something about the little independents." He got quiet thinking. "But Colin would seem the most likely hired gun."

"Not J.B., right? He still thinks you're a revenuer, right?"

"Not J.B. Unless, Colin's filled him in on the details already."

"What now?" I said, holding my breath.

"Well, we can lie here listening for pennies to roll under Hamp's bed," he said, "or you can make good use of your torture chamber."

Since the old rooster wouldn't crow in the rain, I didn't wake up till late. And while the morning broke gray over the woods, a thick gloom hovering about the house, I stood rewinding the sewing thread before Hamp's bedroom door, then snuck in and dressed in my good burgundy wool skirt and sweater for Thanksgiving.

No matter how bad we fought, how bad we hated one another, we all got together for Thanksgiving. That one time of the year. Even J.B. and Colin and their bunch. I didn't dread it like I'd thought I would. Coming out in the hall, leaving Hamp asleep, I gazed out over the woods where the rain looked like smoke and blessed the day that delayed making a decision. Because like the two-day wake and the day of the funeral, a holiday put things off, gave me a good excuse to make up my mind later. But I did decide that if I didn't get the money before Friday night, we wouldn't go to sing; I couldn't chance showing up empty handed. Besides, now that I feared Hamp suspicioned me and Mac, and there could be somebody else out to kill Mac, I had to be more careful about leaving him, despite the slipknots. But Jeanette was back with J.B., and I knew she'd stay with Mac; whether she could keep J.B. or Colin off Mac was another matter. Maybe since I'd learned I had a grandbaby I figured I couldn't leave for good nohow; maybe I figured Mac would soon be leaving without me and wanted to make the best of what time was left.

I stood in the hallway a minute, breathing in the musty damp of the brittle gray walls, then went on in the kitchen to build a fire to dry things out. In the box behind the woodstove, I found only a few litard splinters, a couple of sticks of pine, and one turn of oak. I'd have to remember to nag the boys to bring in some more that evening. I hated nagging them, would rather get the wood myself. But today even the lack of firewood didn't bother me too much.

The wood smelled fresh-split and green from the damp but caught fire right off, filling the kitchen with slow crackling and little feathers of smoke, fire ticking up the pipe as raindrops hissed down.

For some crazy reason, the smell of burning tar reminded me of my mama and daddy cutting cord wood with a crosscut saw. One on each end of the long jagged-tooth saw, pulling and pushing the griping blade across the log in a tug-of-war. Daddy'd have a flat brown whiskey bottle of kerosene in his hip pocket with a stopper wick made of pine straw to dob the saw blade and make it glide smoother.

I would set out in the early fall sun and watch them, waiting till Daddy got the wood split for me to load on the green slat-bodied trailer he pulled behind his tractor. Him and Mama sold firewood on the side only during fall, and while we worked, I'd dread school coming up, the cooling air and the warm tar smell a reminder that I'd soon have to leave them for whole days, a dull chubby-faced me setting in the school room, waiting for the bell so I could go home. At school I was somebody I didn't know, somebody I only felt, my blood running thick and slow, face white as paste; at home I'd play out the rest of the evening, romping through the woods, bright-faced and quick.

Daddy sold firewood to the school, and when I was in the second grade, my room was close to the woodpile, and I'd set listening to the *chut chut chut* of his tractor while the teacher talked and walked up and down desk rows. I'd quit breathing, like it'd make her stop, so I could hear him chunking sticks of wood to the great circle of woodchips and bark set off on the sandy yard. And one time, for no reason that I know of, Miss Rosen held me up to the jalousie window to watch him, and he didn't look nothing like my daddy—not at school, he didn't. He looked fairer and younger; at home, he was dark and chunky, level-shouldered and sharp. His change seemed like one more of the mysteries that takes place when little girls sleep or go to school.

I put on the coffee, smelling it grow rich as the pot on the eye started to sing, then perk p*loop ploop ploop*. The taste of satisfaction set mellow on my tongue. I didn't turn on the radio, just stood staring out over the rain-bright woods. I could make out the copper pipe of the still shining through the blackgums. Hamp had moved the still nearer the house and set a round oak block at the edge of the yard where he could whittle while he waited for a batch of whiskey to run. The block looked lonesome and wet, the still like the outhouse, a reminder of how backwards we were. I felt a sadness rise up inside. How Hamp had dropped fighting with J.B. over the dope patch wasn't like him, and he seemed to be brooding more and more here lately, not firing off but keeping it inside. He'd even slept later than usual this morning. And though I dreaded him, his blow-ups, I didn't feel all that scared, just sad, like something was coming to a end. Would dope end up like moonshine, going out of style when something else come in? What, though? What was left? The leftover feeling of pity for Hamp from last night woke in my heart. But I didn't love him no more. I loved Mac, despite the fact that he could hang Israel, all my boys, though I trusted him not to. Not just that exciting kind of love I sang about, but a deep aching love, something grown between us. And after yesterday, after taking him back home with me, I felt even closer. What would come of it, I didn't know. But I'd know this time next week.

I rinsed out the grits pot, kept turned upside-down on the cookstove, and filled it half full of water. Didn't have to measure the water or the grits like I used to; I went by the greenish water mark on the inside of the pot, poured in what I knew was a cup of grits. For just two, I'd have to learn all over again. Did that mean I was going with Mac? That I'd made up my mind?

When the grits was simmering good, I put on the sidemeat

and listened to it sizzle, smelling the salty smoked fat mix with coffee and burning oak. Then I scooped enough flour in my wood bread tray and cut in the lard, added the milk and stirred till the dough was dry-gummy, sprinkling enough flour to make it knead without sticking to my fingers. I sunk the heel of my right hand into the soft warm dough and kneaded, end over end, then pinched off big rounds and rolled them and laid the balls out in rows on the dented, brown waiter that no longer shined. I couldn't remember it new and shiny, couldn't recall when it turned colors. I didn't care no more.

I was either going to Nashville, or with Mac, or to my mama's. I was going to sing, or marry again, or take up the birthing business.

I can go now, I can go now. I stopped rolling biscuits, stunned to know—really know—that I could. What was to stop me? But which would I do?

I dipped my fingers in the grease can and pulled them out, pressing the balls of dough with the backsides, furrowed prints. Then I slid the waiter in the oven, of a sudden feeling too hot with the sweater and the oven and the fire.

Why had I stayed so long? The boys. Yes, that and not knowing where else to go, what to do, what I could do. And I thought maybe I'd been better off before I had choices, before I knew better, just like the women me and my mama saw every day.

Nate Henderson had give Mama two turkeys he'd killed when the leaves started turning—one for me and one for her— to pay us for treating his leg when he come down with the gangrene. How he got two turkeys, he said, was by shooting the last to fly up first from the flock. Turkeys are dumb, don't scare and fly till they see danger ahead and generally don't look back. My froze turkey floated belly-down in the sink of water, a big bubble, to thaw. I drained the water and checked the bloated bird for pin feathers, then covered it with tin foil, and as I took the biscuits out and cut the heat, I slid it in the oven. I'd be cooking all day, meals back to back.

I heard somebody easing along the hall, then through the kitchen door, and thought it was Hamp. "Come fix you a plate," I said, taking the biscuits up and stacking them on a platter.

A head ducked to mine, kissed my cheek. I turned quick. "Mac!"

He grinned and shuffled over to the woodstove to set in the chair left for him. "Where's Hamp?" he said low.

"Still sleeping." I put my finger to my lips to shush him. "He'll be up any minute. What're you doing coming in here early to set?"

"I could hear you; I wanted to see you." He looked silly with his hair sticking up, his blue shirttail hanging out. "I've been lying there wondering if you still love me, now that you know..."

"That you could ruin my boys?"

"I haven't caught anybody. Understand?"

Was he trying to tell me to warn Israel to quit while he could? If I did, would I blow Mac's cover as a revenuer?

He changed the subject. "Where did you get the name Merdie?"

"My daddy named me after a French woman that saved him from the Germans during the war."

"I love it, I love you." He grinned.

"Shh."

He set, watching me. And I felt silly cooking for people who'd gobble it without so much as a thank you, silly with Mac seeing me go through all the hassle, us both knowing it was over, our life the way it was. We'd both been through something and couldn't go back, didn't want to. We'd changed while the rain kept up the same pace, the world outside, even and bland.

After everybody got done with breakfast and went on about

their doings, Mac still set there, watching me cook. We didn't talk because Bo Dink and Little Noah were in and out; Hamp was hanging around like the houseflies, swarming low, trying to escape the coming cold and sure death. Shots from the deer rifles were regular pinging over the woods.

By the time I put the cornbread dressing and yams in the oven, I was tired and sweaty, anxious to get shed of the skirt and sweater, but at the same time anxious to look my best for Thanksgiving. For Mac. I didn't want him feeling sorry for me, linking me with Hamp; I didn't want him feeling sorry for me being stuck in the kitchen all day.

I started to rinse out a syrup bottle to give back to Mr. Tinion, who always divided up cane syrup with us after grindings, but when I thought about Mac watching, I chunked it in the papersack of trash by the cookstove.

Around dinnertime, J.B. and Jeanette come up with her younguns, who went to knocking the rocker backs against the front porch wall and rattling the window over the sink. (Israel always did hate to see those younguns come.)

J.B. stomped up the hall and into the kitchen, nosing into my cooking. Picking up pot lids, peeping in the oven. Silly as he looked, same old but clean white t-shirt and slicked hair, he seemed a double danger to Mac, now that I knew.

"How you, J.B.?" I said, shoving past him to the stove.

"Shaking like a dog shitting peachseeds." He crossed the kitchen with his thick neck scrunched and leaned into the door jamb, scrubbing his back like a hog.

No harm in him today, I decided, relieved that at least I wouldn't have to worry about him telling that I sang with the boys—he'd forgot. And as long as he believed Mac was a revenuer, Mac was safe.

Colin and Lucy come in, right behind J.B. and Jeanette, her and her bunch of girl younguns plundering in the front rooms, looking for my boys or something to lift. Colin stuck his dark welted face through the door and eyed Mac, then me.

"How you, Colin?" I said.

He snorted at Mac, a sneer pushing his marked cheekpads to his hard black eyes, then lumbered across the back porch.

Uh huh! Proof that he thought of Mac as a horseshit revenuer. Mac had to be wrong about him being the one out to get him, but if he wasn't, then who? Not J.B., there was no mistaking that J.B. still thought of Mac as a revenuer, not to be took serious. But Hamp did, and he'd probably think a drug agent was the trick. Oh, Lord!

Lucy slouched into the kitchen right after Colin left. Her silky purple frock rustling as she moped to the sink and drew a glass of water; sunk eyes closing, she tossed two aspirin to the back of her throat, then swigged some water. Her usual signal that she didn't feel up to helping out. I didn't want her to, Jeanette neither. But there was no danger of Jeanette getting in the way of my cooking.

The rain fell slower as the day wore on.

Soon as J.B. and Colin went out with Hamp to his camp around the still, Jeanette set at the table and told about how tough it was to be a telephone operator, what her boss lady said and what she said back. You could believe about half of it.

"Merdie," she said, "you ever tried a mayonnaise cake?" Her round face looked slick, her dark hair flat.

"A mayonnaise cake?"

"A gal works with me give me the recipe," she said. "Can't taste the mayonnaise. You can get it on sale at Wal-Mart this week, eighty-nine cent a quart."

"I'll try it sometimes." I finished cubing the apples and tossed the chunks with pecans, oranges and bananas, thinking about Israel who loved fruit salad—he had to be hungry by now. He hadn't eat to my beknowest since I'd fired off at him about the baby. Next time, I'd talk, not about Emmacee, but about drugs.

Jeanette rattled on, while Mac set this way and that, twisting from the woodstove to the wall.

"You want me to get one of the boys to take the revenuer to be-excused, Merdie?" Jeanette said.

He got up and hobbled out, and I knew he hated having to take that. But he probably did need to go. I thought it was really kind of funny, him being a prisoner of his own free will. He was spoiled now and couldn't tolerate her not knowing he was free, maybe hated her not knowing he was a drug agent instead of some horseshit revenuer.

When he was good and out the door, Jeanette set up straight. "He's mighty stuck up for a revenuer. I tried to keep him comp'ny, talking to him just like anybody else, and he ain't said pea-turkey. Some people you just can't be friendly with." She sighed.

I felt all at once like laughing, like giving the whole thing up, but I went on and made the tea, a gallon, bitter-black and sweet. Pretty soon it would all be over. But I couldn't picture how it would end: me and Mac going, or him going and me staying— him maybe found out and dead—or me and the boys going to Nashville. I thought about Israel again, about Emmacee Mae and the baby, and wondered if I really had choices.

The long eating table wouldn't hold us all, so I set up my cook table on the back porch for the younguns, my boys throwed in, all except Israel who ate with us in the kitchen: me setting between Hamp and Mac, so I could feed "the revenuer," J.B. on one end, next to Mac, and Colin on the other, Lucy and Jeanette across from us, with Israel between them. Lucy and Jeanette didn't get along.

I started to scrunch Little Noah in a extra place to keep him away from Lucy's girls on the back porch. I could see the biggest one from where I set, straight blonde hair sliding over her eyes, squinting at Little Noah, next to her. Wouldn't be all that ugly if she'd act right. She didn't say a word, just ate slow, chewing slow, but I knew she was thinking up some meanness to get into. I had all ideas Bo Dink had already had things to do with at least one of them. If Little Noah hadn't, I didn't want him getting a taste now. Bad as drugs.

I fixed me a plate, then one for Mac, and started feeding him, while everybody passed bowls and ate.

J.B. put in for Colin, who set with his back to the door, a good head higher than the rest, to tell the story about how he'd butchered a gator with a strand of haywire and a teddybear inside; about how he hunted gators in a little john-boat, him barefooted and snatching them from the water and rassling them down, to either be killed or tagged and took to the Florida Everglades. The only time him and the other hunters got to kill a gator, according to Colin, was when it was a real danger, had done eat up some youngun or somebody's pet dog. J.B. got tickled and like to choked, ducked his head toward Mac and went to wheezing. Colin laughed, low in the throat, a grin making on his flat lips.

J.B. straightened up, like he was looking for something fresh to get choked over. Guess what? "You ever shoot fish, Mr. Revenuer?"

"All the time," Mac said and I fed him some tea to shut him up.

"Shore you ain't a game warden?" said J.B., punching Israel and winking.

Mac yanked his head back and tea trickled down the buttonhole plack of his blue shirt. "No, I'm a hit man."

"A hitman!" J.B. slapped the table, grinning mean, eyes scouting out one and then the other for some go-ahead. "Who you hit, man?"

"You, soon as I shuck these ropes." Mac's head was still tilted like he thought I might put the glass to his mouth again.

"Hear that, y'all?" J.B. said, getting stiff and walleyed mad. "Y'all hear that?" He meant Hamp, who never looked up. "See how come me to want to jump his ass ever chance I get?"

"Now, J.B..." Jeanette whined, reaching across the yams

with her moley white hand.

J.B. raised his fist like he was fixing to slam the table and socked the air, just short of Mac's face. Mac jerked and skittered the chair. J.B. laughed like he was satisfied he'd come out the winner and watched Hamp for praise and, getting none, went on eating.

Hamp shook his head, eating fast, glittery eyes low over his plate. He always held a biscuit or a piece of cornbread in his left hand to shove food to his spoon. When he wanted more tea, he rattled his ice, and I jumped up to refill his fruit jar. He wouldn't drink out of a glass, said it didn't hold enough tea. Same old fruit jar always set on the window sill over the sink.

"I declare if Merdie ain't got her hands full," Jeanette said, dipping pot likker to her turkey dressing.

J.B. snorted.

Hamp grunted.

I handed him his jar and set, fed myself for a few minutes to throw her off the subject.

"I don't know how you do it, Merdie," she started again.

J.B. belly-laughed and reached for another piece of turkey, gnawing over his plate.

"Colin," I said, hoping for some clue to prove or disprove him as the hired gun, "have you got to go back to Florida next week?"

"Soon as I can get right. Run that turkey buzzard down here, J.B." His hard eyes settled on his brother.

"You boys got your dope gathered yet?" Hamp kept eating, broad shoulders hiked from his propped elbows.

The turkey platter stuck, one end in my hand, the other in Colin's, under Hamp's nose.

Nobody said a word.

I could feel Hamp heating up; my hands started shaking. I should have known he was waiting to get everybody together to bring it all up.

"I say"—he got louder, eyes cutting from his plate—"you

boys got your dope gathered yet?"

"Yes sir." J.B. rimmed his teeth with his tongue, blanched face popping sweat. He looked at me. "Who put you onto us, old man? A little songbird?"

Israel, who'd been eating low over his plate, now gazed up, chewing slow, eyes flashing from me to J.B.

"Knock that fly off the taters, Lucy. Will you?" Jeanette's bosom rose and fell like a fan was blowing under the tail of her white blouse.

Mac fingered the slipknot on his wrists.

"I don't see no difference in dope and moonshine," Lucy said, raising her flat face.

Hamp hooked his thumbs under his belt. "They's a big difference, gal."

"Let's don't talk about it today," I said, feeding Mac some yams.

Hamp flicked his eyes my way. "Shut up and see to your boy, woman."

My hand froze at Mac's mouth; I knew he couldn't swallow the last bite. His knee hit mine.

J.B. laughed, went to eating, maybe glad to have the heat off him. Then he stopped.

"Somebody's fixing to find out I'm still the man around here." Hamp shook his jar, rattling the ice, and I got up, nerves in my knee caps jumping, got his tea and come back.

If I'd told right then that Mac was a drug agent, it might have took the heat from Hamp off him and at least I'd have known if being a revenuer was all Hamp had against him. But, supposing they didn't already know that Mac was a drug agent, those two apes at the ends of the table would tear him apart. Besides, I didn't know if Hamp was out for me or J.B. and Colin. I could tell they hoped it was me. I hoped it was them.

Somehow we got done eating and everybody scattered out,

226

leaving me and Mac in the kitchen. We didn't speak till I was
drying the plates, until there was enough noise in the hall and
on the porch to drownd out our talking.

Jeanette and Lucy would be napping.

I watched J.B., Colin, and Hamp go out to the still in the
drizzle. The rain was letting up and time had started to tick
down again.

"Let's go tonight, Merdie," Mac said low.

I kept on washing dishes, gazing out the window at Hamp
whittling where he set on the block before the braiding flames
of a fire. J.B. walked around a little, kicking at the dirt, then
backed to the fire with Colin. "We got time, don't pay Hamp
no mind," I said.

"Merdie," Mac said—too loud, "I don't think so. I think he
knows about us, anything's apt to happen now."

"He was going on about the dope, not us." I didn't believe
that, I just needed more time.

"It's not just Hamp, you know that." He was talking real
loud, taking chances. "What is this with you?"

Israel's car radio was running wide open on the side yard;
Lucy's girls squealed and laughed.

"I don't know what you mean," I said.

"You do."

"I ain't made up my mind yet." I twisted round quick, hands
in the dishpan. "My mama just died, for Christsakes!"

"What's that got to do with anything?"

"It's got everything to do with everything."

"Does that mean you're staying?"

"I've got a grandbaby..."

"So what?" He stood up, face red.

"So I don't want to leave him to starve."

He got low, hung his head, shuffling in front of the woodstove.
"You're not going with me, are you?"

"I don't know. I need more time."

"Tell me if you're not and I'll go."

"Maybe you should."

"Merdie," he said louder, "why do you keep washing dishes and clothes and milking that cow for this bunch of fools?"

"Fools?" I almost hated him. "You're talking about my boys."

"Yes, them too. For all I know one of them could be in cahoots with the sheriff."

"You better just let it go, Mac."

"I can't." He come closer, two feet behind, while I turned to the dishes seeming to grow on the counter.

"Don't you know women don't do all this anymore, only to get treated like dirt?"

"The women I know do."

"I mean women in general—out there." He raised a finger from the clasp of roped wrists and pointed west.

"I've got a tv, I know."

"You don't watch tv," he snapped. "I've been here two whole months and I haven't watched tv either."

"I don't like to watch, I like to do."

"You don't go anywhere—shopping or anything."

"I have what I need, anything more is greed." I felt stupid for rhyming words, stupider for sounding clever. "Going to sing's going somewhere."

"Jeanette's more in touch with the outside world than you; even she knows that bootlegging's a laugh." He kept to the same spot, like a wall was between us. "You have no connection with the outside world, don't keep up with what's going on."

"I can think for myself, thank you."

"Then think!"

What I thought was how wrong I'd been about me and Mac thinking alike, that harmony of minds, about mama and daddy. I thought about how everybody expected too much of love.

"Little Noah," I hollered out, "come take the revenuer to be-excused."

That night, it was still rainy and cold and I slept in Hamp's room. Without another word, I'd told Mac to go. I did not know if he'd do it or not; I had no way of knowing, had give up guessing. But if he went now, I decided, I was mad enough not to hurt bad for two or three days.

I tried to keep my mind on the choices, like I'd dropped going off with Mac as being one of them. That night, I didn't even consider trying to get the money from Hamp for our manager. I'd done tried twice when I knew he was out and away from the house, and one of those times the money bag was gone. Which made me think for sure he knew I'd tried to steal from him, whether or not he knew about me and Mac.

If Mac stayed this time, what happened to him was not my fault. I tried not to think about one of the boys being in cahoots with the sheriff, as Mac put it. My back ached, my feet cramped from standing in my good shoes all day.

Little Noah had ended up going off with Lucy's biggest girl and I had all ideas he was hooked. I listened for him to come in. Israel and Bo Dink had loafed off that evening too, hadn't come back, and I wondered if Israel had stopped by to see his baby. But I was satisfied the both of them had gone to Reba Suggs' beer joint in Jasper, where they'd get drunk and hook up with some whore or other, then take the Bakers Mill Road home to keep from getting caught by the law. And sorry as I felt for Emmacee Mae, I just about despised her, couldn't picture her as my daughter-in-law, how she'd fit in at the table next Thanksgiving. Oh, Lord!

Yes, Mac, I thought, I do know other women out there don't put up with what I do, but they're not here, and I'm doing what I have to till the time comes. I've raised my boys the best I know how, helped bring a blue-dozen baby girls into the world to go through just what I'm going through, unless they're blessed with not never knowing the difference.

229

Injun Gal and Jean Stover—even Emmacee Mae—looked like they were just as happy when they got done with labor and birthing, some reward for what they'd just been through. And I knew they caught hell, a lot more hell than I'd ever caught. Maybe when people got past struggling to raise a family and make a living, they got bored—like me. Emmacee Mae, Jean Stover, Injun Gal weren't bored, weren't looking to go nowhere.

Still, I fell asleep trying to figure how to get the money. I'd made up my mind that me and the boys would be going to Nashville.

XIII

ut it all started over the next day: the rain, me tying up "the revenuer"—him sulking—and staking him out for me to milk, to cook, then parking him in the sideroom so I could wash. Rain or no rain, I had to wash, to dry what I could on the back porch clothesline.

But my old washer picked that hellacious morning to break down. First it overflowed and then it just quit, slick water standing on the back porch floor. I'd washed three loads of sheets and heavy dungarees, set to sour sopping wet in my clothes basket. I hung up some of the sheets on the line strung end to end of the porch and let the others go. You could smell them sour and starchy-blue through the hall where the gray light from outside hardly made a dint in the leftover dark. Cold rain whipped from east to west, soaking the drape of white sheets.

Israel come in, tracking mud, and I made it a point not to ask the whereabouts of Bo Dink and Little Noah. Me so mad I couldn't see straight. If I got started now, no tellings what I'd say or do. I went on about my business, straightening up behind everybody, and kept out of the way. I'd burned the breakfast biscuits and the scorch smell pressed down in the damp.

From the time I'd woke up, morning had stayed the same shade of gray, like daylight stretching. By ten o'clock, I was wore out, as much from being on the outs with the revenuer as anything. How would it all end? Would it end?

J.B. wandered in and went to tinkering with my washer, had it pulled out in the middle of the porch floor where Israel and Hamp had to paw the wall of sheets with their dirty hands to get around it. I didn't say a thing, but I knew J.B. couldn't fix his hair, much less my washer. He was bored, that's all, fixing to make a joke out of my washer, then leave the guts scattered from here to kingdomcome.

I stood in the kitchen door watching them, while watching the revenuer across the hall in the sideroom. He was laying on the cot and mostly what I could see was the soles of his boots. I wondered if he could see me; I wondered what he was thinking—how stupid I was probably—but I didn't much care.

J.B. got the back off the washer, him laid out and grunting as he poked inside with a screw driver. Wasn't long before Hamp pulled up a chair to the shadowy streak running between the porch wall and the washer and went to quarreling with J.B. over what was the matter with the machine. The belt or the pump? Hamp cussed at J.B. a couple of times, but J.B. still laid on his back, grunting with his belly pooched in a white t-shirt. Cold vapors puffed from their mouths with every word, a double thrust to their cussing.

Israel, right in front of me, kept peeping around the back of the machine. He'd scratch his head and study the inside, stooping with his hands on his knees. He was a good hand generally to fix stuff, if you could get him to do it. "Reckon it's getting any fire to it?" he asked J.B.

"Shit!" Hamp yelled across J.B. "You don't know beans about washing machines, boy. Get on out from here." He chuckled, walking the rocker closer and blocking what little light there was between the wall and the washer.

Israel didn't pay him no mind, went on studying. "J.B., let's check for fire, first."

"You got fire, boy," Hamp hollered, "you got fire."

Israel bunched his pants at the knees, squatted, and reached under J.B.'s back, feeling for the cord. He pulled it up, feeding the black cord through his fingers as he stepped back, till he got to the socket where the washer cord hooked to a brown extension cord. The whole rig plugged in behind the screened dish-safe in the kitchen. He held the plug and socket a minute, then hooked and unhooked them a couple of times.

"Put that down, boy," Hamp bellowed, stomping his foot. "Can't you see J.B.'s tinkering with the pump?"

"The belt," J.B. said and grunted.

"Ain't no fire here," Israel said, tapping the hookup like a mike.

I could tell the revenuer could see me; his head was cocked on the pillow. I could feel his eyes. Looked like night in the sideroom, and I thought about us, how it was, how it might not never be again. I wondered if he thought about that too.

Hamp was still quarreling with J.B. about what was wrong with the washer, while Israel kept hooking and unhooking the washer cord from the extension cord. He tapped the socket like it might bite. "Ain't getting no fire."

"Put that sondabitch down," Hamp yelled. "J.B.'s getting the pump off."

"The belt," J.B. grunted.

"Fire'd help," Israel said.

I glanced over behind the dishsafe and sure enough the extension plug had jarred loose from where the washer had frammed against the wall. I stepped over, reaching behind the safe, and plugged it in just as I heard Hamp jump up, hollering,

"Sondabitch! If nothing won't do you but to prove they ain't no fire, stick it in your mouth."

Israel yelped like a hit dog on the highway.

Hamp and J.B. pulled up chairs under my sheets, slugging whiskey from the same bottle and laughing.

Israel, so pale he was purple, set under the light in the kitchen for me to check his tongue. His shaky arms were crossed on the back of a chair, feet hooked behind. His tongue was a bloody pulp, with one blue burn hole in the middle of the crease. His blood shot eyes stared up at the light.

"You'll live," I said, backing up. "I could put some Methiolate on it but it'd burn you up." I didn't know what to say; maybe I'm sorry. But I didn't. I'd let Hamp take the blame, and if what happened had shocked some sense into Israel, then praise the Lord, praise the washer.

Israel scraped his boots on the floor and reared the chair. "Anybody'd listen to that old man oughta lose his dern tongue." He spoke low and tongue-tied.

"How come you do then?"

On the back porch they laughed out, my old rooster squawked, a bottle thudded to the dirt.

"Ain't got no better sense than to listen." Israel laughed too, at hisself.

"Go on," I said, "get out of here."

"Can't," he said. "One day I will though."

"One day has a strange way of slipping into two."

"You don't believe I got it in me to quit being the old man and them's gopher."

"Gopher?"

"Yeah, you know: Israel, go for this, Israel, go for that."

"I'd like to think you've quit."

"Well," he said, "go ask the sheriff where I told him to shove it when he tried to sic me on the revenuer." He sucked in and fanned his mouth, feeling his tongue with his tongue.

By that evening the rain was over. In the sky, a scattering of white sheep-like clouds were driving the dark thunderheads west, air like it was coming off ice checking in from the north. I set out for Emmacee Mae's, taking the revenuer with me to look in on her and the baby.

I guessed she thought I'd come after my money, or maybe she was mad because my Israel hadn't been by. She was up and fussing, bad blistered from laying in the sun, and grumbling about the baby. "Don't never draw a quiet breath," she said.

I picked him up, sopping wet, and changed his diaper. His little navel was all red and festered, pooched out like a risun. I trimmed the stump of dead skin and thought about my own navel, how it'd been hooked to my mama, and started to cry. I touched mine, under the squirming baby on my lap, still gazing, blurry-eyed, at him kicking and squalling. A healthy new wail against my old muffled sobs.

The tv was wide open on a show where people laughed from the same record all the way through. Each go round, one woman cackled like a satisfied hen after the others quit.

"Emmacee," I said, looking down to hide my tears, "you've got to keep the navel stump cleaned around with alcohol till it sheds."

"I can't do that, can't stand to look at that thang." She was eating a mustard sandwich, standing in front of the tv, one thick, frayed braid snaked over her shoulder.

Mac set in a chair by the door and stared out.

I finished with Little Israel and put him on my shoulder, patting his back. I'd be the one cleaning him every day. "You giving plenty of milk?" I asked Emmacee.

She stared at the two wet spots on her white "baby" t-shirt. "I reckon I *am*, can't keep a dry stitch on my body."

The baby screamed, kicking his thin red legs. I bundled him

up in a faded flannel blanket. "Emmacee," I hollered above the racket, "where's Bobbie Jean?"

"Can't keep up with her." Emmacee bit into the sandwich, watching the tv, and swigged some tea.

"Emmacee," I shouted, "I think this baby's starving. When did you nurse him last?"

"Huh?" She looked mean at me.

"I said, when did you nurse the baby last?"

"I can't keep up with it." She saluted me with her glass, then drank some more tea.

"Well, young lady," I said, "you just get over here and do it now."

"Don't you tell me what to do, you ain't Grannie."

"I mean it, Emmacee." I took the baby to her, rocking while he screamed. "I'll take him to the welfare if you don't."

She put the glass down, swallowing the last hunk of bread, snatched the baby and yanked up her top. "You ain't taking my baby nowheres."

"If you don't take better care of him, I'll show you." Tomorrow I'd have to come up with something else to scare her into taking care of him, till finally, I figured, I'd be taking him home with me.

"Come on, Mac." I walked out the door.

Now, it looked like the boys would be going to Nashville alone. I'd reduced my choices to staying with Hamp or going to my mama's house. And I was mad, but at least not so tore up over what to do.

We traipsed through the woods the way we come, bright sun strong in the cold, no sound but the crows cawing over the swamp. Much as I hated to tell him that one of my boys was maybe out to get him, I had to. If the sheriff had tried to get Israel to kill Mac, he wouldn't stop there. Mac sucked in and darted his eyes about the woods, like he expected every pine to have a hired gun behind it. So did I.

When we got back to the house, Mac, tied up again in fake

knots, went to his room, and I started sweeping. Sweeping around Hamp's bed a long time—even the spider webs over the spindled iron bedstead—before I got on my knees to check for the money bag. Two cardboard boxes of old clothes set to the side of a clean streak in the dust where the money bag had been drug out. No doubt now that Hamp knew. As I stood up, it hit me that our manager probably wouldn't be interested in the boys without me. And maybe I didn't even need to chance stealing the money, because the boys might not could go even if they would. Still, I had to try.

But Little Noah hadn't come in yet.

When Little Noah did come in, he had his shirttail hanging out. He'd always been the tickiest one of my boys. I couldn't get him to poke it in his britches. But that wasn't what mattered. Poor little fellow couldn't sing, and I'd made up my mind to make him sing that night, to go to Top Twenty with or without the money, whether or not our manager got mad.

Before Jeanette got to the house to set with Mac, I went back through the business about the guns in the boys' room—told him not to take no chances if J.B. or Colin come by, if Hamp acted the least bit spooked. "If I was you, I'd hit the woods, first dark, and high-tail it out of the flatwoods." He was sweating it out, I could tell, but I couldn't tell if he'd go. Me and the boys took off anyhow, me strung out on one of my pep talks about making it to the Bigtime, Nashville, Tennessee, and them letting me have at it. My heart wasn't in it, was at the house with Mac.

We had to go out of the way, toward Fargo, to drop the load of shine for the barber, us done pushing it because Jeanette'd had to work late at the telephone office.

"Bo Dink, you drive." I patted the seat between me and Bo Dink. "Israel you set here."

"Not my car, you don't." Israel shifted gears to first and

aired his burnt tongue.

"Stop the car and do what I say." I pulled a sheet of paper from my skirt pocket, while Israel, snorting and braking on the dirt road, got out and switched places with Bo Dink.

Bo Dink stripped gears along the three-path buggy road between cold rustling palmettoes toward the highway. Israel all puffed up and pouting, staring hard into the sun.

"Now look here, Israel"—I tapped the sheet, printed in pencil, c's and prompts over the words to a song. "I wrote this for you, a Christmas song. You're gonna do it tonight."

"The hell you say! I ain't making no fool out of myself." He stuck out his tongue. "Besides..."

"Yeah, you are, dammit!" I didn't feel one bit like cussing, not mad, just desperate. I'd use whatever weapon I had to turn him, to turn them.

By sundown, frost was done making on the grass along the shoulder of the hardroad, the car heater chuffing hot around my feet. I could put my hand on the window glass and go cold inside, where fear for Mac had my stomach churning.

All the way to Valdosta, the deerhunters' trucks kept going around us, clearing out of the woods before dust-dark, like they went right by the law. And it come to me out of the blue, that one of them could be after Mac. Easier to picture in my head, because I didn't know them personal, and what I did know of them, made it real. My heart sank till I thought about how Hamp hated them, and they hated him, how he'd lay them low before they laid Mac low. And I saw Hamp in a new light.

When we got to town, my jaws were tired from talking and singing Israel's new song, and I knew the boys were as sick of hearing me as I was of hearing myself. Just words.

Bo Dink pulled up to the Top Twenty, and J.J. was standing out under the long green canvas over the walkway, cars parked bumper to bumper in every row like they'd wrecked.

He was bundled up in a tan jacket with fur around the collar, hands sunk deep in the pockets, his beard running into fur. When he saw us, he swaggered over to where we'd parked, close to the door.

"Thought y'all wadn't coming." The skin on his face was chapped from the cold. "They waiting in there, listening to the jukebox."

I got out, Little Noah stumbling behind me. "Poke your shirttail in, hon," I said.

He strutted on off, strapping his guitar on, and slung it to the side. Israel and Bo Dink drug their guitars out and stepped in behind me, going up the walkway. Jukebox music was thumping against the gray brick walls of the building. We went on around the side to the back door, cold wind coming strong off the north corner where Little Noah was leaning like he didn't give a dern.

J.J. opened the door and the music sailed out on a warm draft of beery smoke. The light inside was rose as a smoky sunset.

"Let's sing like we mean it, boys." My teeth were chattering so bad I couldn't hardly talk. But I was relieved our manager hadn't said a word about the money—yet.

He stepped back for me to catch up. "Go on in the dressing room and put on the red dress and makeup, just like last time." He started to walk off across the table-studded room, one boot toe snagging. "And start out with that new song of yours"—he snapped his fingers and cocked his head—"what's it called? 'Can't Go Back Without You,' that's it."

"I kind of thought I'd try something different." I could tell he figured I'd wrote another song by the way he grinned and walked off. And I had—not just Israel's Rudolph song—a song that would make me or break me.

In the dressing room, I put on the red dress, scratchy balls and all, and then the makeup, but this time I left my hair hanging, parted on the side. Show him I had some say-so.

Soon as I got to the main room, J.J. strutted up to the mike

239

and went back through all the old lies, plus some—now I was fixing to sing at some concert with George Jones, Lord help me! I trotted in, smiling, and stepped up on the stage and went to running my mouth, the boys flamming around behind me where the steel guitar player was sliding on his steel thimbles, the drummer bumping about, settling in behind drums hung like washtubs.

"Pass me one of them guitars, boys," I said, reaching back as I held to the mike pole. Didn't want to act too sure of myself, just sure enough. Much as people doubt you, they don't want you doubting yourself. I strapped one of the boy's guitars on, chording while I talked. "This here's a little song I been working on awhile now"—*lie* bleeped in my head. I'd wrote it in my mind that rainy night I went back to Mac. A song to make me or break me. Slow, strong and sweeping. I took a deep breath, plunging into the song like icy water.

They say the moon pulls heavy
on the unlit night
as it slides quicksilver
like a bead out of sight

They say you go to craving
and you can't get enough
till the grip lets go
and the moon scrolls up

On dark of the moon...oon
when the world ain't right
when the night ain't lit
and my heart ain't light
I'll come back to you
and make it all right
and we'll make love
yes, we'll make love

Dark of the Moon

through the long black night

Looks like to me
that gra...vi...ty
pulls more than planets
Pulls people too—is fate—
I just can't wait

We'll make faces at the moon
when it comes back around
and we won't care
if it slides underground

After the last line of the chorus, sang twice, I held my head down, looking at that old smoked-brown guitar, through a swarm of clapping, tears making in my eyes, and didn't look up till I'd timed the applause to last longer than before. Counting the whistles and hoots as double time. Then I looked up at the crowd sunk in red beery smoke, and still didn't know if the song had made me, but I knew it didn't break me. Now I had to sell the boys.

"I prechate it," I said and somebody at the bar whistled. "Thank you," I said, unstrapping the guitar and passing it back. "Now, my Israel's got one for y'all. Put you in the Christmas spirit." I cocked my head. "Come on up here, Israel." I stood to the side while he stepped up to the mike, his face stiff as clay, the same color. His lips poked out. He just stared out and went to picking, then singing, a tune not all that different from one of them funny songs Ray Stevens sings, but the words were Israel's because I'd wrote them picturing how he'd think.

All the time he was singing, half-talking—more Mel Tillis than Ray Stevens with his tongue burnt—the crowd was laughing—not to poke fun, mind you! I could tell that Israel could tell they liked the song and him. He was grinning with his white teeth showing. But when they let up clapping, he went to

241

jabbering into the mike about Christmas and all that "crap." I didn't care, long as he was feeling good and making the crowd feel good. Then I looked over at J.J., setting in a booth by the platform; he motioned for me to take the mike.

I stepped up next to Israel. "What you say, Israel, we do one for all the lovers in the house?"

"Woman's in love with love..." He hogged the mike and belched. "We got any lovers in the house?"

Everybody clapped, a bunch of men at the bar in the back hooted and whistled. Israel rocked and grinned. I was so happy, I didn't care what J.J. thought; I didn't care if my own son was making light of me, his way of handling attention. Giving back good as he got. He didn't show no signs of stepping away from the mike, so I went on into a Patsy Cline number, him picking right along beside me and pitching in on the chorus.

Everybody clapped at the end, just like they did when I sang "Dark of the Moon." Same thing. I didn't look at J.J. I could feel him puffing up over me singing the old stuff.

"Dim lights, thick smoke, and loud, loud music"—I started out singing by myself, and the crowd clapped while the boys and the band joined in like we'd planned it. But the steel guitar, sharp and long-noted, hadn't warmed up good before the crowd went to drinking and wandering—"You'll never make a wife to this home-loving man."

That was one song the other boys would blat out with me, and Israel looked like he'd be trouble to shut up now, because I'd raised them on that song and they didn't have to think the words. Even Little Noah could sing it.

By the time we got to the end, the crowd was setting at attention, a bunch of them dancing on the board square off the bandstand, so I picked up the chorus and sang it again, tapping my paper-stuffed shoes, one and then the other, dropping my part just enough so the boys could be heard good over me and the steel and the drums. Israel still hogging the mike.

Seeing how the crowd loved that song, it dawned on me that

they'd love anything we sang loud and fast and familiar, and all I had to do to get the other boys singing loud and fast was pick old stuff they'd teethed on. Their faces were blank and calm as I'd ever seen them. Pick something they didn't have to think about and I was in control of them and the crowd. Long as I made the crowd believe they were having a good time, and that we were, they didn't care how we sang or what.

Everybody went to dancing and clapping with the music when we got to the next number and I skipped break, finally getting the guts to look at J.J. He was reared with his arm on the booth, tapping his fingers. He smiled and nodded and warm waves started up from my toes. Now, he'd take the boys with or without me. We sang half a dozen more numbers and then I called a break.

Some woman set in the booth with J.J., so I started not to go over, but when she slung her head and laughed, I made out Katy Land's fluffy hair. Well, well, that would about wrap up us singing at Top Twenty. Katy was back. I didn't much want her to see me in that getup—she didn't never put on airs, didn't have to, not with that voice. But if she was gonna be sucking up to my manager and taking over my gig, I might as well go on and have it out with her. At least let her know I'd been there.

I set in the booth across from her and J.J. I wasn't studying the boys right then, this was girl to girl. "How you, Katy?" I said.

"Hey, girl, how you been?" Katy placed her warm, light hand over mine on the table and squeezed. "You sounding good, girl, I swear. Where'd you get that moon song?"

"I wrote it." Of a sudden, the song seemed weak and forced. I thanked her anyhow.

"Uh uh uh," J.J. said, wagging his head. "You got some set of lungs, Merdie Lee."

"Where you singing now, Katy?" I cut in—might as well uncover the shit and let it sun.

Her big breasts went to rising and falling under her plain

white shirt—had little pearl leaves on the collar. "God! hadn't you heard?"

"What?" I wanted to crawl under the table and hide my flashing red dress with the scratchy ball boobs. Looked like every other sequin snared a separate light from candles on the cramped tables.

She placed her hands on her hot, pink cheeks, then elbowed J.J. in the gut. He grunted, chuckling, and laid over in the corner. "J.J., you old dog, you don't care enough about me to even brag."

"Yeah, I do." He bumped his head on the wall, grinning like a love-struck boy. "Go on, tell her."

I got ready for some puppy-love news.

"J.J., old devil, just signed me up with Warner Records in Nashville, and I..."

He broke in like he couldn't wait for Katy to keep blushing and gushing and holding back. "Warner's a major label, no little independent you gotta screw to take you."

"God, girl, I can't believe it!" Katy laid her head on the table and grabbed both my arms. "I been singing and fooling around places like this for 15 years or better, and now...finally..." She sounded like she was crying.

"Katy don't let on when she's happy," J.J. said, and she kicked him under the table and he said "Ooch" and nabbed her by the scruff of the neck, pinning her fluffy brown hair while she laughed and gazed up, bliss-eyed.

"You mean," I said, "you, J.J., you're Katy's manager?"

"Fifteen years," she said, "I been putting up with this sonofabitch."

"Hell, tother way around," he said and turned away to keep from showing how proud he was. His oily face looked like a electric Santy Claus's.

"Gotta go," she said, slapping the table, stood and shook the wrinkles from her denim skirt. "Just dropped by to see how J.J.'s taking the news tonight. Wish me luck, girl."

"Yeah, I do, I do," I said and meant it. But selfish just like my mama always said, I was thinking about how long it would take to "make it"—providing I decided to—and about J.J., all I'd thought about him being crooked.

He got up and followed her out, unbogging his belt from his gut, and in a minute he was back, sliding in the booth across from me.

"Why didn't you tell me you was Katy Land's manager?" I asked.

"You didn't ask me." He slid to the corner and crossed his boots on the bench. "Lie. I didn't tell you because Katy Land weren't nothing to boast about then. I didn't tell you because I wanted to set your sights higher—K.T. Oslin high. Got to keep your eyes on the Bigtime, and Katy Land still ain't Bigtime. Know what she's gone be doing for the next two, three years?"

"Singing her heart out on the radio."

He held up a finger. "If she's lucky—making a record and making a hit's two different thangs. More'n likely she's gone be busting her butt keeping up with the big groups, big-name singers on tour, filling in. Stages, you know, you got to go through a bunch of stages to get to the top."

"One more question before I go back on," I said.

"Shoot."

"What am I doing in this getup?"—I clapped my hands over the balls on my breasts, driving the styrofoam deeper into the flesh. "What am I doing dressed up like a hussy while Katy Land dresses in plain old clothes that don't say nothing no louder than she wants heard?"

"Two reasons. You gotta pass the test with me..."

"What test?"

"Let me finish"—he held up one red-pied palm. "You gotta show how much grit you got for doing what you're told, for trusting me and going along with what I tell you to do."

"You mean to say all this suffering, my tits ate half off, and

245

it's a test?"

"Hell no—that dress was all I could come up with, couldn't figger how to fill up the top." The hand flew up again, palm out. "Let me finish. Reason two, you ain't Katy Land, and you gotta have something right at first to make you stand out. Till you get some self-confidence—you done got style. And probably you'll end up like Katy Land and look better natural."

"I better, I hate this dress. She wouldn't be caught dead in it."

"Katy Land broke in in that dress."

We went on and I got Israel singing "Since You've Gone," his voice deep and husky, guitars whanging. He looked like he was right at home: stepping back, serious now, and strumming his guitar between verses. The other boys so caught up in the old stand-bys they didn't even notice when I shifted them over to something newer. And I knew they loved to sing as much as me, it was in their blood, and all I had to do was get them to Nashville.

After one hour of full singing, I wrapped up with "Dark of the Moon," and just like the first time the crowd went to clapping and hollering up, "Do it, Merdie, sang it again!" I called another break, promising I'd sing it when we come on again, and the boys headed for the bar, stopping by tables to talk to people.

I went back and set across from J.J., hell-bent on talking about the boys and the hell with Katy Land and me this time. "Well, what'd you think about the boys' singing tonight?"

He set up, put one bear paw on my arm. "Lord, Merdie, that song's awright. Didn't strike me at first, but it's awright."

"Israel—what about him?"

Looked like J.J. was trying to keep from smiling; he stared at me, the paw going with the arm across the booth back. "He ain't the best, but he ain't the worst neither."

I knew that was real praise. "They good enough to make it to Nashville?" I drummed my fingers on the gritty table top.

"What you mean by *they*?"

"I mean even without me."

"You got the money for the demo?"

"I'll get it."

"Does that mean you won't be going?"

"If I can, I will." I watched Little Noah at the bar. "If I can't though, would you take them anyway?"

He propped both elbows on the table, then crossed his stuffed jacket arms. "You get the money, then we'll talk."

Least I knew he did have some pull in Nashville, and as risky as it was to steal from Hamp, it was riskier not to. If I could get Israel, all of them, out of the flatwoods, they stood a chance. They'd go; I didn't know if they'd stay. Because I did believe J.J. would take them, I just didn't believe they'd be no different than no other half-good groups that had been there and come back disheartened. At least, they'd have the chance to see what they could be, see a different way of thinking and doing, and Israel would be out of pocket when the dope agents come down on the flatwoods. That's all I asked.

But I thought about how I used to sing with my daddy and his four living brothers, all over the county—before money, before I knew what it was, just something rattling in my candy sack—how simple just to sing, unpaid. They used to stand me on a box and stoop over, beating their guitar strings, while I sang, louder than good. My heart wasn't in it after I married Hamp; I thought I wouldn't never sing no more. The music didn't move my soul. And when me and Hamp would go to a square dance, or have one at the house, in the old days, I'd stand against the wall with the other married women and watch the men dance with the girls. I wouldn't even clap my hands, like clapping I'd run a risk of making a fool of myself in front of whichever girl or woman, married or not, Hamp might have a hankering for.

"Merdie"—J.J. leaned close—"you do have one hell of a set of lungs, I want you to know that. And the songs you wrote ain't half-bad. Specially the one you sang tonight. But if you don't go, if you can't, you still got this crowd to keep you in pocketchange. Come first of the year, George Jones'll be in Valdosta, and I'm working on a deal..." He bowed his chest, went slack. "I know you got to be wondering if I'm on the up and up with you. Maybe I am and maybe I ain't and maybe I'm just dreaming. But I know talent when I see it. And you got talent."

And then he went on to tell me about singers come from nothing, making the Bigtime: Loretta Lynn, Patsy Cline...K.T. Oslin. Said he believed I could make it on my voice alone. No guarantees. Said we could sell my songs straight to the big publishers for twenty, twenty-five dollars, and if they were hits, we'd make them rich. If I went and sang the songs myself, I'd be good as there—the Bigtime. Me and the boys. "Little Noah, too," he said, pressing both palms flat on the seat. "They told Willie Nelson they'd take his songs but he couldn't sang worth a shit."

Saturday, I spent the whole cold day mulling it over, not looking under Hamp's bed for the money bag, and not letting on to Mac that I'd changed my mind, that I'd go to Nashville.

That morning we set out walking to Emmacee Mae's, both of us bundled up and breathing the ripe muck air off the swamp.

"Merdie," Mac said, "I've decided to go."

"I expect you ought to." I could feel his breath, a warm mix with the cold. "When?"

"Tomorrow—maybe the next day."

"Go tonight."

"No."

"How come?"

"Actually, considering how many nights I've spent away

from civilization, I doubt one more will make me anymore uncivilized."

"I hate it when you carry on like that."

"Like what?"

"Like you're making fun."

"I'm not," he said, tearing a streamer of moss from a hanging oak limb. "Ok, so I was... Truth is, I need one more night with you."

I could feel heat spreading through my body, and right then I wanted him as much as I wanted to sing. "One more night won't make no difference."

"Didn't I just say that?" He balled the moss and flung it at a sandy gopher hole as we stepped from the woods to the dirt road. "You're a damned addiction, Merdie, I swear."

"Stay tonight then, long as you're willing to chance Hamp and you know I'm not going with you."

"I guess I don't know that." He put his arm around me, pulled me close. "Guess I still hope you'll go."

"I've got things to do."

"I know—the baby."

"Not just that." I really wanted Mac, wanted him more than singing. "I got a bunch of big babies depending on me."

"I'm sorry I called your boys fools."

"If they are—and maybe they are—I made them fools."

"Like hell!"

"I did, Mac, they do what I tell them."

"Yeah, it looks like it. You can't get them to pick up their socks."

"That's just men for you." I stalked off.

"That's just pure lazy." He caught up with me. "Hamp's the bad influence. The quicker they get away from here, the better off they'll be."

We walked on, our unmatched strides finally matching, like we were marching, and I could feel when he was fixing to turn silly.

Whistling, with his hands in Israel's jacket pocket, he crossed the sandy road to the myrtle bushes and set on a pine stump. "Could I interest you in a break, Missy?"

I stood, watching him. "Mac, why are you doing that?"

"Not used to walking fast."

"I've got to get to Emmacee's and get back to..."

"Merdie," he said, crooking a pointer finger and wagging it, "come here."

"Mac, no." I circled in the road, over both our tracks.

"Do you want me to chase you down and let you have your way with me right there on the road?" He whistled like he was calling a dog.

I laughed, already following in his tracks to the stump. Our eyes locked. He caught me around the waist and pulled me into the vee of his legs, his cold head nuzzling into my jacket, and breathed between my breasts.

"You're warm," he said.

"I'm cold—freezing to death."

"I can warm you up." He squeezed my rump.

"Not here you don't," I said, "not here."

"Here." He was breathing fast, hard between his legs. He kissed me, bringing his right hand around to my front and unbuttoning my khaki pants.

I craned my neck, watching the sun ray in hazy palmetto patterns through the tree tops, while he worked his magic till the sun exploded.

Little Israel was dry and sleeping on the mattress with the yellow cat while Emmacee was getting ready to go to the fire tower. Bobbie Jean, setting crosslegged beside the baby, was watching Saturday-morning cartoons. She always seemed older and a shade smarter than Emmacee—gave me hope that, like her, Little Israel wouldn't take after his mama's side of the family—so I wasn't too worried about her staying with the baby for her mama to work.

I showed her how to boil baby bottles and mix Karo syrup with Carnation milk for formula; it was plain now that Emmacee couldn't be trusted with nursing. Besides, her breasts were hard and feverish and she was carrying on, holding her elbows out and shaking her long white hands, sucking in and moaning. I was scared she was coming down with the mastitis. I took a jar of mayonnaise from the frigerdaire and dumped the white clotted gunk in the tiny sink, washed and dried the jar, and stuck a scrap of papersack inside and set it afire. When it burned low, I screwed the lid on, and the jar churned with fine gray smoke, like bottled clouds. I made her lay on the mattress and pull up her shirt; her blue-veined breasts were all swole round and tight. Then I took off the jar lid and put the mouth to one of her tender nipples, and she went to hollering and taking on.

"Lay still," I said, getting ready for them long skinny feet to raise up off the mattress and kick me. She just laid there, nothing but her chalky mouth moving. In a minute, the smoke went to drawing, yellowish milk filming the jar around the curling smoke, her big tit going down like a stuck balloon. After I'd done the same on the other breast, I gave her two aspirins, tried to bind her breasts, and told her to stay there on the mattress another day and let Ethel Henderson keep the tower a while longer.

No, she wouldn't, and no she wouldn't have her titties mashed flat as a flitter.

I'd come over ready to take the baby home with me, was a little relieved I didn't have to. I really believed Bobbie Jean would look out for him.

Mac must have thought so too, as he watched her wash her hands and screw the cap on the bottle without touching the nipple. One less reason for me not leaving with him.

XIV

hat Saturday we didn't have a gig scheduled; another group was singing at Top Twenty for the holiday weekend and the American Legion was closed. We had promised to sing at church on Sunday morning, a Thanksgiving special.

I slept with Mac that night, but neither of us really slept. We were edgier than usual—I'd hooked the latch on the middle room door, I'd put out the thread across Hamp's door, like most people put out the cat, but felt like I'd forgot something, felt like I was in a bed of fire ants—because all during supper that night, Hamp had been talking to hisself, mumbling under his breath, even in his bedroom while he built up a fire. Couldn't make head nor tails of what he was saying. Mac said maybe he'd had a stroke, but I figured he was getting set to show hisself and I hadn't forgot nothing, was just edgy over the letdown of Mac's leaving, which could wind up with a big bang.

But despite being edgy, we made love like two people making love their last, all through the cold windy night, and I didn't really believe it was the end. I didn't really believe he'd go and I didn't really believe I would or that I wouldn't.

"I love you," he said. "Shouldn't you check on Hamp?"

I laid straddled on him, tingling, him sunk deep inside me. "I will in a minute," I gasped.

He was still hard. "I don't care what happens, I'll come back for you. What was that?"

"Chicken on the back porch...the wind...I don't know." I breathed out. "I mean, I don't know about us."

His mouth crushed the words. He started moving slow inside me, bringing up the sweet tingly feeling that had gone. There was always more.

"Go now, Mac." I was on bottom, and we'd come together, a wet spot under my hips, the bed cold as we were hot.

He was still inside me, not hard now. "Not yet."

"Mac, it won't get no easier." My arms locked around him. "Go."

He laughed. "How?"

I spread my arms out flat on the bed.

He got hard inside me and I locked my arms again. "See," he said and laughed, moving in and out, in and out, a slow regular rhythm, more rub than feel-good.

The rooster crowed beyond the wall facing me.

"I've got to go," I whispered. "Hamp..."

"Where?"

"Nowhere... I meant he might..."

We were laying front to back, still hooked like two dogs.

He gathered me closer, almost under him. "No, don't go."

"Don't make me stay."

"One more time." He moved inside me, hard, always hard, a burning now that got lost in the tingling. "Could be a long time."

"Are you leaving?"

"Yes, tonight."

I knew he meant it. As the rooster crowed again, he come again. I rolled over and kissed him and left the room to rewind the thread and go to bed.

In the cold Sunday sun, more Easter-like than Thanksgiving, it felt good to be getting ready to sing at church. Sunshine through the open hall routed every shadow, every recess and corner blowed up bright. And foolish as it sounds, I didn't worry about leaving Mac at the house. Hamp was acting normal, normal for him, back to his old routine of getting up and getting dressed and making the morning coffee, then making a beeline for the still. He probably wouldn't even come in again till I got back. And it felt good not to worry for a change.

The boys went on out to the front porch to wait, and I stopped at Mac's door, happy knowing that no matter what happened now he'd come back or go to Nashville to find me. I hadn't never been so sure of nothing or nobody in my life.

He was laying on the bed with his pillow doubled under his head; he smiled, drowsy-eyed.

"Remember," I hissed, "look under Israel's bed if you need a gun."

He winked.

Right then, I must have believed that things would go on as usual, up to the time Mac would go, up to the time that I could lay my hands on the money. I must have believed I was the only one on the place who could think. That's how I made most of my mistakes: believing that the boys thought the same thoughts that I thought, each of them thinking what popped in my head;

Mac too, thinking only what thoughts I put in his head. And Hamp...

I'd heard that most car wrecks happen close to home. Now, I know why: that ditch or that curve seems harmless because it's close to home where you're safe, where you know the very dirt by smell.

That morning, me and the boys went on into the sunny cold churchhouse and took over the song service.

Little Noah, Bo Dink and Israel were scrubbed clean and wearing starched and ironed white shirts and khaki pants. Their faces shined and they looked smart, like they'd been to Nashville and back since the last time we sang at church.

I was still singing lead, still singing for the most part by myself, but at least I could accept it as fact now. I didn't no more expect the boys to take off singing than I expected them to fly to the moon. When we sang "I'll Fly Away," they pitched in just on the chorus and sang like they meant it. When I got done, they waited till I picked another song, then sang as good as Mr. Anybody on "In the Sweet By and By."

I got to wondering if maybe we hadn't oughta stick to gospel, hearing our voices ring back from the hand-planed, age-stained walls, everybody smiling so sweet in the sunshine.

> *In the sweet by and by,*
> *we shall meet on that beautiful shore.*
> *In the sweet by and by,*
> *we shall meet on that beautiful shore.*

Even little Noah, with his shirttail poked in, was singing like a angel, the way he would in my dreams, his pale face rosy in the holy light.

Then the door opened and in walked Hamp.

First thing that come to mind was what about Mac? Had

Hamp finally made good on his promise to knock him in the head? Had somebody else—say, Colin—give up on Hamp and done the job, sending Hamp over the edge?

Everybody went to whispering.

He just stood there a minute, cold air shooting to the pulpit, while I watched him watch me—scared to sing, scared to quit singing—and I went back through what seemed like our whole lives before we wrapped up the chorus.

He shut the door and set, alone on the front pew.

I didn't know whether to go on and sing some more or leave. I could feel the boys go tense behind me; their voices got tight. I looked at the clock over the black splintering-veneer piano— 11:20. We still had ten more minutes to sing. I didn't say what we'd do next, just started singing "Rock of Ages," clear, strong and mellow, the boys strumming in and letting me have at it like they weren't into this.

> *Rock of ages,*
> *cleft for me,*
> *let me hide*
> *myself in thee...*

Me thinking, *Rock of ages cleft for Mac, cleft for Mac...* Oh, God! I tried looking ahead, through the back window at the winter-dead woods, but I could see Hamp out of the corner of my eye. He set with his feet flat on the floor, hands together between his knees.

I hadn't never sang that strong, a sound that made the hair on my back stand under my white blouse. People have been known to lift a car when they get scared, and I decided that if a half-good singer could stay scared, she'd make it to the Bigtime. But the thought wouldn't hold. What would Hamp do, now that he knew I sang? Why was he here? Had he gone crazy and killed Mac, come after me? I couldn't find a stopping place—

256

Let the water
and the blood
from thy wounded side
which flowed

Rock of ages,
 cleft for me...

I just kept singing, safe in singing. It was 11:35, five minutes of preaching time spent.

Hamp was staring me square in the eye. Not with meanness. His face didn't look mean. Just interested. Like he'd come to hear me.

I was light as paper ash, felt I might float right off, as we wrapped up with "Amazing Grace" and set down, me with Hamp—because I might as well—and the boys at the rear of the church. I listened for their boot heels to stop clicking on the hardwood floor; there was a break in the clicking, then one set of heels clicking back along the outside wall. Little Noah walked around the corner of the pew where his pa was and set between us. He leaned forward with his hands between his knees.

The tall bald preacher, pink in the soft sun, walked up to the pulpit and started preaching and looked like he couldn't help eyeballing Hamp. His pure blue eyes kept locking on our pew.

I don't know what the preacher preached on; I don't know if it was hellfire-and-brimstone or what, to cause what it caused. But when he gave the usual invitation for anybody to join the church, to be saved, Hamp just got up and moped to the front, him white as his shirt, hiking his blue-blue dungarees, and stood by the preacher with his hands at his sides, while everybody sang "Just as I Am."

The preacher looked like he didn't know whether to keep the invitation open or go on and face Hamp, and I knew how he felt.

257

Finally, the song plain wore out, and the preacher turned and pumped Hamp's hand.

Hamp cleared his throat and nodded, eyes wide and taking in the the congregation. "I come to get sanctified," he said, and looked like he was waiting on it to take.

I ain't never been no scareder. *Oh, Mac, are you laying there suffering, are you done suffering?* Little Noah set back against the pew, stiff.

The preacher just stood there: swaying and sweating and lifting his blue eyes to the heavens like maybe Jesus would come down and help. Then he went on and said what he always said when somebody joined the church or got saved, the same thing about how happy Jesus was when one of His sheep come home. There would be a baptizing at Tom's Creek, come spring. And Hamp just stood there, looking long with blared eyes over the church people, like he was still waiting and it hadn't took.

I knew right then he'd gone crazy—Hamp, in church!—and the best I could hope for was that he'd be a humble crazy, maybe lay down somewhere like Injun Gal's old man and not give no more trouble. But then it come to me how most of the mean old men I'd known in my lifetime gave up on meanness and turned to religion when they saw they weren't fixing to be no different and live on forever, and that seemed just as cowardly, just as dangerous, just as sad. A sign of the end to Hamp's rule.

After everybody had shook his hand and hugged his neck, he shambled out of the churchhouse behind me and the boys and got in the car.

Israel drove slow, me in the middle, Hamp with his arm stuck out the window, the first time he'd been in a car in better than fifteen years.

The last time we'd all been in a car together was to go to the stockcar races in Valdosta. Used to go all the time. We'd stay there till twelve or one in the morning, then drive over to the

Silver Dollar in Ray City, Hamp and me going inside, the boys outside, playing around the car; Hamp playing the slot machines, and me out and in, checking on the younguns, then Hamp.

Now we all set in a car again, sun glancing off the smeary glass and our death-still faces. No fighting, no fussing, no life left. As we pulled up to the house, I thought I'd rather die than walk inside. I figured I'd find Mac with his head blowed off.

I let the boys and Hamp go on in ahead while I set the rockers flat on the porch. (I'd tipped them to the wall the night before to keep the dog from sleeping on the cushions.) And I listened hard for anything unusual, my face a white I could see.

They talked a little, washed up. Somebody spoke to Mac. Relief grew like sunshine from my toes to my head.

I went on up the hall, and Hamp was setting in a chair at Mac's door, staring in, like he'd set in church: feet flat on the floor, hands rammed between his legs.

I walked on between them, glancing in at Mac, whose head was sprung, watching Hamp.

Now, I figured Hamp would get the shotgun and come for me and Mac, maybe even the boys.

I listened as I put the dinner I'd cooked earlier on the table, now and then looking up to see Hamp still perched in the chair.

If he'd moved a hair, I couldn't tell it. I had to say it—I had to—but I didn't know what it might set off. "Dinner's ready."

All through dinner Hamp kept the same turned-inward look, maybe checking inside for change; double lines making on his forehead, now and again, like he'd asked himself a hard question.

I tried to eat, I couldn't, and I didn't dare go get Mac to eat. I knew anything could tip Hamp off. I'd rather Mac go hungry than get caught up in what was coming down.

The boys ate, nobody speaking, then went out the front. I

heard Israel's car crank up and wondered if they'd all gone. I hoped so. I hoped whatever had come over Little Noah in church, touched as I was that he'd set with me, wouldn't come over him again. Whatever would happen with Hamp—and something had to—would happen soon.

Me and Hamp set there.

He was done eating and set staring at his plate with his fingers hooked on the edge of the table.

I wanted to get up but I was scared to.

Should I start doing dishes and hope something normal like that would make him amble on out back?

We just set there.

He never looked at me.

I couldn't even see him breathing.

His white shirt stretched across his stony back.

We couldn't set there forever.

He was closest to the door, could get to the shotgun first.

Then I remembered I'd hid his gun under my bed.

But the boys had guns in their rooms, at least two apiece.

He stood up, slid the chair to the table and walked out and across the back porch.

"Oh God!" I let my breath go.

Then I eased up and peeped through the window over the sink, watching as he ambled to the smutty circle under the blackgum and started building a fire. When it was rolling good, he set on the block, whittling, his face still blank but wrinkled from that rising-up question.

I tipped to the kitchen door, looking out to where he set, and dashed across the hall to Mac's room "You've got to go," I whispered, rushing to the bed and groping at the slipknot on his wrists.

He set up, bent double, and slipped the knot on his ankles, hissing rope against sheets. "What's going on?"

"Hamp went to church; he knows I sing."

"Is that so bad?" Mac said. "Looks like he's calm now."

"You wouldn't understand; let's just say he's crazy." I finished untying his elbows. "He joined the church."

"I don't know if joining some church constitutes..."

"Shh," I got still, listening, then heard the soft *tch tch tch* of whittling wood out by the fire. "You don't understand, Hamp hadn't never heard me sing before. Ain't stepped foot inside a churchhouse since he was a boy."

The smoke carried thin through the hall; the sun had switched ends and carried with it.

"While I'm in the kitchen, cleaning up," I whispered, "you go out the front. The boys are gone."

"No, no, not by myself." He grabbed my right wrist.

I heard Hamp chunk a piece of wood on the fire, heard it crackle, and tipped to the door to look out.

Again he set whittling, feet crossed before the fire.

When I looked back for Mac, expecting him behind me, he was laying with his hands behind his head.

"Mac, please," I hissed, holding to the door jamb.

"No," he said low, "not if you're in danger."

"Please go." I tiptoed to the bed and stood over him. "I beg you to go now. He'll be ok if you go." I knew that was a lie.

So did Mac. He closed his eyes, breathing even and slow, listening to the voice inside his head.

The soft, quick whittling stopped, and I tipped back to the door.

Hamp was staring at the fire, his knife held still over a long white hickory stick.

"Merdie," Mac said low, getting up, "if you refuse to leave with me now, I'm going out there and..."

"And what?" I hissed. "*Reason* with him, what? Talk some sense into that old messed up head, what?"

"Tell him the truth," he said, pushing around me.

I yanked his arm. "What truth? That you been sleeping with his wife. God, Mac, you don't understand, you ain't never fooled with nobody like Hamp. You say you love me; well, do you want to get me killed?"

"Why won't you just go then?" he pleaded. "Please."

"I can't right now, you have to go without me. Could be he's just in one of his tempers, now go." I let go of his arm and crept out, and halfway across the hall, a board squeaked.

Hamp looked up.

I stopped.

He went on whittling, the knife dragging along the skin of the hickory rod, sharpening clean as it turned in his hand.

I felt faint but tiptoed on in the kitchen, making lots of normal noise with the dishes. From the sink, I could keep a eye on him. So I'd rush over to the table, gather the dishes, and dash back. On my last trip to the table, I hissed, "Go on, Mac," then went to the window to watch Hamp while I listened for Mac to pass along the hall.

Except for my dishes rattling, the house was still, a Sunday-evening timelessness setting in. When I quit rattling dishes, I could hear the clock ticking up front and the knife snapping on the hickory stick out back.

I stayed there till the sun touched just the tips of the pines and blackgums, then I bleached dishcloths, fumes rising heavy to my face. As I started to bend and put the bleach jug under the sink, I spied one of Little Noah's drawings pinned to the yellow checked curtain that hid the water pipes and junk. I unpinned the sheet of notebook paper, holding it to the window so I could see it better and at the same time watch out for Hamp.

With a pencil Little Noah had drawed everlast one of us, with just enough likenesses that I could pick one out from the other. Even the revenuer and my mama. We were all seated around a long table with him at the left end, a head taller. He was holding a fork up and smiling. Israel and Bo Dink's heads were bowed over flower-patterned plates. Looked like Little Noah had spent more time on those little bitty perfect flowers than all the rest. Or maybe on the food: a big bowl brimming with little o's for peas, a turkey in the center so tall it covered his brothers' chests, other dishes of food that looked prettynear the same. The revenuer was setting beside me, smiling while I fed him. Hamp set at the other end of the table with his head lolled to one side, like he was asleep. Maybe dead. My mama set between J.B. and Jeanette with a cleared space on the table for her elbows. On the other side, next to me, set a straight Lucy, with a straight Colin beside her. At the top of the page Little Noah had printed "The Last Supper" under a arch, maybe a rainbow.

What did it mean? Had he decided to draw instead of sing? Was he saying in his own way that our family was over? Was he trying to get my attention again? Could it be a warning? Something he knew that I was fixing to find out? Maybe he was just drawing, I decided, folding the picture and slipping it in my pocket. Anyhow, if I stretched its meaning, the picture could account for his being missing after Thanksgiving. Maybe he hadn't been with one of Lucy's girls after all, maybe he'd been off somewhere drawing.

There was nothing else to do, and my feet were killing me. I needed to set down, but if I did I couldn't watch Hamp. And he'd been there so long that he seemed part of the block, nothing changing except the hickory stick getting shorter, up close to his hands, a nub, where before it had been sticking under one elbow.

I was shivering cold, but if I closed the door—like a icebox left open—I'd shiver worse from not knowing what went on with Mac or what might pop through. My ears roared from waiting for some blast.

Finally, when I couldn't stand the cold and waiting another minute, I creeped over and flipped the latch on the woodstove door with the toe of my shoe, poked up the hot ashes and crossed a couple of oak sticks on the fire.

As I started to close the door, cast iron grating on the quiet,

I heard something and stopped. I kicked it to with my toe and heard it again, then hurried over to the window.

Hamp was still setting before the fire, but he was gazing at the house. Pocketknife held over the pencil-size stick. "Woman," he hollered, "I ain't gone call you again."

Across the hall, Mac's bedsprings squeaked.

I rushed to the kitchen door, where I could see up and down the hall and the yard off the back porch where Hamp set whittling again.

"Merdie?" Mac hissed. His shadow from the sideroom doorway heaped on the hall floor.

"Stay there, Mac," I whispered.

"I'm going to get a gun, Merdie," Mac whispered.

"No," I said, then hollered, "what you want, Hamp?"

"You." He looked up, his face blank of any meanness, just like in church. "I want you to come out here and talk to me."

"No, Merdie"—Mac's shadow spilled across the hallway and met mine—"don't go."

"I have to."

"No, wait till I get a gun."

"I don't want him hurt."

"Woman," Hamp called, "come see if I ain't good and sanctified this time." He laughed.

"Oh, God!" My face streaked fire.

"Don't you set foot out that door." Mac stepped back, barely inside.

"I have to Mac." I creeped out on the porch, could hear Mac behind me. "Please don't hurt him, Mac, don't come out." My feet felt numb as I walked toward the doorsteps.

"Woman," Hamp called, stretching his eyes, "I say, come see if I ain't good and sanctified." The fire burned bright and high.

"I can see from here, Hamp," I said, edging along the watershelf, "and you are for a fact."

"I'm what?" He looked confused, stood up.

"You're good and sanctified, Hamp."

He set. He laughed. Then he whittled all the way around the point of the hickory nub.

I don't know how long I stood there, but I heard the *tch tch tch* of his whittling, the tick of the clock, the floor joists squeak in the front of the house.

Hamp stared past me, his gaze shooting like a bullet through the middle of the house.

I couldn't look; I figured Hamp had seen Mac coming down the hallway with a shotgun.

But Hamp went on whittling, flames twining like ribbons before him.

Then I couldn't hear another sound anywhere except the clock ticking in my head, the soft snip of wood, the crackle of fire. I didn't dare move, I didn't care how long. Oh, don't shoot him, Mac, I thought, and thought how silly that sounded turned around. How for so long I'd been scared Hamp would shoot Mac.

"Woman," Hamp hollered. He kept whittling, seemed to know I was still there.

"What, Hamp?"

"I want you to go in yonder and get my money bag and bring it to me." He quit whittling, looked up quick.

I thought I'd pacify him by talking. "How come, Hamp?"

He stood and pointed the stick at me, gazing down it. "Don't you sass back at me." He shook it. "I'm setting things to right around this place, now I'm sanctified. Got that?" He set, mumbling. "Now, go get my money bag, woman."

I was glad to have a reason to go, glad to turn around and see where Mac was, to stop my ears from storming while I waited for a gun to go off.

Mac was nowhere to be seen, but as I started in the door of mine and Hamp's room, I heard him slamming stuff around across the hall, not even trying to be quiet, searching for the boys' guns.

I didn't know if I'd go to my bed and get the shotgun I'd hid or to Hamp's bed for the money bag, until I went to his automatically and fished out the floursack of money, hugging it close and hurrying out before Mac could find a gun.

When I come out in the hallway, Mac was still slamming stuff in the boys' room—had they put their guns in Israel's car?—Hamp whittling on like a deaf and dumb man, and the fire rolling good now, with litard smoke rising black against the orange sun.

I didn't know what he wanted with the money, but I meant to get it to him and scram, then go find the boys to come help.

If only Mac would go!

I walked on toward Hamp, him whittling slow and deliberate, charmed by the fire. My feet felt like they'd come off and my ankle stubs were hitting hard on the cold packed dirt, my head floating out beyond the woods where the sun peeped through, a blaze as scarlet as the fire. My knees trembled like the peat batteries in the swamp. I held out the bag.

He took it. He looked up as he opened the bag, strings vanishing. "I'm gone get shed of my sins."

He reached in and pulled out a roll of bills and handed the bag back. Then he went to shelling them off, hundred-dollar bills floating to the fire where they blazed and curled. One floated off to the side of the block and he twisted round, picked it up, and held one end to the tip of the blaze, watching it catch. When the fire singed his hand, he let go.

"I'm sanctified now." Again, he peeled off another bill, and another, watching them burn, till his turned-up hand was empty. "Give me some more," he said.

I tried to hand him the bag. He shook his head like he had the palsy. "Help me, woman, help me get shed of this sin money."

I reached in the bag and pulled out another roll. He took it and started peeling off bills, dropping them on the fire from above, the sun falling violet on his stone arm. "Give me some more." He stuck out his hand, watching the money burn.

I handed him another roll, clutching the bag to my bosom. I could hear Mac cross the hall, thought he was coming, then heard the floor joists squeak in my bedroom.

"Hamp," I started.

"Hand me some more, woman." He stuck out his empty hand, wiggling his stiff, scratched fingers, still watching the fire, watching the bills curl, gray-green, with eyes deep-reaching and repented.

I gave him another roll and balled the nearly empty bag to my bosom, watching him drop one, then another on the fire. He stuck out his hand.

"It's all gone, Hamp," I said, hugging the slack bag.

"That ain't all." He stabbed me with sharp eyes.

"Yeah, it is, Hamp." I'd come this far, I had to go on, to risk all. Nothing made sense but what I was doing. The flickering of the fire made me dizzy. I turned around and walked slow toward the house, then speeded up past the clothesline.

"Woman!" Hamp said. "You lying to me, woman. You lying." He was hollering so loud that his voice echoed "you lying woman" from the swamp. A double threat.

I ran for the doorsteps, looking for Mac up the hall. He strolled out of Hamp's bedroom, face open and lit white.

"Merdie," he shouted, "throw the bag down." He moved toward me, slow up the sun-shot hall.

Then I heard something snap behind me, thought Hamp'd chunked a piece of wood.

"Merdie!" Mac hollered, seeming to stick halfway up the hall.

It all happened so fast, it was slow. A shotgun went off behind me, shots plunking and pinging on the porch wall. Above the settee, orange dots picked the heart pine wall.

I stopped on the doorsteps. "Hamp, you better shoot me if you want me, for I'm long-gone if you don't."

He cocked the gun again.

I didn't turn around, stood holding the bag, madder than he

was.

"Woman, you get back here!" Hamp's voice pitched from his spot by the fire, like he was rooted there.

"Go on and shoot me," I said, squeezing my eyes.

"Merdie!" Mac yelled, on the porch now, face looming like the moon. "Throw the bag down, Merdie, and come on."

"No." I started up the steps.

"I'm gone shoot you, woman."

My ears roared like wind as I kept walking slow toward Mac.

"Hamp!" Mac hollered, coming quick ahead of me and stopping on the end of the porch, facing Hamp like a one-man firing squad. "You shoot her and you're done." His empty hands hung at his sides.

"No, Mac!" I begged. "No!"

"I ain't got no truck with you now, revenuer." Hamp stepped in front of the fire, body squared as he squinted down the barrel of his old rabbit-eared shotgun. "It's her. I can't kill no man, now I'm sanctified, but I gotta punish that woman."

"No, Hamp," Mac said low, "don't shoot her, please don't."

"She's a Jezebel," Hamp ranted. "Whore of Babylon."

Mac turned to locate me, then stepped in front, still on the edge of the porch. "Hamp, I hear me and you's got something in common."

Hamp gazed fixed along the shotgun barrel, feet apart, fire flaring at his back.

"I hear you hate dope." Mac propped on the corner post, his elbow twitching. "That right?"

Hamp got a new grip on the shotgun, aimed at Mac, then at me ducking around him.

Mac stepped in front of me again. "Well, I got to level with you, Hamp, I ain't no revenuer."

Hamp lowered the shotgun to his chest, looking over with wide unblinking eyes.

"I'm with the FBI, a drug agent, and I came here to clean up your woods. Get rid of the dope patches and dope fiends."

Hamp lowered the shotgun to his waist. "Yeah?"

"Yeah." Mac talked off the porch like a neighbor. "Gonna clean up these woods like they used to be."

"You ain't after my shine still?" Hamp tossed his head toward the glinting copper pipe.

"Never was."

"Then how come you to story?" Hamp lifted the shotgun stock with one hand and caught the barrel with the other.

"I couldn't tell, Hamp"—Mac was shaking—"J.B. would've shot me for sure."

Hamp lowered the gun to his side. "You gone take him in, him and Colin?"

"Not if they straighten up."

"Pshaw!" Hamp ducked to the side and spit. "Ain't no straight side to them son-da-bitches."

"A man can change, Hamp."

"That's the truth." Hamp wiped his mouth on his shirt sleeve.

"The one I'm really after for dope-peddling is your sheriff."

Hamp rocked on his heels, studying. "That a fact?"

The barrel of the shotgun flew up as I dodged between Mac and the porch post and chunked the bag to the ground. Mac leaned against the post, covering me with his shadow.

Hamp's eyes cut from the dirt to us. He tilted the gun up, then let it fall by his side. "Tell you what, man"—he backed to the block and set, placing the gun across his knees—"I'm gone give her to you for a Christmas present." He hung his head, shoulders quaking, and went to laughing, then crying, ugly choking sobs that carried through the hall with me and Mac and out the front.

I stopped under the oaks, looking back and thinking about Lot's wife looking back and how it wasn't fair, her being turned into a pillar of salt when Lot was the one at fault, but how she'd been hooked to him by something holy, something it wouldn't do to fault because God could strike you dead on the spot, and then I wasn't thinking at all, and Mac was urging me on across the sun-blazed dirt toward the woods, saying, "Let's go, let's go," watching for Hamp to show through the fiery open hall, for him to show around the shadowy corners of the dead house, and I knew in my heart Hamp wouldn't bother, because I knew Hamp. I knew he was done with me and me with him.

Freedom's not free.

The woods were still and quiet, closing dark, as we come out at my mama's house, frost done forming on the palmettoes and wire grass, a hazing of ice on the heavens, on the stars spinning from trees.

I'd quit crying but kept hugging myself like I was hurt. Mac pulled me close and walked fast across the road. I could hear his teeth clicking with mine. Both of us bare-armed and sniffling.

A stack of split firewood was stacked from wall to post on the right end of the front porch. Mac turned me loose long enough to gather an armload.

I opened the door and went in, the room dark and smelling of dust and cold smut.

He come in behind me and dropped the wood with a clatter and roll beside the fireplace, then went again to the double-paned door, fiddling with the knob. "Merdie, where's the lock?"

"Hamp won't come, Mac, he won't."

"Is there a gun around here?" He stood in the last of the light, a fuzzy shape that might have been the man in the moon, one of my boys, Hamp...

"Mac, please don't, don't... He won't come."

He crossed to the fireplace again and got on his knees, laying sticks of firewood on the shiny, fire-gnawed log left from my mama's last fire. Then he struck a match and lit a splinter, the sulphur smell as strange as his taking charge, as strong as his presence in the room. The tiny flame curled black smoke to the dead light of the low yellow ceiling.

I drew to the fire and stood close to him.

"We'll get warm and calm down, then we'll go." He brushed his hands, stood up, and held me again, both of us staring at the fire that crackled and grew, fluttering orange over us like the sun we'd just left.

"Mac, he won't come here, he won't go nowhere..."

"He might."

"Take my word for it, he won't." I was talking through my teeth. "Too much trouble."

"He went to church this morning, didn't he?"

"That was different. He went to church to get saved— insurance against hellfire."

"I don't get it."

"Hamp's like a lot of old men I know. They find out they ain't so much a man no more, go to dwelling on dying, and get scared. Fact is, they probably figured all along, while they were at their meanest, that when they got old they'd turn to religion."

"A last resort, right?"

"Right."

He rubbed my shoulder. "Sit down." He kneeled on the rag rug, pulling me to him.

My eyes felt dry, like I'd drained my last tears. "Mac, I need to find the boys. I can't let 'em go home and find Hamp like...he could do anything."

He pulled my head to his shoulder, kissed my hair. "Poor Merdie, you try to do everything." He laughed low, nothing happy in it. "How are you going to find them? Walk clear across the woods and check every mile? They're probably already back home for supper."

"Mac, they'll think I've left for good."

"Let them."

I didn't really believe Hamp'd hurt them; I just hadn't never been out of pocket, felt cut off from them. "I can't let Hamp just set there. Crazy or not, he needs me."

"How would you help him?"

"I don't know."

"My truck's parked not far from here, out in the swamp. Soon as we get there, we'll go for help."

"You mean the law?"

"No." He let go of me and shrugged. "I don't know, I guess we could try to get the boys to help take him to a hospital."

"Some kind of asylum?"

"Yeah, some kind of mental facility."

"Hamp don't need no *mental facility*. He is what he is, by his own choosing. And truth be told if he thought he had another chance at it, he'd be the same all over again. Anyhow, he'd die if you locked him up. Not only that, the boys wouldn't let you."

"Merdie," Mac said, leaning close, "listen to yourself. You can't help Hamp or the boys. Why do you keep getting side-tracked?"

"I'm not."

"Why don't we just go?" He got up and crossed to one of the double windows over the porch, peering through the glancing black glass with his hands each side of his eyes.

"Mac, Hamp's not coming...you can forget that." Thinking about Hamp maybe still crying in the dark yard at home— home!—I started crying again.

Mac come back and set on the rug with me. "Don't cry, Merdie, please don't. As soon as we go you'll..."

I quit crying. "Mac, knowing what you know about us, what you've seen since you got here, can you expect me to just go? Could you walk off from your own family like that?"

"I can't say." His square jaw twitched. "But a woman..."

"Look at me, I mean really look at me." I thought I might cry again and discredit what I had to say. "Think about all you've seen, all we've been through, and forget I'm a woman. I've lasted a long time out here with nobody to look out for me.

Yeah, I got a houseful of men to keep the boogers off, but who takes care of who? Think about that, and while you're at it think about all the people needing me, and tell me—could you just go?"

"Merdie, I don't know, I really don't. All I know is I want you with me. Maybe that's selfish, but I want you to go where I go."

I braced myself. "Are you leaving now?"

"Not tonight, no." He pulled me close. "Does it seem to you that question's been asked too much?"

I wanted him to say then and there that he'd never go, never leave me, but what with all the questions ringing in my head, one more would block my brain, and it would be best all around to just feel and let the heavy stuff wait, and maybe tomorrow when the sun come up again I'd ask again, Are you leaving now? and he'd say, No, not ever.

We slept in my feather bed in Mama's sideroom, and throughout the night I'd wake up and think about the boys, about Hamp. Mac must have been thinking about them too, because everytime I'd wiggle, he'd gather me close and put me back to sleep, bed rocking like a cradle as we made love. A long night, longer than I'd ever known, sleep dragging me down with a sweet feeling I could taste and just as quick pushing me up again with a bitter aftertaste. Then I'd forget to be sad, forget that tomorrow he might go, that tomorrow I might have to go back to being Merdie, mama and midwife.

Somewhere in the night, though, after the fire in the living room had died and the doorway turned black, I made up my mind not to never go back. I'd stay here at Mama's, I'd keep a close check on the baby, I'd keep up my mama's birthing business, at least till I could train Ethel or maybe even Bobbie Jean to take over. The boys could come and go as they pleased, and if they didn't want to sing no more, that was fine too. I would. I'd keep on singing wherever J.J. said, for cash and experience. I would make that demo. If Katy Land could do it...

The sun shining through the east window woke me, warm on my cold face, on my arm hooked over the quilts. I had to lay there a minute to figure what was what. Then I felt Mac, felt him spring the bed, set up and get still. Was he leaving? Should I stay there till he was gone? Would it be easier, harder?

"Merdie?" he said, turning with a knee in my back. "What's this?" He stuck a wad of hundred-dollar bills in my face.

"Money," I said, rolling over.

His hair was sticking up, his eyes were red. He looked rough as he had the first time I saw him. "Where did it come from?"

"My bosom." I took it and set up.

"So, you actually did snitch Hamp's money?" he said.

"I earned it." I started counting the bills—one hundred, two hundred, three...up to six. "Mac, I have to stay here—I mean at Mama's. I'm going to take over her birthing business. But I aim to make that demo."

He slapped his forehead and laughed, vapors trailing cold from his mouth to the scrolled iron bedstead. "But when did you...how did you slip that money out of the bag?"

"I took it out just before I chunked the bag off the porch."

"You're a born thief, Merdie." He kissed me and then we scrunched under the cover, front to back, the tops of his feet warming my cold soles. "Doesn't the Bible say *Thou shalt not steal*?"

"He who comes to the table first eats best," I said.

He laughed, molding to me.

Then I asked, "Are you leaving now?"

He talked into my hair. "Not this second, no."

"You know what I mean."

"Yes to both."

I could feel tears like blood rush to my face. "I expected you would; couldn't see how you could stay."

"Between dodging hired guns and trying to raise bees or bootleg, I wouldn't have much of a life here."

"The hired gun part might not be as much of a problem as you think."

"Think you've taken over Grannie's power too, don't you?"

"Maybe—I know I can keep the boys from bothering you. But the other—how you'd make a living—I don't know."

"I do."

"What about us, aren't we enough?"

"You answered that question a few minutes ago when you said you intend to make that demo."

"You love being with the FBI that much, huh?"

"Don't know that I'd call it love, but it's my job—more like your birthing business, I suppose." He sucked in, waiting. "I have to travel, Merdie, but I'd like to call where you are home."

I felt a warm peace seeping in. "I'm sleepy."

"Then go to sleep, Missy," Mac said, rocking me in our cradle one more time.

About the Author

Janice Daugharty is the author of *Necessary Lies* and a collection of short stories titled *Going Through the Change*. She lives in Valdosta, Georgia.